CAP

Opa
mattress,
rope, she was uncomfortable, hungry, thirsty, bruised, and humiliated.

When the admiral sat down beside her and placed a huge hand on her breast, she felt her loathing for him mounting into fury. He pulled aside the torn silk of her dress to fondle her more intimately, delighting in the soft, cool touch of the gentle swelling. She stared up at him with cold, hard eyes that were on fire with her anger.

The hand left her breast and went to her chin, and he leaned down and kissed her full on the lips. Opal bit down hard with sharp teeth. There was a trickle of blood at his lower lip, seeping into his thick beard, and his eyes were very angry. But he was still forcing a smile, and he said gently, "No, dear lady, that is not permitted. The first lesson you must learn is the helplessness of your position. The second is never to fight me. And the third is to accept whatever indignity I may choose to perpetrate on you, and accept it willingly."

The hands were at her breasts again, the caress of an ardent lover. His fingers were crawling lightly, down to her stomach, under the skirt of her dress, finding her thighs and parting them. He cupped her naked flesh, a finger probing, as he whispered, "Do not be afraid, dear lady. I will not mark that beautiful body; it would be an act of desecration, would it not? But you must learn to pleasure me. And you will do so quickly, for my patience is very short. . . ."

Other Pinnacle Books by Antoinette Beaudry:

Tropic of Desire
River of Desire
Desert of Desire

Strands of Desire

CHAPTER ONE

There was perhaps no place in the world more dangerous than Algiers' Casbah. And yet, to a visitor who did not know it well, it was a very romantic sort of place, too.

The romance came from the twisted, cobbled streets, so narrow that the sun never reached their rutted surfaces, streets that were filled with colorful movement, crowded with artisans squatting on the steps of their stalls: coppersmiths, goldbeaters, jewelers, ivory carvers, weavers of cotton, wool, and silk in the brightest colors imaginable. Donkey carts, oxen, mules and camels mingled with people in the crowded streets.

There were tiny brick archways everywhere, leading to secret alleys, and steep steps leading up and down over the hill. Over the whole scene hung a sort of mystical air that was quite indefinable, but somehow fascinating to the stranger who took his life in his hands when he ventured between the ancient walls.

There was music everywhere in the Casbah, played on native strings in innumerable coffeehouses, a counterpoint to the constant click of the pieces at the backgammon tables where Berbers, Arabs, Touaregs from the Haggar, Riffs from their mountain fastness, black men from the Fezzan, Egyptian merchants, Lebanese drug peddlers, Moroccan bandits and desert nomads all sat together, smoking their water pipes. Small children ran lithely among them, carrying brass trays of coffee or strong tea, and the air was always ripe with the smell of hashish.

Sometimes there were dancers in the streets, the women of the Ouled Naïl tribe, dressed in ankle-length, shapeless gowns made up of brightly colored bits of cloth stitched together; their bodies dripped with long rivers of beads that hung around their necks, and their splayed desert feet were bare. They had been sent here by their fathers to earn their dowries by dancing and prostitution in the bustling metropolis. They would work here for a few years, convert their well-saved earnings into gold in the form of personal jewelry, then return to their desert tents as very rich women. Then their fathers would begin the marriage bargaining, sending excited word from one encampment to another: "A young girl of great quality, and very rich, seeking a husband of merit, beautiful as a gazelle and a virgin still. . . ." On the wedding night, the virginity would be faked with copious applications of wood ash, and though the husbands knew all about this, they never objected; the image was more important than the fact.

So they danced in the streets, and enticed any passerby who might have a few coins in his pocket into their dark little rooms, where as befitted their elevated station in life, they were waited on by very young girls of a caste lower than their own.

The Casbah was dangerous because it was not only the haunt and hiding place of the huge Algierian underworld, it was also the pleasure ground of the Barbary pirates who ruled the southern Mediterranean coastline from Morocco to Turkey, terrorizing shipping, claiming these waters as their own and demanding tribute from the European powers to leave their shipping alone—a covenant that was not always kept.

The Barbary States, named after the Berbers who lived in most of them, were four: Algiers (the most powerful), Morocco, Tunis, and Tripoli (later to be known as Libya). The Berbers were a violent and volatile people, arrogant, undisciplined, fierce fighters, and certain that their future lay in the judicious use of their gunships and their scimitars. They maintained pirate lairs in every little cove along the coast, and from these they preyed on European shipping whenever they felt like it, treaty or no treaty. The price of their restraint was very high.

For the last five years, the United States, concerned for the safety of its shipping in this great international sea, had been paying the bey of Algiers, nominal head of the Barbary States, very handsomely for a tenuous peace that was frequently broken. In this year of 1800, the exact figure was $992,463, though Congress had set aside only $80,000 for the purpose. And this annual tribute was constantly being augmented by special ransoms for American sailors taken prisoner in raids on U.S. shipping.

The European states were likewise being bled. France was paying $200,000 yearly, England $280,000 (but the British had a secret clause in their treaty with the bey that stipulated quite simply that they would not object to the occasional sinking of one of their competitors' ships). England was the only naval power in the world strong enough to put an end to this nonsense once and for all, but England's prime minister, Mr. Pitt, was above all a very pragmatic man, and he knew—just as President Adams did in America—that bribery was far cheaper than war.

So the fighting was only sporadic, and the Barbary States were technically at peace with the rest of the world. But peace formed no part of their philosophy; they were fighters, to whom violence was the only acceptable way of life.

The Casbah was the off-duty haunt of these pirates, a place in which to throw their booty around and enjoy themselves. They liked the coffeehouses, they liked the dancing girls, they liked the brothels. They could be recognized instantly by their swagger, as well as by their dress. Scorning the Moslem gown and baggy pantaloons, they wore instead uniforms taken from enemy seamen they had killed: dark blue coats, tight European breeches, even high boots, as well as their own scarlet waistcoats, with an astounding variety of hats. They all carried scimitars and daggers, and a wide assortment of guns, and drunk or sober they were very dangerous people. The local inhabitants gave them a very wide berth, though they themselves were by no means averse to a good fight to break the boredom of their lives.

To European gentry making the Grand Tour, the Casbah was a mandatory place to visit. From Gibraltar, a safe British fortress, they traveled to Marseilles, Naples, Malta, Athens, Constantinople, Beirut, Alexandria, Tripoli, Algiers, and back to Gibraltar with a sigh of relief, for the return journey to civilization and tall tales of their adventures in their clubs.

The Casbah sometimes seemed to be filled with these travelers: English, French, Spanish, Dutch gentlemen, sometimes accompanied by ladies. They were always escorted by armed dragomen from the luxurious hotels of Algiers, built on the waterfront below the high mountain on which the Casbah had sat for three hundred years. But these daring souls were always careful to leave the Casbah's exotic confines long before dark and return to the pampered safety of their ships or their hotels.

But now, at nearly six o'clock in the evening, a young English girl was wandering here, unaccompanied and unafraid, quite unconcerned even though she was hopelessly lost in a maze of passages that seemed to lead nowhere but back to themselves. She had already bought herself a beautiful pendant of very heavy silver inlaid with beads of coral, turquoise, and enamel. Looking at the tiny diamond timepiece she wore on a silver chain at her breast, she thought that it was high time she found her way back to her hotel.

Her name was Opal Grant. She was twenty-one years old and very lovely. Her skin was white and lucid, her hair quite thick and almost black, piled up high on her head under a flowered bonnet from which it escaped enticingly. She wore a chemise-dress in pale, oyster-colored silk, very high-waisted, the low-cut back and the hem trimmed with ruches. The gown was decorated with tiny flowers of crepe de chine to match those on her bonnet. She wore long white gloves that covered her elbows, and she carried a fan with which she tried to brush away the persistent flies. Her gently swelling breasts were modestly covered but nonetheless quite apparent to the hungry eyes that stared at her wherever she went.

A European woman alone in the Casbah? It was unheard of! Surely it had never happened before!

Her beauty was startling. Her dark eyes were very large and solemn, her lips were very full, her nose almost imperceptibly snubbed. There was a bright intelligence on her face, and perhaps a kind of overconfidence, too.

She was the stepdaughter of an English nobleman, Sir Neville Grant, second secretary to the Foreign Ministry in Mr. Pitt's government. He was the scion of an ancient and honorable family that could trace its origins back to the sixteenth century, a history filled with distinction and renown.

Opal was here alone for very private and compelling reasons that she tried, not always successfully, not to think of; for when she did, a kind of trauma swept over her and destroyed her emotionally, all of her happiness disappearing with the advent of a single thought. So, by the strength of her very considerable will, she forced those secret memories to the back of her mind, into the dark recesses from which they surfaced with dreadful persistence once in a while and left her trembling in the throes of a weakness she would not accept, troubled with mixed and frightening emotions, not the least of which was a kind of sexual frustration that drove her to distraction.

When those memories came to her sometimes, late at night in a sleepless bed, her hand would stray between her thighs, and she would moan softly to herself. The image that came to her on those alarming occasions was of a powerful and virile man whom she both feared and hated. And yet, how could that be? She had once loved him, very dearly. Could love so easily turn to hate? A hatred brought on, indubitably, by so prosaic a thing as a liquor distilled from grapes. The memory of that hard and rampant flesh forcing its way into her still brought nightmares, and she would weep uncontrollably, knowing that there was no escape from her stepfather's evil image.

Now, in the darkening Casbah, she was well aware that

she was being followed; it had happened to her before, in Malta, Alexandria, Tunis. But this was the Casbah, and she was not aware of the important difference. This was a place where the police, the soldiers of the bey, patrolled fearfully and only occasionally, and were always very careful to say, in every coffeehouse, on every street corner: "We come because we have been ordered to come. Leave us alone and we will leave you alone. We are all brothers."

There were men behind her whom she had seen before, an hour ago, two hours ago. Little groups of men, and women, too, were following her wherever she went. She walked on from the Street of the Leather Workers to the Street of the Goldsmiths. A legless beggar followed her, propelling himself along with calloused knuckles on a wheeled board. Two young men were beside him, scarcely out of their teens, slightly bearded and dressed in long grey gowns. The beggar had accosted her once, saying to her in broken English, "Missy, you come with my sons?"

He had continued talking in Arabic, and the two boys with him had laughed. She had tilted her head imperiously and had gone on her way.

And they were still there behind her. The crowds were thick, but it seemed to her now that many of them were gathering around this group, laughing with them, agreeing to whatever it might be that they were saying and somehow becoming a threat she could not identify. She was uneasy, but would not allow herself to be more than that, forcing the idea of fear away from her and insisting to herself that apprehension would be quite ridiculous. In the hotel she had heard from other travelers of the Casbah's fearsome reputation, but on a busy, crowded street, surely no harm could come to her?

She was negotiating with an ancient goldbeater for a particularly beautiful pendant. It was a fish, a tiny good-luck charm intricately worked with great artistry. The old man spoke a tolerable kind of English, and she said to him, frowning, "The old beggar there with the two young boys, they seem to be following me. Would you please tell them to go away and leave me alone? They're really offensively persistent, and it's not very nice to be stared at so blatantly."

"Yes, missy, I tell them. But better first you take pendant, two hundred piasters, cost much more, but for you, good price." He slipped it into a little velvet-lined box, snapped it shut and wound it with string, and said: "There. But remember, is good luck, you open it before you get to hotel, luck fly away."

There was good reason for his concern. He had skillfully palmed the little gold carving, slipping it quickly into the rag around his skinny waist, and the box was empty. Opal counted out the money for him.

"Thank you. And will you now tell those people to stay away from me?"

He grinned ferociously, his teeth yellow and broken. He said, "They liking you, missy, they want make jigga-jig."

"Jigga-jig? It is not a word I am familiar with, I'm afraid. I do not speak Arabic."

He answered her with a vulgar gesture, raising two calloused fingers and moving them up and down. She colored, and he repeated happily, "They *liking* you."

She moved away, but they were gathered tightly about her now, the beggar and his two sons in the forefront of a small, expectant crowd of men and women, all of them shouting happily and refusing to open a path for her. The beggar was shouting louder than any of them, addressing his Arabic to her, and the goldbeater translated for him. "He say his sons take you now, you go room back of my shop, they make jigga-jig two-three times, they don't kill you, you go back to ship, is good."

Opal said coldly: "Kindly tell them that I never heard a more revolting suggestion in my life. I am leaving now."

The wrinkled old eyes were still bright with his laughter. "No, missy, you not leaving. Foreign missy in Casbah she do like Casbah people want." He said sharply, indicating, "You go my room, if not, they taking you here."

Now desperation was on her. Everyone was talking at once, their eyes on fire with an emotion that was not friendly. Some of the women were ululating, their tongues moving back and forth rapidly as they shrieked out a high-pitched, quavering tone to show their pleasure and to offer their encouragement. One of the women stepped forward, took hold of Opal's gown, and ripped the flimsy material away, exposing her breast. Opal gasped and tried to cover herself, but one of the two young men moved in on her and seized her, twisting her around as the legless beggar shouted his instructions. Her head was tucked under a foul-smelling arm and there was a hand at her breast, mauling her. The crowd milled around them, almost hysterical with the prospect of a rape on the street, and one of the women pulled up her skirt, shouting "*Imsika*, take her!"

A patrol of the bey's police passed by, two soldiers hand in hand like lovers, and they stopped to watch. Not daring to interfere, instead they too took pleasure in the spectacle of a foreign woman's humiliation.

Opal felt strong hands at her bare hips, and the terrifying touch of naked flesh against her body. She screamed and screamed, twisting herself this way and that against the monstrous power of the hands.

And then, suddenly, there was a flurry of activity. Opal was conscious only of a fist crashing into the stomach of the boy who held her, and then the flailing of a cudgel that struck her assailant squarely across the bridge of his nose, breaking it instantly. She heard a very deep, masculine voice talking quietly insistent Arabic and recognized the loathing in it, and the authority as well. Then she was lying on the ground and the crowd was fading miraculously away. There was only a very handsome young man bending over her, helping her to her feet, and saying anxiously, "Are you hurt badly, ma'am? Can you stand? If not, I will carry you."

She struggled to her feet with his help, and tried to take firm hold of herself. She was a woman of considerable courage, and she broke down only momentarily, leaning into his strong chest and shuddering. His arm was about her, seeking to comfort her, and he said again, worried, "Were you hurt, ma'am, badly?"

She shook her head, unable for the moment to speak,

and composed herself desperately and said, "No, sir, I was . . . more humiliated than hurt. And I thank you for . . . for helping me."

He looked down on the recumbent body of the man he had struck; the blood was pumping out of his nose, staining an already filthy gown. He said grimly, "For if you were, I will teach this fellow another lesson, one that he will not quickly forget."

"No . . . If you could . . . escort me away from here?"

He answered gently, "Yes, I think perhaps I should." Some of the people were returning, wondering at the rashness of this young man; a fight against such odds in the Casbah? It could so easily cost him his life! Yet they eyed the tall, muscular figure with a great deal of respect. He said quietly, "Yes, it is better that we leave this den of iniquity at once, before these vulgar fellows summon up a courage that is fleeting, but often quite dangerous."

The shock was beginning to take hold of her now, and he felt her trembling. He said quietly, "Let the tears come if they must, ma'am, there is no shame in it."

She shook her head. "No. I will not weep, even though . . ." Suddenly, the tears came gushing, and she sobbed as he led her away. As they walked slowly together down the Street of the Coopers, the smell of teak chips and sawdust all around them, he said, "My name is Jason Farn, ma'am. If I may know yours?"

"Opal Grant. I am making the Grand Tour, and I went into the Casbah, and . . . oh, God!"

He held her tightly. "Alone?"

"Yes, I fear so."

"If I may say so, ma'am, without disrespect, that was a very foolish thing to do."

"It will not happen again, I assure you."

"And you are English, I think?"

"Yes. And you, sir, by your speech, are American?"

"I am indeed. I'm a journalist, a correspondent for Mr. Fenno's *Gazette of the United States.* I'm sure you must have heard of it."

Opal shook her head. "No, I'm afraid not."

He smiled. "One of our better fledgling newspapers. The war between America and Algiers is over, though without a doubt a new one will be upon us soon, and meanwhile my assignment is to report on the Algerian scene. It is a very violent one, as you discovered to your cost."

"And I cannot begin to thank you, Mr. Farn, for what you have done for me, and at such great risk to yourself! I was very close to being—permanently injured."

"I thank God that I chanced to pass by. And your ship?"

"No ship, sir. She was the *Ever-Ready* out of London, but I chose to stay in Algiers for a while and be picked up by the *Empress of India* when she docks here, and sail with her back to Malta, a place I find quite charming."

"Ah, the Grand Tour indeed. But I find it hard to believe that you are alone, without an escort on this wonderful journey, so far from home?"

"Quite alone, Mr. Farn."

They reached the Secondary Gate to the Casbah, the one that overlooked the harbor far below them. He asked her the name of her hotel. She told him it was Le Grand Hotel des Etrangers. He summoned a carriage and took her there. The sun was setting when they reached it, casting a splendid glow over the ships tied up at the waterfront and gilding the high stone walls they had left behind them. She looked back and murmured, "In this light, even the Casbah is beautiful."

He nodded, smiling. "And I am glad that even now you can recognize its beauty. Does it mean that you have recovered from your terrifying experience?"

She too smiled. "Not quite, I'm afraid. But well on my way to complete recovery, knowing with the deepest sense of gratitude that I have you to thank for it."

"It is I who must thank you, Miss Grant," he said gallantly, "for the opportunity, unhappy though it was, to meet with a lady whose courage seems to be as remarkable as her beauty."

She felt the rush of blood to her face as he walked with her through the spacious lobby and up the stairs to the third floor where her room was. He took the key from her and hesitated before inserting it into the lock.

He was twenty-seven years old, ruggedly good looking, with a look of strong virility that was pleasing to a susceptible woman. He was very muscular, a man who liked to keep himself in prime condition. His chest was broad, his shoulders were powerful, his waist taut and his hips slender. He wore blue canvas breeches and high jacked-leather boots, with a flowing, open-necked white silk shirt and a broad cummerbund of dark blue cotton around his middle, a heavy ash cane slipped into it. There were humorous lines about his mouth, a trifle sardonic perhaps, as though he found the world around him to be idiotic in the extreme.

He said carefully, conscious more than ever of her great beauty, "You must rest after so harrowing an adventure, which surely must have left you deeply disturbed. Would it be helpful, perhaps, if I were to sit with you for a while, in your room? What do you think, ma'am? If we could talk for a while, it might take your mind off these unhappy events, which are best forgotten as quickly as possible."

Her heart was beating very fast, as fast as his. She raised her eyebrows and said, "In my *room*, Mr. Farn? Oh no! Though I thank you for your concern. Really, a lady must not entertain a gentleman in her bedroom! It would not be proper at all!"

Jason laughed happily. "Not *proper*? That is a very English sort of phrase, is it not?"

"Until recently, Mr. Farn, the Americans were English too, I think?" She smiled softly, utterly charmed with him, and her heart seemed to be fluttering in an agitation all its own.

He took both her hands in his and whispered, "Perhaps for a few moments only? And I will swear to you that my intentions are honorable. Or at least not dishonorable to any unacceptable extent. For a little while?"

She was sorely tempted. In her present condition, with the memory of outrage still on her, surely he would make no improper advances? Of course, he was an American, but even so, he obviously still had gentlemanly instincts.

And if he did try to take advantage of her? She felt faint at the very idea. She shook her head slowly, and he kissed her hands, brushing them very gently with his lips, and said quietly and very seriously, "I would like so much to know you better, Miss Grant. Will you at least allow me to call on you tomorrow? By then, I dare hope, you will be feeling much, much better."

He wanted so much to take her in his arms, but he restrained his emotions and touched her gently on the cheek with his fingertips, a gesture of genuine affection. There was a wonderful light in her eyes, and she nodded. "Yes, I would not like this to be our last meeting."

"We could go to one of those delightful little coffee-houses down on the waterfront, and watch the great ships while we talk. Would you like that?"

"Oh yes, very much!" She hesitated. "And you are right, by tomorrow I will be very much better, I am sure of it. I am not weak, Mr. Farn. There have been circumstances in my life that have . . . hardened me more than I would really wish."

The remark puzzled him. He looked into her lovely eyes and thought he saw a veil passing over them, as though to obscure a painful memory. He wondered about it, but before he could speak, she said very seriously: "I owe you my life, Mr. Farn. No, more than my life. And you must understand how very grateful I am. It is a debt that can never be paid."

He still held her hands, as though they were precious to him and he could never let them go. She whispered, "When I think what could have happened to me . . ."

He was conscious of the half-sob in her voice, and he said quickly, "No! You must not think of it! Not now, or ever. It is best forgotten!" He smiled. "May I suggest that this is one of the secrets of happiness, which we all need in a sad, sad world? To forget the bad, however difficult it may be, and remember only the good?"

"Yes, yes! I am sure that you are right!"

He said, musing, "There was a river in the underworld of the ancient Greek gods and goddesses, called Lethe."

"Ah yes, the river of forgetfulness."

"There was great comfort for those who slowly rowed their boats along it."

"Yes."

"Tomorrow, then? At noon?"

"Tomorrow, at noon. I will be ready."

He wanted so badly to embrace her, to hold her tightly to him. He was deeply conscious of her torn dress, tied into place over her breasts. Remembering the sight of her half-exposed body, he yearned to touch her now.

He laughed again. "I will wait for you below, in the lobby, and send you word, as is *proper*. And I cannot tell you how eagerly I await our meeting again! May I say, Miss Grant, that you are a truly wonderful woman? May I tell you how deeply you move me? May I hope that tomorrow will be only the first of many meetings?"

She could not answer him, so great was her emotion. He kissed her hands again quickly, then unlocked the door and opened it for her to let her enter. "Goodnight, Miss Grant."

"Goodnight, Mr. Farn. And again, my wholehearted thanks."

He felt the blood draining from his face and a curling sensation at his scalp. Close beside him, through the tiny crack of the doorjamb, there was a movement. He tried not to look, but the instinctive glance had been enough. A bright touch of scarlet and the polish of well cared-for leather; the redingote and high black boots that the English gentry wore? It was the tiniest vision through an infinitesimal crack, and he dared not look again, but he knew that someone was hiding behind the door.

"*Alone*," she had said, and "*no escort*."

Yet there was a man in her room. A husband?

He was very careful not to change his expression. He said, still smiling, "It is *Miss* Grant, I dare hope? Not *Mrs.* Grant?"

She raised her lovely eyebrows. "I am not married, sir."

A lover, then! If, indeed, she spoke the truth. His heart

sank, but only briefly, and he said to himself fiercely, "So be it, then! I will take her away from him!"

A lover waiting! And where the devil was he when he was needed, up there in the Casbah? Skulking now like a coward behind a half-open door!

His smile was false now, and he was not accustomed to deception. She knew it, somehow, and it both puzzled and worried her. She said, "Till tomorrow, then."

"Yes, tomorrow. Goodnight, Miss Grant."

The change in him was almost imperceptible, but he was not adept at hiding his true feelings. Opal, worried, stepped inside the room and closed the door; he heard the click of the lock.

As he turned away, his heart heavy with an unexpected kind of pain, he heard her scream. It was a scream of sheer terror, and it was quickly cut off. He did not stop to think. He turned back and hurled himself at the door. It withstood his first assault, and he stepped back and drove his raised foot into it, bursting it wide open, charging into the room.

There were four men in the room, Algerians. Two of them were throwing a length of canvas over her head and roping it around her, while a third danced on the edge of them, yelling his instructions.

The fourth was a man of entirely different aspect. The three were waterfront scum, dock rats, dressed in rags, but he was wearing a scarlet waistcoat—not a redingote at all—and high leather boots up to his thighs. He was tall and very handsome, of enormously powerful build, his European-style breeches well cut, but all European similarity stopped there; the waistcoat was pure Berber, heavily embroidered with gold thread, and under it his muscular chest was bare. He wore an ornate leather belt around his narrow waist, with two daggers fastened to it in highly decorated sheaths. He was fiercely bearded and moustached, and his eyes were very dark and flashing, large eyes that any woman would have been proud of. He was a man of magnetic, almost hypnotic attraction, and those angry, mocking eyes were fixed on Jason as his underlings wrestled with Opal, seeking to contain her struggles as they wound the rope around her.

Jason sized up the situation at once. There were four of them, and he knew where the real danger lay. Leaving Opal to her trials for the moment, he threw himself at the obvious leader, striking for the head before attacking the limbs. He drove his fist into the throat and saw him go down, and then turned to one of the men holding Opal and seized his long, filthy hair, spinning him round and driving a fist into his face, sending him sprawling. He tackled a second of the dock rats, but then there was a strong arm around his throat, strangling him and holding him firmly. The man he had attacked was on the ground, blood spewing from his nose, but his arms were around Jason's feet, imprisoning him.

The leader's furious eyes stared into his own. He struggled against the throat hold and could not move.

There was a curved dagger in the leader's hand, and the sharp point of it was at Jason's side, just above the hipbone. The strong forearm was pressing at his throat, and he was beginning to lose consciousness. He heard the angry voice, somehow controlled and all the more menacing because of it.

"Before you die, pig, know my name. I am Sinan, Admiral Sinan. When you go to your Christian heaven, you will tell your foul God: 'I was killed by Admiral Sinan!' Sinan, Sinan, Sinan! Remember the name as you begin, slowly, to die."

The dagger was being slipped into his side, and the pain was intolerable. Jason screamed uncontrollably and fought unconsciousness, and then he felt the twisting of the blade as it was withdrawn. That handsome face was leering at him, very close, and the voice came to him out of limbo.

"A slow death. In a few hours you will bleed your life away. In those hours, reflect on the name. *Sinan, Sinan, Sinan,* an Algerian gentleman of quality and an admiral in the fleet of His Excellency the Bey. You die at the hands of a nobleman; it may be consolation for you."

Then there was only blackness, with no consciousness at

all, and he was only half aware as the coma came over him that he was shrieking, "Opal! I am here, I will save you!" But the sound that came from his throat was an incoherent croak. There was nothing in the room but a galaxy of shooting stars, each and every one of them pounding into his side and driving him into the throes of complete delirium.

The whole world was black, nothing but utter darkness.

CHAPTER TWO

Jason tried to ease his body into a more comfortable position, wondering whose were the hands that were restraining him, whose was the voice, a woman's voice, saying to him in Arabic: "No, you must lie still now. You are hurt. Lie still, do not move. I will bring a doctor."

The sun was streaming in through the window. How could that be? It should be setting now. What time was it? And what was he doing here, lying on the floor of a room he could not recognize? Above all, who was *she*?

He stared up at her. She was a child, perhaps twelve years old, dressed in a simple black cotton shift, and there was a man beside her, a cheerful young man whose happy face he well remembered from a distant past. The man was saying: "Jason! Don't you know me? I'm Pratt, Pratt Wilson, your friend! If you desert from the marines, they'll hunt you down and you'll die on the gallows or at the yardarm! But I'll help you, Jason, if that's what you truly want to do . . ."

Jason whispered, "Pratt? Pratt Wilson? Is it truly you, dear friend?"

He was speaking Arabic, and the girl answered him, puzzled, "Pratt? No, *ya hawwajer*, my name is not Pratt. Pratt is not a name at all. I am Suri, a servant."

"Suri?"

"*Na'am, ya hawwajer*, Suri."

"And where is Pratt?" But Pratt was a figment of his imagination, a memory, no more, and he had vanished.

"There is no Pratt, *ya hawwajer*. There is no one else here. There is only Suri, a servant."

The clouds were moving across his mind, and moments of lucidity came to him. "But there was a lady here, an English *Sitt*. I cannot remember her name, but she was here."

"Yes. This is her room. She is gone now."

"Gone?"

"Gone. I do not know where. She has gone."

"I must find her, Suri."

The pain was insufferable, but he tried not to moan. He put a hand to his side and found a pad there, caked with dried blood. The young girl whispered, "I stopped the bleeding, *ya hawwajer*, or you would have died. I tore my dress and made bandages."

"It should have killed me . . ."

"It takes a long time for a strong man to bleed to death."

"How can I repay you, Suri?"

"There is no need."

She was coal black, from the southern Sahara perhaps, and there were twin burn marks on her forehead that proclaimed her a slave. He said, "You have saved my life, Suri. It will not be forgotten, nor go unrewarded. Tell me what it may be that I can do for you."

She hesitated, her child's eyes were wide with excitement. "You wish to reward me?"

"Yes. In whatever way I can." It was hard for him to talk, and his voice was hoarse with the pain.

Suri whispered, "Sandals."

"Sandals?" He did not understand what she meant, but she nodded eagerly. "Yes, I have never had sandals, never in my life. Will you buy me some?"

His heart was breaking. He tried to struggle to his feet and could not. Her hands were at his shoulders, forcing him to lie still. "No, you must not move. I will find a doctor for you."

He took her small hand and lay still on his back, letting the nausea pass over him. He said at last, "And will you tell me where your home is, Suri? The desert, I think, the *sahara*?"

"Yes. I come from the sand hills of Ain Sefra."

"Ain Sefra? That is a very long way. Will you help me once more?"

"Of course."

"I must go to the Casbah."

"The Casbah?" She said fiercely, "You do not need the Casbah now, you need a doctor."

"There is one there whom I can trust, and friends there I must talk with now."

"Very well, then." She was tiny and very slight, but she was a nomad and her muscles were strong. She helped him to his feet, and he swayed unsteadily for a moment. He was a big man, more than six feet tall and weighing a hundred and eighty pounds, but she supported him down the stairs and out onto the street. She called a gharry, and sat with him in the carriage as they drove up to the Casbah at the top of the hill. She was very solicitous, peering into his eyes and finding the pain there.

"Where in the Casbah will you go?" she asked.

"The Street of the Brothels. Number ten."

"Ha! I know it! The lady Munia. You can do nothing for her now."

"No, but she can do something for me. She is a friend."

"You are a gentleman, an *effendi*. And your friends are whores?"

He smiled. "Some of them, Suri."

"Munia is from the tribe of the Ouled Naïl. I do not like the Ouled Naïl."

"Munia is not like most of them. She is a fine woman."

Suri said nothing. When the carriage drew up at number ten she jumped down and hammered on the door. It was answered by Munia herself. She was a splendid figure of a woman, no longer very young but still handsome and passionate, full-figured and robust, with startling black eyes and fine, smooth, olive-colored skin. There were tribal tattoos on her forehead, and her nose and ears had been pierced to take fine gold rings. She was well dressed in a long gown made from strips of different-colored cotton. She gasped when she saw him, and said, "Jason! You come to me like this? More dead than alive?"

The two women guided him into one of the rooms and laid him down on the nearest cot. It was a dancer's bench, only a foot or so wide and two-and-a-half feet from the ground, carefully calculated measurements that had been devised for the ultimate in sexual fulfillment. Munia looked at the black girl and said sharply, "Go now! You are no longer needed."

But Suri was still holding on to Jason's hand, and he whispered to her, "Yes, go now, and I thank you. In a day or two you will hear from me again. There are things I must do now, but . . . In a day or two. Will you trust me?"

"Of course. And are you in good hands now?"

"Yes. I am still in good hands."

Her liquid eyes lingered on his for a moment, and then she left. Munia pulled aside the breeches and the bloodied shirt and said scornfully, "A knife wound. It is nothing."

He sighed. "Is Doctor Assad here?"

"How should he be here? I run a brothel, not a hospital." She grimaced. "He is here only at night."

"Then will you send for him, please?"

"As you wish." She raised her voice and called, "Osman!" When a ten-year-old boy came running, she said, "Go and find *Hakkim* Assad at once. But first, have them bring hot water and oil."

The child ran to do her bidding. While they waited, Munia stripped him completely and bathed his body and rubbed oil into it, tossing the filthy rag away in disgust. "Pah! A black girl's rags. Have you no shame? What happened to you?"

"I was stabbed."

"What, I am blind? I can see that! Who was it, an angry husband?"

"A man I must find, Munia. And you will help me find him."

"Perhaps." Not changing the tone of her voice, she said, "Why is it, Jason, that in all this time, three years and more, you have never loved me?"

He wondered about that himself, and could not find an answer.

The doctor came and examined him casually. Grunting, he said, "A knife wound, nothing else! Why do you need a man of my high qualifications for such a trifle?" He probed, finding the depth of the wound. "A certain amount of internal bleeding. It is to be expected. External too, and you should have bled to death, but you did not. Good. I have a certain yellow powder greatly favored by the Europeans which is really quite remarkable. But you are in pain, I think. A wound like this . . ."

"Yes. In pain."

The doctor turned to Munia. "Copious draughts of strong hashish then, but only the best."

"I have *only* the best here. This is a very high-class house, as you know." She told the boy to bring a water pipe. He fetched one and piled the hot coal onto its ceramic bowl, filled with good Algerian hashish. The doctor said, gesturing, "Inhale deeply. There is nothing in the world that will take away the pain so quickly, I promise you." He grunted again. "It will also make a man of you once more. Have you smoked hashish before?"

Jason shook his head. "I have more sense, Doctor Assad."

"One of its many blessings is that it is a very powerful aphrodisiac." He glanced around the room, small, neat, and clean, washed with lime to which blue antimony had been added to keep most of the flies away. There was a single grated window, curtained in brilliantly striped cotton, a geranium in a clay pot on its sill. There were three leather chairs, because sometimes customers paid to watch the gyrations of the dancer at the bench. Copper plates inlaid with silver wire decorated the walls, and there was a large painting of a Turkish pasha copulating with one of his women, as two young girls crouched beside him, assisting his efforts.

"Deep into your lungs," the doctor said. "And when it has all gone, the boy will bring you more."

Jason nodded, watching the smoky bubbles course their way through the scented rosewater in the jar. He hated the taste of it, but he knew that its analgesic properties were very strong.

The doctor forced his yellow powder into the wound with his scalpel, which was rusting a little at the edges. He made a pad of fairly clean gauze and bound it firmily over the wound with a bandage around Jason's waist. Then he rose to his feet.

"In a day, sir, you will be on your feet again. Not yet quite whole, but very much better."

When he had gone, Munia knelt down by the cot and fondled Jason's naked body. The amber mouthpiece of the pipe was between his lips, and he was breathing deeply. His wound was already beginning to feel numb, and he knew that he had to speak to her quickly before he passed out.

"Who is Admiral Sinan, Munia?"

The caress of her hand stopped, but only briefly. "Sinan?" she asked. "I do not know this name, Jason."

It was a lie, and he knew it. He said gently, "I think you do. I think you know every scoundrel in the whole of Algiers."

"Then tell me why you wish to know about him."

"Because he was the man who wounded me."

"Then you are lucky to be alive. *I* am lucky that you are alive." The delicate, butterfly touch of her hand began to make itself felt. She went on, "Admiral Sinan is the chief of all the bey's spies. Here in the Casbah, in Algiers itself, Casablanca, Tripoli, Constantinople, even in France and England, and yes, in America too, his spies are everywhere. He is a very dangerous man, Jason."

"And are you too one of his spies, Munia?"

She laughed. "No. I am a spy for the Americans. The money is much better."

"Yes, I always thought you might be. So will you help me, Munia?"

"If you will tell me how, and I can, yes."

His voice was beginning to falter, and he saw two of her crouched beside him now, four hands exploring his body. Hazily, he told her what happened at the hotel, and she listened gravely, reaching from time to time for a cloth to wipe the sweat from his face and chest.

"I must find this Englishwoman, Munia. It is for this that I need your help. To find her, I must find Sinan."

"And he will kill you!" she said fiercely. "I know this man, Jason! This time, he will kill you! Already, he will know that you did not bleed to death, that someone came in time to save you. Perhaps he even knows where you are at this minute."

"Then if he does," Jason said as steadily as he could, "you must throw me out on the streets, Munia." He tried to sit up, and she pushed him back angrily. "No! You know that I will never do that!" She sighed heavily. "Very well, if you must. Though I am a fool to help you find another woman."

She rose to her feet and stood looking down on him, and she whispered, "You are so beautiful a man, Jason. And can you tell me why I help you when it means I may never see you again?"

He tried to smile, and could not. The images of her were swinging around his head now. He whispered: "Yes, I can tell you that. It is because, as I have always known, you are . . . you are a woman of quality, Munia."

He could hardly hear her voice. "And I am a woman in love, I think. And you . . . The pain has gone?"

"Almost."

"I was sure of it. Smoke more, all the time that I am gone, or it will come back, worse than before."

"Gone?"

"I go to speak to people, and to listen to them. I will come back in a few hours, and we will see what can be done to find your woman."

"Not . . . not my woman . . . Munia."

"Sshhh." He was not aware that he had been shouting.

She said softly, "Sleep, and smoke again when you waken, and wait for me."

He was fighting the coma that was trying to take hold of him, a drugged forgetfulness, and he was barely conscious that she left the room. The amber mouthpiece fell from his lips. The child Osman was there at once, rolling up the long, decorated tube and removing the charcoal from the bowl.

He awoke in a while, thinking that perhaps he had slept for ten minutes or so, and tried to clamber off the cot but could not. The boy was beside him. Jason said hoarsely, "How long . . . how long have I been here, child?" There was no light streaming in through the window. Osman said fearfully, "It is night, *effendi.*" He was frightened; his mistress had been gone a very long time.

Two of the girls came in and peeked at Jason, and then a big black man in the traditional scarlet and gold of a eunuch came in and chased them away. The eunuch raised the lid of one of Jason's eyes and peered into it, and said, his voice deep and melodious, "Good, good."

But Jason's world was swimming back and forth wildly. Yet he was wide awake and very conscious, and he wondered why the eunuch was moving so impossibly slow, as though time itself had slowed down. But thank God, there was only one of him now! Though the scarlet of his uniform was almost blinding in its intensity. And then, to his shock, the eunuch was feeling him, and he said softly, "Good, your strength is returning too. Soon the mistress will return, and no doubt send you one of the girls to relieve the tensions that are in you. It is good." Then he was gone in a blaze of blinding light.

Jason slept again, and when he awoke he found that his sanity had returned. The pain had come back too, but he gritted his teeth and found that he could bear it.

And Munia was there beside him. He stared at her in the light of the tallow candle, and focused his mind by a strong effort of will. The words were tumbling over in his mind, but before he could speak, Munia said softly, "I have found out what it is you have to know."

He swung his legs off the narrow cot, gasping at the sudden seizure in his stomach, wondering where his clothes were. But Munia gently pushed him down again, and she whispered, "No, the time is not yet. In a few hours, but not now."

She pushed him gently back, and he lay down as she dropped once more beside him in that peculiar crouch of the Ouled Naïl, squatting on her heels with her knees pressing against her breasts. She was very calm. She said quietly, "The English lady, her name is Opal Grant—"

"Yes, yes, I know that!"

"Listen to me! Did you know that her father is a famous English milord?"

"No, I did not."

"Then listen to me, and learn. Her father is an English milord who lives in a place called the House of Parliament, I think. He is a very powerful man in the government of England. The bey, Karim Abdullah, knows who this great milord is, and he knows too that Opal Grant is his daughter, and so the lady has been taken to be a hostage."

"A hostage?" Jason was aghast.

"Yes, a hostage. You know about the tribute that England pays so that the bey will not sink their ships?"

"Not only England," Jason said grimly. "Our own vessels too. Yes, I know about the tribute."

"America pays much more than England," Munia went on, "though England has more shipping, and the bey wants to raise the English price. He believes that if he has this milord's daughter as hostage, there will be one strong voice in the English government that will say yes, we must pay the bey what he wants."

Jason did not know the Arabic word for blackmail, and he said instead: "Persuasion."

"Yes, persuasion. There will be a meeting soon with the bashaw of Tunis, the emperor of Morocco, and the bey of Tripoli, and our own ruler, Karim Abdullah Bey, wants to tell them that he has this English lady a prisoner, and will ask for more money from England, for the tribute. As you know, perhaps, he must have all their votes before he can do this."

Jason said tightly, "This means, then, that she has been taken to the bey's palace?"

"No, not yet, though she will be. Not to the palace here in Algiers, but the summer palace on the island of Djidji. She is on board the *Habou*, which is Admiral Sinan's flagship."

His voice was tight with emotion. "She is on board a pirate ship? And how sorely has she been treated, do you know that too, Munia?"

"She has not been harmed."

"Not harmed? But that is impossible!"

"No. Karim Abdullah wants her for himself. He is very fond of European women. There are many of them in his harem. And this is well known. Not even Sinan will dare force her."

"And she has not gone to the bey yet?"

"Not yet."

"Allah be praised that there is still time!" He tried to rise again, but her strong hands were at his shoulders once more, forcing him down to the narrow cot again.

"No, Jason, the time is not yet. The *Habou* is tied up at the docks, taking on crew."

"Then I will go there at once!"

"What, at midnight? Are you mad? You will find fifty armed guards there! If you must go aboard that ship, where they will kill you instantly, there is only one way."

"They are taking on crew, you say? Then I will sign on with them! If I dress as a Berber, and try not to talk too much—my Arabic is fluent, I think . . ."

"It will not be necessary. Sign on, yes. But there will be several Europeans looking for work as deckhands, without a doubt. The docks are full of derelicts from England, France, Holland, men who cannot go home because of the crimes they have committed, men who will do anything for one meal a day. Only in this fashion, Jason, will you be able to board that ship. What you do then is in the hands of Allah."

"And they will be taking on crew again? When? At sunrise?"

"At sunrise. Will you be strong enough, if you sleep for a while?"

He said fiercely, "I am strong enough already, thanks to your care, Munia."

"But there is time on our hands now, some hours. If we must waste them, then let us do so intelligently."

She stood up and stripped off her gown, and as he looked up at her naked body, smooth and oiled, hairless in the Moslem fashion, he whispered, "You are a very lovely woman, Munia, more lovely than I could ever have imagined."

"Yes. And I will enjoy you now. And you will enjoy me, too."

"I am wounded, and not strong. It may be that I cannot do you justice."

"The hashish that is still in your blood will do me justice. And you are strong, very strong." Her hand was at his manhood, clutching him fiercely, and she whispered, "So beautiful a man, a *strong* man . . ."

She threw a thigh over him and stood straddling him, her feet planted on either side of the dancer's bench. It had been made specifically for this purpose. She took him in both her hands and guided him into her, lowering herself firmly on him. He was an iron rod within her. She whispered, "Now, you lie still . . ."

She began the dance for which the women of the Ouled Naïl were justly famous. With her hands behind her head, keeping her head and her feet still, her body began to tremble, her shoulders rippling first. Then the quivering moved slowly to her full, upright, pointed breasts, as Jason thrust at her and screamed, "Munia! You are killing me!" The oscillation moved down to her stomach, expanding throughout her body. And then, infinitely slowly, as though deliberately prolonging his ecstasy, it moved to her loins and her thighs, and the muscles that held him so tightly imprisoned were quivering too, draining him as he flooded into her.

She still would not leave him. Her body arched, her head

thrown back so that all he could see of her upper torso was the beautiful contour of her splendid breasts, outlined with the golden sheen of the candle. Her oiled body was vibrating furiously, rippling, pulsating, quivering and driving him to distraction. The dance was the culmination of all that she had been trained for since her infancy.

She was satiated at last, and she collapsed atop him, flattening her breasts on his chest, kissing him on the mouth and whispering to him, "There are still more hours left for us."

He could hardly speak. He said hoarsely, "Will you tell me why I am lying under your lovely body like this, when I should be searching for my enemy, Admiral Sinan?"

"Because, my love, my Jason, you will not find him till the morning, which is not yet upon us." She smiled, mocking him. "And are you strong enough to fight a man like the admiral?"

"If I am strong enough to survive what you have just done to me, Munia, I am strong enough to fight a thousand Sinans."

"You must sleep now, or in the morning you will be a wreck of a man, worse even than you were when you came to me. Come, we will go to my own room now. This is not a good bed for sleep. It was not made to sleep on."

She took him to her own exquisitely feminine room, with a huge brass bedstead in it covered with a patchwork quilt. He was able to stand without great difficulty, and even walk with some assurance. The wound in his side was throbbing, but only slightly. He lay beside her on the bed and slept, conscious of the warmth of her presence.

He awoke once at the sound of a quiet tapping on the door, and felt Munia leave him and go to answer it. Half asleep, he heard the deep voice of the eunuch whispering, "A matter of importance, mistress," and fell asleep again. Then she was beside him, and she took him again in his sleep, and when he awoke he touched her cheek and found that it was moist. *Tears?* From so strong a woman?

He whispered, "Munia . . ."

"Ssshhh. Do not talk now, Jason. Soon you will find

your English lady. We have loved each other for the last time, I know it. The first, and the last." She was weeping. She whispered, "Please, be silent. Let me enjoy my sorrow. Let me weep because we did not become lovers long, long ago . . ."

Jason could not answer her. He fell asleep in her arms.

Shortly before sunrise, Osman brought them strong coffee flavored with *khel,* the cardamom seed that was a stimulant in itself.

Munia whispered, "A pipe of hashish, Jason, before you leave me forever?"

He shook his head. "No, it is not the false strength of a drug that I need now. My mind must be clear for what I have to do." He took her hand in his. "But will you do one more thing for me?"

"Of course. Anything."

"Will you go to my bank for me? It is the Ottoman Bank on Sharia Malakal. The manager there, Yussuf Pasha, is a friend of mine, and if you give me pen and paper I will write a letter for you to present to him. I must go to the docks, and I dare not wait for the bank to open and perhaps miss the *Habou*'s sailing. But there is urgent and important business I must attend to, a debt of honor. Will you do this for me?"

"Of course, Jason, of course. I know Yussuf Pasha very well, he is one of my best customers."

"Good. I will give you a letter to him. Draw out all of my money, leaving only a token amount to keep the account open. And then . . . There is a poor child at Le Grand Hotel des Etrangers, a servant, the black girl who saved my life. You saw her when we came here. Her name is Suri. Go to the Street of the Sandalmakers and buy her the finest pair of sandals you can find, of camel leather with water buffalo soles, dyed red, perhaps, and decorated with gold and silver wire."

Munia said, puzzled, "*Sandals?* For saving your life?"

"Yes, sandals," Jason said firmly. "And then, go to the hotel and find out who her owner is. She is a slave. The owner is no doubt Asula Effendi—"

"Another of my customers."

"Good. With the money from the bank, buy her freedom."

But there was a veil over Munia's eyes; he had first become aware of it when he mentioned Suri's name, and he remembered the hatred in her voice when she had said, on their arrival here, "Go now, you are no longer needed." The Ouled Naïl did not like the blacks, who had sorely mistreated them.

He said gently, "I wish to buy her freedom, Munia, however much it may be. I do not know the extent of my account, but it is quite considerable, and will be more than enough." He broke off, staring at her. Something was wrong, and it was more than hatred of the blacks.

Munia touched his arm and whispered, "Suri is dead, Jason."

"*What?*" The blood was draining from his face.

"She is dead."

"How? In God's name, how?"

"Her throat was cut."

"Sinan?"

"Perhaps. Or one of his men."

"Oh God, dear God . . ." He sunk his head in his hands and tried to fight his anguish. "She was perhaps twelve years old," he whispered. "She found a dying man in one of the rooms and brought him back to life . . ."

"I know."

He looked up at her, not trying to hide his tears. "And does this mean that Sinan knows I came here?"

"Yes."

"Then you too are in danger."

"Yes, without a doubt. But there are now ten armed men in my house, the brothers, sons, and cousins of my eunuch, good fighting men, all of them. If Sinan sends his men here it will be to their cost."

"Oh, God . . ."

He was smitten with grief for the child who had saved him. Munia said softly, "Come. You must go now, before the *Habou* finds its crew and sails without you."

"Yes."

She embraced him and whispered: "It is goodbye forever, Jason. My heart is breaking."

He said quietly: "You are a woman of quality, Munia. I will not forget you."

"Go now to the ship. Tell them that you were once an American marine, as I know you were. They will hire you instantly. And then—everything will come from Allah."

"Yes, from Allah. He is good, sometimes."

"Do not throw your life away too easily."

"I will not. It is precious to me."

"Remember always that if you must fight, then tomorrow is better than today. The heat of the moment leads to mistakes, which must not be made with men like Sinan."

"Yes, that is true."

"And will you marry her, Jason?"

He smiled. "Perhaps. I do not know. She is not my lover, Munia. It is simply that . . . I tried to save her, and I failed. I must try again."

"Cost what it may?"

"Yes. And this time I will succeed, though I do not know how."

"Goodbye then, my love."

"Goodbye, Munia. I cannot thank you, there are no words . . ."

She watched him as he left the Street of the Brothels and walked down the hill toward the harbor. He was moving well, only stopping once in a while as the pain seized him. But he was forcing a steadiness on himself that augured well.

He found the *Habou* tied up at the wharf. It was a fine twenty-two-gun cruiser, its sails furled now against the bright blue sky. There was a crude trestle table set up on the dock close by, and a grey-bearded Algerian was sitting there on a wooden bench, half asleep. Two Berber touts were striding up and down, calling out to the world at large: "Good food on board, and a share of the booty! Three meals, three, every day, for any skilled sailing man who wants to improve his standing in the eyes of his fellows by signing up for the *Habou*, the finest of all our ships. Three meals a day, and French gold for the asking if you know how to fight as a good man should! Three meals every day!"

There were a dozen dock rats lounging and paying very little attention to this come-on; they had heard it before, sometimes to their cost. But one or two hopeful, ragged men were hesitantly lining up at the table, and Jason joined them. When his turn came, he said to the bearded Algerian: "Farn is my name. I am an ex-marine who deserted and now looks for work. As a deckhand perhaps, *ya habibi.*"

"*Habibi?* I am not your friend, nor ever hope to be." He looked Jason up and down, noting the quality of his clothes, his fine bearing, and his strong muscles. He blew his nose on his fingers and wiped them on his gown and said, suspiciously, "Why should the likes of you seek work as a deckhand?"

"You spoke of a share in the booty. You spoke of gold, and when I hear that word I become the best fighting man in the Mediterranean."

"An American?"

"Yes."

"I do not like the smell of Americans."

"And for my part, I do not like the stink of Berbers. But I will fight alongside them, if only to show them how an expert can handle a sword or a gun in a good battle."

"A marine, you said."

"An ex-marine."

"You know how to climb rigging?"

"A marine, *ya habibi.*"

"And where did you learn to speak Arabic?"

"In the whorehouses of the Casbah," Jason said, mocking him.

"Ha! Very well, then. One good meal a day, as much as you can eat. Good gruel made from millet, with sometimes a piece of meat in it. And if you acquit yourself well in the fighting, you get a one-thousandth share of the booty taken, at the discretion of the captain. You treat the officers with respect, you learn the ship's rules, if you kill a fellow seaman without good cause you get flogged. Tell me your name again."

"Farn."

The Algerian wrote it carefully down in his notebook and handed it over. "Make your mark here."

Jason took the stub of pencil and made a cross against it, just as the others did, and stepped onto the gangplank. A moment later he was moving across the broad, noisy deck of the *Habou* in search of the bo'sun, his new and temporary master.

CHAPTER THREE

Opal was in despair.

A day and a half had passed since her abduction, an interminable time passed in contemplation of the dreadful fate that she was sure was in store for her. She was lying on a greasy mattress in a tiny cabin, her hands and feet bound with short lengths of rope. She was uncomfortable, hungry, thirsty, bruised and humiliated—and fearful of the future.

The tall, striking-looking man who had commanded her abductors came to her cabin only a few hours after she had been unceremoniously dumped on the narrow cot. She knew him as the man she had heard saying, "Sinan, Sinan, Sinan, remember the name as you die. . . ."

There was a strong and painful image in her mind of Jason Farn lying on the floor, dead because he had tried to save her from this abomination. When the admiral sat down on the bed beside her and laid a huge hand on her breast, she felt her loathing for him mounting into a fury. He pulled aside the torn silk of her dress to fondle her more intimately, delighting in the soft, cool touch of the gentle swelling. She stared up at him with cold, hard eyes that were on fire with her anger. She would not deign to struggle uselessly; she suffered his unspeakable attentions in silence.

He was smiling, almost laughing, as though he found great humor in her predicament. He was wearing a brass-buttoned scarlet coat with a white cotton shirt open at the throat, tightly fitting black breeches and high black knee-boots with large, loose turnovers at their tops. His waist was narrow and taut, his chest and shoulders powerful. A fearsome-looking scimitar hung from a broad leather sash, and in his ornately decorated leather belt there were two daggers and a revolver; one of the daggers, she was sure, had been used to murder Jason. And still he smiled, an imposing and attractive man whose face was marred only by the cruelty in his eyes.

He spoke to her in English, in a well-modulated and educated voice, with no trace of an accent. He said, mockingly, "You cannot know how much it pains me, dear lady, to see you trussed up like this. It's most ungallant of me, is it not? But I fear it is necessary until we put out to sea. I cannot yet spare the men to guard you, and I am convinced that a woman of your undoubted spirit might find the closeness of the wharf a little tempting. Escape is quite impossible, but you might not consider it so. And therefore, until we sail, you will remain tied up. It will not be for much longer. Once we are under way, I will allow you the run of the decks, to take the fine sea air as you please. Will you enjoy that?"

She still would not answer him, nor struggle to avoid his caresses, but bit her lip and held her peace. He rolled her tiny nipple back and forth, the tips of his fingers gently sinking into the resilience. He bent his head and kissed her breast, and suckled on her for a while, and she trembled; in spite of herself, she felt the nipple hardening under his tongue, and she thought, shaking: Bound as I am, he can do what he wants with me, and I am powerless. . . .

"There are a hundred crude and savage men on board," he said softly, "but they will not harm you, they have been warned. And shall I tell you why?"

He sighed. "It is not, as you may think, so that you will be mine alone, alas no! My orders are to take you to His Excellency the Bey, Karim Abdullah, the ruler of Algiers and of the Barbary States, and he wants you . . . intact. You *are* intact, I assume? An English lady of such tender years? Even I myself may not take you until the bey has first had his pleasure with you, though after that it is my hope to enjoy you too. But meanwhile, there are many other pleasing ways, are there not, in which we can amuse ourselves together? You might perhaps find them strange at first, though perhaps you will learn to enjoy them too. And may I say that I have seldom seen a more lovely young woman in all my life, a life that has been spent with very many lovely women."

The hand left her breast and went to her chin, and he leaned down and kissed her full on the lips.

Opal bit down hard with sharp teeth. But then she felt his thumb and finger pressing into her cheeks, crushing them against her teeth cruelly, forcing her to open her mouth again. She gasped with the pain of that dreadful hold, and she thought she was about to faint. There was a trickle of blood at his lower lip, seeping into his thick beard, and his eyes were very angry. But he was still forcing a smile, and he said gently, "No, dear lady, that is not permitted. The first lesson you must learn is the helplessness of your position. The second is never to fight me. And the third is to accept whatever indignity I may choose to perpetrate on you, and accept it willingly. Will you learn these lessons?"

She fought back the tears, and he released the strong grip on her face. He was laughing now, not a cruel laugh but filled with a kind of perverse delight that he seemed to want to share with her. The hands were at her breasts again, the caress of an ardent lover. His fingers were crawling lightly down to her stomach, under the skirt of her dress, finding her thighs and parting them. He cupped her naked flesh, a finger probing, and he whispered, "Do not be afraid, dear lady. I will not mark that beautiful body, it would be an act of the vilest desecration, would it not? But you must learn to obey me in all things, and to pleasure me in the ways that are open to us." His voice hardened. "And you will learn to do so quickly, for my patience is very short."

His hands were all over her body now, and he said, frowning, "It is too much to expect that I should hold so lovely a flower in my hand and not enjoy its fragrance." His voice was hoarse with his desire for her. "Your thighs are as smooth as the finest silk, your breasts are the purest alabaster. . . ."

Somewhere above them a bell sounded. Sinan took a long deep breath and said ruefully, "And I must leave you now. A ship cannot be well trimmed without the presence of its highest officer." He was smiling again, mocking her. "Can you bear to be parted from me? It will not be for too long, perhaps. And you will be thirsty now, I think, no?"

Opal turned her face away and would not answer. She shuddered as she tried to control her anger; the touch of his hands was still burning in her loins and the humiliation was more than she could bear. She turned back to look at him, hating that confident smile, and said coldly, "The ship's *highest officer*? You are scum, sir, and nothing more than that."

She expected him to strike her, and braced herself for the blow, which did not come. He laughed shortly, went to the corner of the tiny cabin, and picked up the huge clay water jar there as though it weighed nothing at all. He stood above her, smiling broadly. "Open your mouth, dear lady, a lovely mouth that holds so much promise of pleasure."

She turned her head away again. He tipped the heavy jar slowly, letting a stream of water pour down onto her hair, then traced a line with it down across her breasts, to her thighs and back again, and then up-ended it completely in a strong deluge over her. He put the vessel back in its place and opened the door, turning back to say quietly, "In a little while we will be at sea. I will send a man to release you then, and he will take you on deck for an hour or two, after which you will be returned to your cabin under guard. And tonight, I myself will bring you food and drink, and we will explore together the pleasures we spoke of."

He was gone.

Opal turned onto her side and tried to fight the cruel ropes that bound her. But the knots were sailor's knots, expertly tied, and she knew that she could not escape them.

She lay still, and thought with tears in her eyes of the agreeable young American, Jason Farn. "I would like so much to know you better, Miss Grant," he had said, and had spoken of watching the great ships together from one of the little waterfront cafes. And what had become of him? Dead, she was sure, on her own account, in a gallant and hopeless effort to save her from the fate that was overtaking her now.

She could hear the shouting through the barred porthole, and soon the rolling of the ship, the heavy creak of timbers, the cracking of the sails as they filled out, telling her that they were moving into rougher water.

An hour later, the door opened and a skinny young man peered in at her. He was very pale-faced and mean-looking, with an immature growth of beard, an untidy moustache, and a shock of unruly hair. He was dressed in ragged European clothes, a coarse linen shirt that might once have been white, with dark blue canvas breeches, bare legs, and leather sandals. There was a revolver in his belt as well as an opened clasp-knife. He scratched at his face as he stared at her, and said, "Eh, we do look a mess, don't we?"

An Englishman! From his accent, Opal thought he might be from Devonshire or Cornwall.

"I be Clayton, mum," he said, "come to take ye for a stroll on the decks, compliments of our fine Admiral Sinan. And I brought ye something to cover y'rself with, to hide y'r near-nakedness from the lascivious looks ye'll see out there." There was a heavy dark cloak thrown over his thin shoulders. He held it out for her to see, grinning ferociously at her. "A fine cloak, hardly a tear in it anywhere."

He knelt down close beside her. "We've all been warned, mum, not to lay a hand on ye, and that's a thing that personally I'd rather be found dead than doing, taking advantage of an innocent girl just because she's lying there all trussed up like a porker ready for the oven." Nonetheless, he clutched at her bare breasts for a moment and whistled. "Ah, they're good, aren't they now?"

Opal said furiously, "Cut me free, Mr. Clayton! That's what you were sent here to do, isn't it?"

"Aye, it is so." He laughed, showing his yellowed, broken teeth. "And that's what I'll do." He drew his knife and sliced through the ropes that bound her. She discovered that her feet and wrists felt completely numb. He helped her to her unsteady feet.

"Rub y'r hands together, mum, and ye'll bring some life back into them, and I'll dry ye off. Y'r soaked to the skin, ye'll get the pneumonia." He used the cloak as a towel on her, contriving to slip a hand under her skirt as he did so. She slapped his hand sharply.

"Eh, a little touch never hurt nobody."

She wrung the water out of her hair into a puddle on the wooden floor as he rubbed her body down vigorously with the cloak. She looked at him curiously. Surely he could not have been more than eighteen.

"You're English, Clayton?"

"Aye, from Torquay, and I've been a good sailor, man and boy, ever since I ran away from home these ten long years since." He looked glum. "Ten years, seven of them with the Barbary pirates. I started with them as a cabin boy, and seven years later . . . that's what I am today. A cabin boy."

Opal said scornfully, "And how can an Englishman work for these savages, will you tell me that?" He was still drying her, rubbing the coarse wool of the cloak over her body in long, rhythmic strokes. He grinned cheerfully. "It's easy," he said, "and it's a lot better'n starving on the docks, I can tell ye. And I've had a bellyful of that too. Ye'd be surprised what a man can put up with if he's hungry enough. Now, try and walk a few paces, mum, and see if the blood's started running again in them fine and glorious legs."

She moved around a little, and he steadied her, his hopeful hand searching for her breast again. She pushed it away mechanically. "And where are we going, Clayton, do you know that?"

He seemed surprised. "I told ye, mum, we're going on deck."

"No. The ship."

"Oh. Well, we're off to the summer palace at Djidji, that's an island down the coast a ways, and if this wind holds we'll be there late tomorrow morning. It's a place of great luxury. I've seen it. There, and if ye feel strong enough now, we'll take our exercise on deck." He held out the cloak for her. "Here, put this around ye and button it up. As I told ye, we've all been warned to be on our best behavior, but there be some rogues aboard, drunks, half of them. If they get a look at them fine tits o' yours they'll be rolling ye in the scuppers and to the devil with the lash that'll be waiting for them. Here, button it up tight around ye."

The cape shrouded her. It smelled strongly of some kind of cheap perfume, and Opal wrinkled her nose at it. "It smells disgusting!"

Clayton laughed. "I took it, on the admiral's orders, from one of the ladies."

"Ladies?" She said sharply, "You mean there are other ladies aboard this dreadful ship?"

"Only in a manner of speaking, mum," Clayton said. "It's not really the truth to call them *ladies*. They're whores, a dozen or so to service the men. The rougher ones among the sailors can be kept in shape if they can get pleasured once in a while. But they're a sorry lot this time out, not a single one among them I could get my pecker up for. Shall we go, mum?"

They went out into the narrow corridor, up the companionway, and into the fresh air of the late afternoon. Opal had her first sight of life aboard a Barbary pirate ship. She found it to be startling in the extreme.

The deck of the *Habou* was broad and untidy, cluttered with barrels of gunpowder, coils of rope, great stretches of canvas being stitched, nets being repaired, kegs of rum and arak. (The Berbers were Moslems, to whom alcohol was technically not permitted; but these were pirates, to whom the laws, either of the state or of the Koran, mattered not at all.)

Opal stared up in wonder at the great white sails that billowed out above her against a bright blue sky in which cotton puffs of cloud were drifting slowly, a picture of the utmost beauty which made her almost forget her present and very real dangers. The ship's motion was a very gentle one, a very slight roll with almost no dipping at all as the vessel ploughed into a moderate sea; the sound of the waves breaking against the wooden hull was a soft and caressing one, almost a lullaby, interspersed with the cries of a hundred gulls. There were porpoise breaking the water all around them, their dark arched backs appearing in unison, disappearing and reappearing once again. To one side, the placid blue water stretched out to infinity, empty of any other ships. On the other, the stark cliffs of the shoreline were a few miles away, climbing up to high, forested mountains. A few small boats slipped quickly through the water under amber-colored sails.

But when she turned her attention to her more immediate surroundings, she was glad of her uncouth bodyguard's presence.

The men around her were the most ill-assorted rabble of villains she could ever fear to set eyes on, a motley assortment of a dozen different nationalities with only one thing in common: They all looked evil. They wore rags of every conceivable type, torn scarlet, blue, green coats, with canvas shirts and ragged breeches, filthy trews or loincloths. They all carried guns, daggers, scimitars stuck into their belts, and they looked as though all they wanted to do was use them. Many of them were hopelessly drunk already, and two of them were fighting with knives drawn, rolling over and over on the deck. They stopped fighting momentarily to stare at her as she passed, and then continued their struggle again.

Further down the deck, a half-naked, screaming sailor, tied to a mast, was being flogged. Opal gasped at the sound of the rope and at the blood coursing down his back. Clayton grinned at her dismay. "A thief, mum. He stole another sailor's earring, and thieving's not a thing to be tolerated aboard the admiral's flagship."

There were other men high in the rigging, swarming like monkeys as they worked on the sails, letting out the reefs as the strong wind took them.

She heard a voice behind her, a laughing, mocking voice. "Enjoy your freedom, dear lady! Allah is good to us today! The sea is calm, the wind is fresh, the sky is blue."

She turned. Admiral Sinan was on the bridge above her, his feet widespread, his powerful hands gripping the railing as he stared down at her. "Soon," he shouted, "soon we will be together! Take comfort in the thought!"

She turned away. Clayton went with her to the stern, and she looked at the wash behind them that seemed to point to the distant shore. She could still hear the sharp, vicious thud of the flogging, but there were no more screams now. She was bleeding for him, and she whispered, "Oh God . . . how much more?"

The young boy looked at her in surprise. "How much more of what, mum?"

"The flogging."

"Oh, that." He shrugged. "Thievery carries forty lashes, but he won't live through it. He's a Tunisian. They're very weak people, the Tunisians, the weakest of all the Berbers. He'll die before they reach thirty, you'll see. Would you like to watch?"

"No! I do not wish to see it, it's—hateful!" She tried to detach her mind from it, and stared up at the rigging to watch the men there, not believing that they could move from rope to rope with such ease and assurance. The tops of the masts swung slowly from side to side with infinite grace. Gulls wheeled and screeched high above them, sometimes dropping down into the water with incredible speed, like plump arrows, coming up quickly with fish in their beaks. One of them landed on the rail close beside her, ignoring her as it began to tear a fish apart.

The sound of the flogging stopped, and there was a great

burst of raucous laughter. She heard the jubilant shout *"Talateen, talateen!"* Clayton grinned. "There, what did I tell ye, mum? Ye know what *talateen* means?"

"No. I do not speak Arabic."

"It means thirty. He died at thirty lashes." Opal began to sob. She heard the laughter and more shouting, and the splash as the body was tossed overboard. She said quietly, "Clayton?"

"Yes, mum?"

"As a fellow countryman, will you help me escape from this hell-ship?"

Clayton laughed heartily. "Escape? And how would ye do that, mum? Jump overboard and swim to the shore, five miles away or more? Can ye swim so far?"

"No, of course not!" she said tartly. "How would I know how to swim?"

"Then how?"

She gestured hopelessly. "I don't *know*, Clayton! A small boat, perhaps?"

He could not stop laughing. "So! I'll lower a boat for ye, and ye'll row it five miles to the beach in heavy seas, and be picked up at once and brought back aboard again in time to watch me being flogged to death like that poor devil there, for failing in my duties. No. There's no escape for ye, mum. I'll take ye back to y'r cabin now, and when the time comes, at about four bells of the first watch I'd say, the admiral will come to ye and take the pleasures he's set his heart on. And the only advice I have to offer ye is, don't fight him. He'll not take easily to any resistance."

She said desperately: "As an Englishman, Clayton! Help me, I beg of you!"

"No, I will not!" He was grinning suddenly, and he said, "Ye'll not have to worry about y'r cherished virginity, mum, he'll not take it. The story's all over the ship, the bey himself wants you a virgin, and not even the admiral will dare go against the bey's orders, it'd mean his head. Mark you, there's a great many ways a man can takes his pleasure of a woman without breaking through that little shield. And the admiral's always fancied himself as something of a ladies' man, he's very adept in these matters. He'll enjoy ye, mum, in more ways than ye can imagine. But don't worry about it none, ye'll still be a virgin when the bey gets his hands on ye."

"Clayton, I beg of you! If it's money you want—"

"Money? My life is more important to me. Come on."

He took her back down the companionway and locked her in the cabin. He found a box to sit on, and took up his position outside her door.

Opal discarded that dreadful, scented cape, and tried to cover herself by tying the torn threads of her dress together. She wondered, as her fingers worked, how she could avoid the trauma that was in store for her.

The bey of Algiers, the most feared ruler in all the world, wanted her, and he wanted her intact. Sinan had said it, and so had Clayton; in God's name, was the news of her supposed condition all over the ship? She shuddered.

She was not a virgin.

She lay on her back on the bunk, and thought with gentle melancholy of the three men who had lain with her.

There was Manos, the young Greek who had seduced her so expertly on the ship that was taking her from Constantinople to Athens. She found herself in love with him after only four days of his company. He was a man of astonishing good looks and great erudition, who whispered to her of the Greek gods and their loves as he maneuvered himself into position between her thighs, spread to receive his thrusting. He told her of Calliste, "the fairest of women," as he worked his loins to drive her to distraction. She fancied she could still feel his seed flooding into her. He had left her in the port of Piraeus. She had found an envelope on her dressing table in the morning, a short note that read: "For Calliste-Opal. Love is without price, but how will a beautiful lady live without money? I am a rich man, and it pleases me to share my wealth with those who have given me pleasure." There were fifty thousand-drachma notes enclosed with the letter. In tears, she had scattered them on the waters of the harbor.

Before him, there had been the slight and delicate Italian, whose name she could no longer remember. He was a student from the University of Florence, who had recited to her in mellifluous tones from the works of Dante. After a week, he had left a single red rose on the empty pillow beside her, and no word at all, even though he had loved her so passionately.

And before that, a man she had once loved but had grown to loathe; she trembled when she thought of him. It had been the most important, the most disastrous, and the most traumatic of all her experiences.

He was her stepfather, Sir Neville Grant, second secretary to the Foreign Ministry in Mr. Pitt's government, the scion of an ancient and honorable family that could trace its ancestry back to the sixteenth century. He was tall and slim, with a strong and athletic build that overindulgence never seemed to destroy, ruddy-cheeked, grey-whiskered, and desperately handsome, the secret incubus of uncounted London ladies. Unhappily, though he was a man of remarkable brilliance, too much good Spanish brandy was ruining him, though he would not admit its encroachment and held it valiantly in check. He could still make a powerful and sometimes furious speech in the hallowed, timbered chambers of the House, all of the members hushed, hanging onto his words as he gesticulated violently, making his points. Sometimes, there would be muttered comments about him from the floor.

"He's drunk again."

"Yes. And if he were not, this Act would be thrown out."

"And he stands firm, with nary a slur in his voice."

"Not even his logic impaired."

"When he dies, there'll be no need to pickle his bones in alcohol, they're already saturated."

Sir Neville was a powerful man, both physically and intellectually. In addition, he was bigoted, outspoken, and blessed with a devil-may-care attitude that endeared him greatly to London's sophisticated society.

He had been married to a lovely young Brazilian woman

named Margherita, who had milk-white skin, glorious auburn hair, and eyes almost the color of emeralds, a woman of the most voluptuous beauty, with whom he had fallen head-over-heels in love. She had been married before and had a very young daughter named Opal, a rather quiet and introspective child, seeming far older than her three years, with curly hair and bright, dark eyes that enchanted him. After a whirlwind courtship, he had married Margherita, and had embarked on four years of the most exquisite happiness with her.

Then, when Opal was seven years old, Margherita had succumbed to the measles. Before she died, she gave considerable thought to a very pressing question that concerned her lovely daughter.

In Margherita's native Brazil, race, color, creed, meant nothing at all. But her fifteen years' sojourn in London had taught her that here it was of the utmost importance among the upper classes to which she belonged.

And now that she was close to death, she worried about it.

She was a woman of very strong character, a character that Opal had inherited. As Sir Neville sat beside her in those last few hours, she took his hand and whispered to him, "Neville, dearest Neville . . . I must leave you with a thought that I fear will torment you sorely, but it is an obligation I cannot avoid. I must tell you that my mother, in Brazil, was . . . well, really, quite dark." She frowned. "No. I will not minimize the shock to you that I know it must be. She was *black*, Neville. My first husband, as you know, was English too, and I had hoped, for Opal's sake, that she would grow up to be . . . to be as white as I am. But she is beginning to show signs of her heritage, I fear. But please, dear Neville, love her none the less for it."

Sir Neville, that very English gentleman, could only stare at her, glassy-eyed, quite overcome by a feeling of impending disaster. The blood drained from his ruddy face.

And then Margherita died.

Sir Neville was in shock.

Thereafter, he would look Opal over surreptitiously every time she passed him, looking for a snubbing of her nose, for a thickening of her lips. Her skin was still no more than slightly olive when she was seventeen years old, her hair still straight and not crinkled at all.

She herself knew of the taint in her blood. A long time ago, Margherita had told her of it, saying fiercely, "But it must always be kept secret, denied even when it becomes apparent. This is England, not Brazil where these matters are of no consequence! With the best will in the world, the English have a certain contempt for colored blood, and you must not expose yourself to that contempt, ever!"

Frankly, Opal thought it was a lot of fuss about nothing. But with a kind of instinct that her mother might be right, she kept the secret, though she was sure that it mattered nothing. She grew into a very beautiful young woman.

She would stand in front of the mirror in her bedroom and examine her naked body, touching her breasts, which were firm, with very small nipples that responded quickly to her touch. She would turn her body and examine her hips, only slightly callipygian. Her legs were long and straight, smooth and unblemished.

She would retire to her bed, but sometimes she woke up in the night from her erotic dreams to find that her hand was between her thighs, her fingers caressing and bringing herself to climax with most un-English passion.

And then, there came that awful night. . . . It was an explosion of perverted passion of a kind she could never have imagined.

She was eighteen years old.

She had just bathed herself in the hip-bath that the servants had carried into her bedroom and filled with kettles of hot water, and she had dressed herself in a night-chemise and a woollen robe, her long hair hanging down over her shoulders, still wet from her bath. She had gone to the library to find a book she wanted to read, the poems of Robert Herrick. And her step-father was there, quite drunk but still working capably on a speech he had to make on the morrow in the House.

She pulled up short. "Oh, I'm sorry, Father," she said. "I didn't mean to disturb you. I didn't know you were still up."

He tried to focus his eyes on her. "It's no disturbance, child," he said, "to see my daughter."

"I'll only be a moment, Father. A book I need . . ."

"Take your time, child, you don't disturb me."

She crouched down at the shelves, searching. Her robe was half open, the neckline of her chemise very low on her breasts; Sir Neville fancied he could see a nipple, and he shifted his position slightly. The curve of her breast was outlined by the flare of the candles on his desk. Those same lights picked up the line of her profile, her forehead, her nose, her lips, her chin, and the line of her throat, sinking down to those enticing depths.

Sir Neville said heavily, "Your lips are getting to be so thick these days."

"My *lips*?" She turned to stare at him, startled.

"Pour me another brandy, child."

"Yes, Father, of course."

She rose to her feet lithely, took his empty glass and poured half an inch of brandy into it.

"No. More. An inch from the top. Don't you even know how to pour a brandy for a drinking man?"

Opal filled the glass and held it out to him, but he did not take it. Instead, he reached up and laid a hand on her breast, clutching through the cloth of her robe. She drew back in shock. He dropped his hand and seized her wrist and held it, drawing her closer to him. His voice was hoarse as he said, "Yes, thick lips, the lips of a nigger woman."

"A *nigger*? Father, please!"

His other hand was at her breast again, slipping under her robe and fondling her naked flesh. She gasped and tried to pull away from him, but he had risen from his chair and was bending her back over its arms, pulling her robe open and ripping the chemise away from her, exposing her upper body completely. She screamed as his lips began to suckle on her, while his hand ripped more of her chemise, and she shouted, "No, no, no! I'm your daughter!"

She fell to the carpet, and he atop her. He screamed, "No daughter of mine! A nigger woman! Good for one thing only! A nigger woman in my family!"

His lips were still at her tender breasts, his teeth searching out the soft undersides, and his hand pulled up what was left of the torn chemise, exposing her loins.

He fumbled with the drawstring of his breeches, breaking it in his excitement, and shoved them down to his knees.

Then he was between her soft thighs, forcing them apart with his knees. She screamed again, "No, no, *no*! I am your daughter!"

He did not even hear her in the paroxysm of his excitement. He seized her slender leg and threw it over his shoulder, and bore down on her, his naked muscle probing and finding the entry, thrusting himself into her with enormous and frightening power.

He screamed, "Lie still, damn you!" and thrust at her, filling her completely in one massive plunge. She caught her breath at the sudden, sharp pain, and then lay still, moaning softly, suffering the incursion as he began the slow, rhythmic motion of his loins. There was no thought in his drunken mind save the need for complete satisfaction, and he held himself back for as long as he was able, gritting his teeth in an effort to prolong his ecstasy. Finally he flooded into her. She lay quite still, thinking that the end of the world had come.

For a long while they did not move. Then he withdrew from her, flopped over onto his back, and said hoarsely, "Go to your bed, child. I will come to you again, very soon." Then he was fast asleep, and even snoring.

For a little while Opal lay still, not even covering herself, lying on her back beside him and staring dry-eyed up at the flickering shadows on the timbered ceiling.

Soon she pulled herself together and clambered to her feet. She pulled her woollen robe about her, and stared down at the man who had raped her, a stranger to her. She went upstairs to her room and locked the door.

She slept, weeping for her lost virginity. And in the morning, she left the house forever.

Now, Opal lay on the bunk of the *Habou*'s tiny cabin, and knew that more trauma was in store for her.

She thought: *He believes I am a virgin, and will save me for the pleasures of the bey of Algiers. But the other pleasures he spoke of?*

She was not naive enough to believe that the masculine demand for satisfaction was merely a matter of parting the thighs.

CHAPTER FOUR

High up in the rigging, Jason, searching the decks far below, had found her.

He said to his neighbor on the rope, an ancient Moroccan named Fousa, "The woman below there, friend. The lady, did you see her?"

The old man laughed. He was wearing baggy cotton pantaloons, a greasy red turban and a heavy leather belt with two daggers in it. His feet were bare, his scarred chest thin to the point of emaciation. He said, "You think I am blind when a beautiful woman passes by? I am not so old. She was brought here by the admiral's men, trussed up and with a length of sailcloth over her head. The rumor is that she's to be taken to the bey, an addition to his already considerable harem."

He was skillfully splicing a broken rope, working the spike swiftly with gnarled old hands. He showed his broken teeth in a wide grin. "But she is English, they say. And what would a man like Karim Abdullah want with an Englishwoman when there are so many good Arab girls at his beck and call? I had an Englishwoman once. I found her as satisfying as a watermelon."

"And the young man with her, who is he?"

"His name is Clayton," Fousa said. "A child of no quality at all except that he is very fast with his dagger. An Englander too, and not to be trusted, the kind of man who smiles and smiles until you turn your back, and then . . . that's when the knife is in his hand and between your ribs.

He kills, not for profit as a good man does, but for pleasure." He grunted. "I like a good killing as much as anybody, but I want to find profit in it. I'm an honest man."

The sun was setting, and the sound of the four bells of the first dog watch came ringing up to them from the wheelhouse. They heard the bo'sun's shouted, angy orders, and the new crew began to clamber up the rigging for the next shift. Jason was off duty for a while, to begin work again at eight bells, two hours from now. He knew the time was short for what had to be done; still, he could not make the first move till dark.

The seamen who had come off watch were lining up with their tin plates at the galley, being served a gray-colored swill made from ground millet, half-rotting vegetables, and a few pieces of unappetizing meat trimmings. But Jason did not join them. Instead, he wandered with apparent aimlessness around the boat, searching out what he would need, and he found it at last: an array of six large water casks lined up on the lower deck aft, secured with ropes and netting against rough weather. They were in view of the galley, but soon the flares would be lighted inside there, and this portion of the deck would be in relative darkness.

He continued his search, down the companionway to where there were a few small cabins, then down the ladder to the next level, where he knew there would be a few more. There were two very narrow corridors here, and in the second he found Clayton sitting on a box outside a closed door, paring his nails with his knife. The boy looked up at him with piercing eyes as he went on.

Now he knew where she was.

He went back to the water barrels and waited impatiently for a little more darkness. It fell very rapidly at this latitude. The wind was rising, and there were storm clouds gathering on the western horizon. He leaned on the railing and watched their ominous approach, worrying about them.

The flares in the galley were being lit, and he knew that the time had almost come; still he forced himself to wait.

At last, he quickly cut a length of rope and a patch of the netting, and fastened the net to one of the barrels with a couple of clove hitches. He prized out the bung and tipped the barrel over, watching the water drain out along the waterways and down through the scuppers into the sea.

This was the crucial time. If anyone should see him now he would have a fight on his hands, and his wound was still paining him. But soon the cask was empty and he had still not been observed. He drove the bung back home with the heel of his hand, hammering it in firmly. And now his preparations were complete. He walked back to the ladder, and went down to the lower level corridor. There were three tallows burning there now.

Clayton stared at him as he approached, his eyes wary and suspicious. This was not an area where deckhands would normally be seen. He rose to his feet and stood with his wiry arms at his side, waiting, balanced on the balls of his feet like a good fighting man, and Jason thought of Fousa's words: *He will smile and smile until you turn your back*. There was indeed a smile on that thin, pasty-colored face.

Clayton put out a hand and began to speak, and Jason smiled broadly and said, "I'm sorry, friend . . ."

He seized the boy's forearm and swung him round. As he saw Clayton's other hand go for the heavy revolver in his belt, he took hold of his scraggly neck and slammed his head back hard into the woodwork. He bit his tongue till the blood came at the sudden surge of pain in his side, and wondered if the wound had reopened with the sudden strain. But Clayton was lying at his feet, unconscious, and Jason found the key in his pocket and opened the door. He dragged the body inside quickly, and pushed the door shut as he tried to accustom his eyes to the dim light of a single candle. Then there was a shadow moving swiftly from the bunk, and he heard the astonished whisper. "Jason? Oh God, Jason, is it truly you?"

"Yes, it is I. Ssshhh . . ."

Opal ran to him and threw her arms around him, tears streaming down her face. She could not control the sudden emotion that swept over her. "I thought—I was sure that you were dead!"

He held her tightly, his strong arms around her, pulling her slim body close to his. "We have only a moment or two," he whispered, "and you must listen very carefully now." He spoke quickly, but she could not contain her excitement in spite of his urgency. "But what happened, how did you get here, how did you know where to find me?"

"All that must wait! Listen! We are three miles from shore, perhaps a little more than that, too far to swim, even if you knew how, which I doubt."

"No, I cannot."

"But you *cannot* stay aboard this ship. So we must leave it at once. I have a buoy on the lower deck, ready to toss over the railing as we jump into the sea with it."

He heard her gasp of alarm. "Have you the courage to do this? There are heavy trials ahead of you if you stay here much longer."

"Yes, yes! I have courage, I will do whatever you say!"

"Then come." It seemed to him essential that she know the difficulties, and he would not hide them from her. "We have to climb the ladder to the lower deck," he said, "and go aft where the galley is. There will be men there, and they may see us. They may challenge us, though I think not. They are simple seamen concerned only with getting as much food in their bellies as they can. We will pay them no attention at all, you understand?"

"Yes! I understand! Go on!"

"We will walk quickly, not running, which would betray us, to the stern. It will take only a moment or two, and I will be with you, my hand on your arm all the way. When we reach the water barrels there, one of which has been prepared and is our buoy, I will tip it over the railing instantly. And we will follow it overboard."

She was trembling with the thought of it, but her trust in him was absolute. He went on, "You must remember that the ship is under full sail and the wind is strong now, and what this means is, unless we follow it instantly, the buoy will be out of our reach even before we hit the water.

Though I can swim strongly, even dragging you with me, if we delay we may never reach it, and we will find not safety but a watery grave. There is netting on the barrel, there are ropes. Find a good grip and hold on tightly."

She was trying to stifle her fear, and he knew it. He smiled. "An adventure. Think of it as an exciting adventure."

She had one fearful, whispered question. "And the drop to the water?"

"Ten feet or so if we chance to hit the crest of a wave. If not, perhaps twice as much. Are you afraid?"

"No! As long as you are close beside me!"

"I will be. Then come. Remember that our safety depends upon our speed. We *must* not lose that buoy!"

"We will not on my account, I promise you. Oh, Jason!"

He was alive, and come again to rescue her! Her heart was pounding wildly as he held her. He was conscious that her budding breasts were almost naked; she had tied up her torn dress, but it gave her scant covering. He broke away from her, embarrassed by the surge in his loins, and put his hand on the latch of the cabin door, stepping over Clayton's body.

And then there was an iron grip at his foot, twisting it round savagely with such speed that he was hurled to the floor. He heard Opal scream, and then Clayton was astride him, straddling his chest, a knife in his upraised hand, descending toward Jason's throat as he seized the wrist and held it, twisting it around as he heaved his body off the floor. In spite of the awful onslaught of pain in his stomach, he was immensely stronger than the English boy. He reversed their positions immediately and thrust down on the fist that held the blade. Clayton dropped it at once, and it was instantly in Jason's hand. A moan came from Clayton's half-strangled throat: "Mother of God, save me now . . ."

Jason shifted his grip. He was aware that Opal had picked up the clay water jar and was holding it out like a weapon. Clayton was motionless. He touched the knife to the jugular vein and said: "A moment more of anger on me now, and you will have taken your last breath."

"Mother of God, I'm dead."

"But no . . ." Jason hesitated, looking into those frightened eyes and taking pity on them. He said, holding the knife steady, "An Englishman, by your speech?"

"Aye, from Devonshire. And you're a Yankee, a damned American. So kill me now, Yankee, I'm not afraid to die! Just make it quick."

"Your name? Clayton, I'm told?"

"You want to know a man's name before you murder him, is that it?"

"And how old are you, Clayton?"

"Eighteen, if it's any business of yours."

Jason said carefully, "I am tempted to kill you, Clayton, sorely tempted, there's a rage on me now that would shake Jesus Christ out of his complacency. But I find I can control it. I will not kill a child for his foolishness."

"I'm not a child, I'm a grown man."

"And a very foolish one. We are leaving here now. Will you give me your word that you will not raise a cry when we have gone?"

"No. I will not." There was a grin, suddenly, on that undernourished face; all the danger had gone, and Clayton was shrewd enough to know it. "And even if I gave you my word," he said, "it would mean nothing at all, for I'm a scoundrel at heart."

Jason lugged him to his feet and sighed. "Then in that case . . ." He drove a skillful fist at the boy's jaw, caught him as he fell, and deposited him gently on the timber planking of the cabin floor. He took Opal's hand. "Are we ready?"

Opal set down the jar. "Yes," she whispered. "Yes, we are ready for whatever lies ahead of us."

"And you are not frightened?"

"I will tell you a white lie and say that I am not!"

Jason threw open the door.

Admiral Sinan was there, his hand on the latch and a

look of startled surprise on his darkly handsome face. His fierce profile was lit by the dancing yellow flames of the corridor tallows.

Jason did not waste a single one of his precious moments. He struck out hard and fast with his fist, driving it into his powerful adversary's throat, an expertly aimed blow that sent the admiral reeling. As he went down, Jason grabbed at the revolver in the ornate leather belt, reversed it, and dealt him a blow to the back of the head that he would remember for the rest of his days. He knew that Berber heads were hard as cast iron, and he struck hard, remembering the awful events in the hotel room, with Sinan's thugs wrestling Opal to the ground.

He waited no longer, but took Opal's arm and ran with her to the companion ladder and pushed her ahead of him. He turned back as she climbed it and saw that the admiral was unconscious but already beginning to stir. At the top, they walked aft quickly. There was no one by the water barrels. The flares in the galley were burning; there was a new watch there now lining up for their swill. But here, in this tight corner adjacent to the railings and the pounding seas below them, all was in darkness.

He picked her up bodily and sat her on the rail, and whispered fiercely, "Do not look down!" He lifted the oak cask and tipped it overboard, and shouted, "Now!"

His arm was around her as they fell and struck the water, and Opal screamed out her shock, her limbs flailing in near panic. But the arm was a band of steel around her. He yelled, "I have it, I have it!"

The barrel bumped heavily into her head, and she almost lost consciousness, but he was quickly winding a rope around her waist. He shouted, gasping but calmer now, "Hold on, never let go of the net!"

She saw, to her astonishment, that the ship was more than a hundred yards away from them, its great sails majestic against a lowering sky, and then it was gone. Jason was already on the other side of their improvised buoy, reaching over it with strong arms and holding onto her tightly. He shouted, "There, I will stop it from rolling. Find a comfortable hold on the netting. There is a rope around your waist. You cannot sink!"

The monstrous waves were tossing them up and down in a great rhythmic cadence, and the violence of the motion terrified her. This was an alien environment for her.

Opal reached over the cask and clutched at Jason, finding great comfort in his presence. He was laughing. He said happily, "There, we are safe! Within the hour we will be washed ashore, and then, who knows? We will be *free*, and dependent upon our own wits for survival, a very satisfactory condition indeed! Are you frightened?"

"No."

"And are you fairly comfortable?"

"Yes."

"You are a wonderful woman, Miss Grant!"

"And you, Mr. Farn, are a wonderful man!"

"Your wet hair, streaming down over your shoulders, is a sight that charms me greatly."

"It must look awful."

"No! I find myself hoping for a break in the clouds, so that in moonlight I may see you better."

But he looked back over his shoulder at the angry clouds. The wind was changing. He said, "There is a loose end of the rope around your waist, can you find it?"

"Yes, I think so." She groped for it. "Yes, I have it."

"Pass it over to me."

She tried to drag the waterlogged rope up and could not.

"Inch by inch, travel your hand along it."

She did as he told her, and then his hand was on hers, finding the rope and dragging it over the barrel; she felt it tightening about her waist as he heaved on it. He said clearly, "I must tell you, Opal, the wind is changing. We should be carried ashore in an hour or so, but if it swings round a few degrees more, as well it might, it will take much longer. Are you strong enough to hold on?"

"With you to help me, I am strong enough to hold on till kingdom come!"

His answer was lost on the howling wind. The cadence

of the waves was mounting to a furious up-and-down motion of the utmost violence, and at the crest of the dreadful waves she tried to make out the dark silhouette of the shoreline. It looked further away than ever; was it only because of the darkness? No, they were being swept inexorably out to sea. There was only a great watery emptiness all about them, rising and falling from tremendous heights and dropping down again with stomach-turning suddenness into the unfathomable depths of the great waves. And all the time, she heard the howling fury of the wind.

They were alone on the high seas, supported only by an empty oak barrel, and very close to death.

The minutes slipped by, and then the hours, as they hung over the cask like wet rag dolls. The shore line had disappeared altogether; there was nothing in their sight except rhythmic mountains of furious water.

And then, the full ferocity of the storm hit them.

It picked them up and flung them from one wave to another, and down into those terrifying depths again, where the waters rose above them for ten, twenty, even thirty feet, with frightening crests high above their heads. It seemed that half of the time they were under water, gasping, their lungs bursting. The barrel was a cork on the water, but it was still supporting them. Jason shrieked, "Courage, Opal! We are still safe! An empty barrel cannot sink!"

She could not answer him. She wanted to say, "As long as we die together," but her mouth was full of water. The black clouds seemed to be touching the waves that rose up to meet them, and the darkness was absolute. For an hour, or two or three or perhaps even four, they were tiny and insignificant toys swept this way and that on the power of the sea.

There was a shadow looming over them, black against the gray of the sky. Could it be a mountain, out here in the middle of nowhere?

And then, from under the water, a barnacled reef came up with terrifying power, and smashed their barrel to splinters. Opal tried to scream but could not; she was under ten feet or more of rampant water. She was conscious only of a strong arm around her, and there was another hand at her face, covering her mouth and her nostrils so that she could not breathe, though all she wanted to do was gulp in great draughts of seawater and die, just to ease the intolerable pain in her lungs.

She lost consciousness completely, although she was trying to cry out, "Jason, Jason, where are you?"

She was lying on her face on hard, dry sand, and there was a strong pressure on her back and she was vomiting seawater. She tried to move her head, and unknown hands were there instantly, twisting it to one side again, and a comforting voice was coming to her out of limbo. "No, do not move your head . . ."

She fell into a coma again. When she awoke from it, strong arms were around her, dragging her into shade from a very hot sun that was burning her. The first thought that came to her was that she was half-naked, her lovely silk dress in shreds that did not hide her body at all, her breasts quite exposed. But gentle hands were there, seeking to draw up the material and hide them, as though her modesty were all that mattered now! She stared up into Jason's eyes.

"Are you conscious? Are you aware now, dear Opal?"

It was very hard for her to speak. "Yes, yes, I am conscious, I am awake. Jason, oh Jason . . ."

His hand was gently touching her cheek, but there was a look of extreme anxiety in his face. He said gently, "You should, in truth, rest now, you were nearly drowned, and I blame myself for it. But I cannot allow you any rest at all. We must move away from here, at once!"

"Move? No, I do not . . . not want to move now . . ." She saw that they were on a wide and empty beach, where a few tall palm trees leaned out over a gentle surf. A few yards behind them was the beginning of a dense forest, close by the mountain that towered up towards the hot blue sky. She shook her head helplessly. "No, I want to sleep here, wherever we may be, and know that you are beside me."

"No, we cannot!" He was staring up at the mountain, a look of anxiety on his handsome face. "As for where we are, I will confess that I do not know. But when we were washed ashore, I saw a lone cameleer among the trees of the mountaintop there."

"A cameleer?"

"One of the bey's soldiers. He watched us for a while, well hidden, as he thought, among the shrubbery, and then he rode away. It means that very soon there will be a patrol searching for us, and so we must find a place to hide until we can decide what to do."

All she wanted to do was sleep! But he was reaching for her, grasping her shoulders. "We *must* hide, Opal," he said. "And now!" Her eyes were drooping, exhaustion overcoming her. His arms were around her, pulling her close, and there was great comfort in his embrace. He said quietly, "We must hide in the forest from the immediate danger, for the rest of the day, perhaps even longer. When we know it is safe, we will return to the beach at night and find a village. We will steal a boat and sail to Gibraltar, which must lie to the west of us, wherever we may have landed. Gibraltar is a British fortress, and you will be safe there." He smiled. "It is a fine solution to this pressing problem."

How assured he sounded! He even laughed softly as he helped her to her feet. She was still a little unsteady, and his support was a great comfort to her. They walked up the slope of the beach and into the dense forest, and laboriously began to climb the mountain, hand over hand, searching out roots for handholds.

The moon was very bright. They found an eminence and looked back. There was a patrol of a dozen soldiers on horseback where they had been swept ashore. One or two had dismounted, and were bringing staves of the broken barrel from the surf.

Jason and Opal watched them for a while, and then began the long climb again. At last they came to a great stone lighthouse, lit by charcoal fires, that stood at the edge of the promontory. Jason stared at it and whispered, "Oh God, *no*!"

Opal's eyes were wide, mirroring his apprehension. "You know it?"

He nodded. "Yes, I know it. We are not on the mainland at all! We are on the island of Djidji, where the bey has his summer palace! I have brought you to his threshold!"

He was aghast. She took his hand. "It was not you who brought me here, Jason. It was the wind and the tide. All you did was save my life. And we are still free to decide our own destinies."

He took a long, deep breath. "Yes," he said. "And that is how it will remain." He scratched his head like a puzzled schoolboy, a gesture that somehow touched her deeply, and said at last, "Well, in truth it matters very little where we are. Nothing has changed, and our plan will remain the same. There are fishing villages all along the coast here too, and plenty of unattended boats to be found." And then, incongruously, "Are you hungry?"

"I am starving. I feel that I have not eaten for a month."

"Yes, and I am too, another discomfort we share together. And there is nothing to eat here on the mountain."

"Then we will stay hungry. It is a very small thing."

"Yes, you are right, a small thing."

They continued on their way up the mountainside, and found a cave at last, small at the entrance but large inside, with promising tunnels that led down into the depths of the earth. There was a tiny ledge in front, and Jason lay there on his belly and watched the shoreline, bathed in the brilliant light of the moon. There were many soldiers down there, searching.

"There are more patrols than I expected, and we may have to stay here longer than we planned. By tomorrow, I think they will have given up on their search of the beach, and if so . . . they will move up here. That is when *we* move down *there*. So now we must rest to recover our strength."

He stripped off his jacket and laid it down for her, and

said gravely, "It is no feather mattress, but will you accept it as a bed?"

She was looking at him with very solemn eyes. "Thank you, Jason. But will you not need it? The night will be cold."

In the darkness, her semi-nakedness was all the more enticing. As she sat down on his jacket, he stripped off his cotton shirt and slipped it over her shoulders, ignoring her half-hearted protests. She was so glad to be modestly covered again. He pulled it down around her waist and rolled up the sleeves for her, and said, laughing, "There, a night-chemise as good as you have ever worn, though perhaps not as delicate as those you must be accustomed to."

She touched his bare chest. "And now, you . . . you will freeze to death."

"Never. The night is warm enough." He hesitated. "And there is great warmth in your company."

She lay down on his jacket in the sand, and found his hand, and whispered, "How can I ever thank you, Jason? There are simply no words to tell you how I feel."

"No words are needed. Will you sleep well tonight?"

"Yes, I am sure of it. Our adventure has left me exhausted."

"Then close your eyes. I will be close beside you."

"But first, there is so much you have to tell me!" They whispered together like children in the dark of the night. "How did you know where to find me, how did you contrive to board that dreadful ship?"

He laughed softly. "I am no stranger to Algiers," he said. "I have been here many times before. And I have friends in the Casbah, where everyone knows everyone else's business, even the most closely guarded secrets. The sale of information in the Casbah . . ." He sighed. "Only a few years ago, we were at war with Algiers, and today, the French and your own people are convinced that a new war will break out very soon, perhaps with America again, so the spies are constantly at work. It was not difficult to find out what had become of you."

"But what brought you here in the first place?"

"I was a marine once. This time, I came here on the *Philadelphia*, a flagship of the U.S. Navy, the famous Captain Bainbridge in command. You have heard of Captain Bainbridge?"

"No, I fear not."

"Well, he's one of the most highly respected of our officers. He was bringing America's yearly tribute to the bey of Algiers, nearly a million dollars, and if this were not enough of an indignity for so great a man . . ." He broke off, scowling at the memory, and went on, "As a correspondent for the American press, I was present when Captain Bainbridge handed over the box containing all the money. Karim Abdullah, the bey, made the captain stand there like a messenger boy while he had it all counted, three times, to make sure it was correct. And then he ordered Bainbridge to sail in the *Philadelphia*—the most honorable of all our ships!—to sail to Istanbul with routine dispatches. Bainbridge protested, of course, but the bey is a monster, a cruel and arrogant man, and he said to the captain, 'You will do as I tell you to do, or your ship will be sequestered, your officers and crew imprisoned and held for special ransom. Remember, Bainbridge, that you are my slave, as all Americans are my slaves.' These were his precise words, Opal, well recorded, so that posterity may know how easy it is for the Arabs to blackmail us if we allow them to do so. And there was nothing the skipper could do save accept this further humiliation. The *Philadelphia* sailed for Constantinople. I myself stayed behind in Algiers."

"I am so fortunate that you did." Opal's hand was tight in his. "And then . . . how did you find me so quickly?"

"My friends in the Casbah helped me."

He told her almost all that had happened, without mentioning Munia, who had discovered the secret for him. He told her of the time he had spent in forced inactivity, waiting for a partial healing of his wound; of the deadly game of Berber politics; of his signing on with the *Habou* as a deckhand.

He was crouched over her in the mouth of the cave, the moonlight catching the rippling muscles of his bare chest as she looked up at him. She held tightly onto his hand, and whispered, "And your wound? It cannot have healed so quickly."

"Not yet, though I am well on the way to recovery." There was an expression of the deepest anguish on his face. "If a serving-girl, a young child, had not chanced to enter your bedroom—I think it was the damaged door that aroused her curiosity—then God alone knows what might have happened to both of us. Out of the goodness of her heart she helped me back to life when I was surely bleeding to death. And for her pains—she was murdered."

"Oh God . . ."

"By Sinan, the evil Admiral Sinan, or his men."

He fell silent for a while, remembering the sandals poor Suri had wanted. He sighed, and said at last, "But now, you must sleep. Tomorrow, or whenever it may be, there will be a hard journey ahead of us." He smiled again, trying to comfort her. "In an adventure of this nature, we must take one step at a time. We have a good hiding place, a point of vantage from which to watch the beach, and we will see what must be done next."

"And you must sleep now too, Jason."

"For a little while, perhaps."

She whispered, trembling with a curious kind of excitement, "Will you lie close beside me?"

"If I may. If it will not be too . . . too intimate."

"So that . . . if I wake, I will not feel alone."

"Very well, then." He stretched out his long limbs at her side, and murmured before he closed his eyes, "Sleep well, dear Opal."

"Goodnight, dear Jason. And my thanks."

"Ssshhh. Sleep."

She closed her heavy-lidded eyes, and felt safe. He was careful to avoid too close contact with her, just holding onto her hand to assure her of his presence. But after a little while he drew closer and put an arm across her, holding lightly onto her shoulder, squeezing it once affectionately. Soon, he put the hand at her waist instead, and let it rest there for a while.

Was she truly asleep?

He found that there was an unaccustomed lump in his throat as his hand crept upward and found her breast. She made no movement at all, and soon he slipped the hand into the deep V of the shirt and trembled at the touch of her naked flesh, so soft and smooth and resilient yet firm. The pounding in his loins was intolerable, and he gently eased himself still closer to her, his strong manhood against her hip; she did not stir.

He was not accustomed to indecision, and yet he could not drive away an awful feeling of guilt as his fingertips fondled her. Her tiny nipple hardened under his touch, light as a feather, and her breath came a little faster. His delicate caress moved down over her stomach and found her soft thighs, and then the junction between them. She still made no move. He held his hand there, quite still, and let his mind wander into fantasy. At last he whispered, his voice hoarse, "Are you awake, dear Opal?"

There was no answer, and he slowly withdrew his intruding hand, ashamed of what he was doing. Then there were slim fingers around his wrist, moving it down again as she parted her thighs very slightly. Her voice was very, very small. "Yes, I am awake. And I will not resist you, Jason. I owe you so much, so very much, all that I can give and more."

She heard him catch his breath. "*Owe* me?" He froze. He said huskily, "You owe me nothing, Opal!"

She knew that she had used the wrong word, that without even thinking she had wounded him deeply, and she bit her lip till the blood came. But the damage was done, and he moved his hand away from her and laid it again at her waist. He almost turned away from her, but there was nothing in his character of sullen anger, and so he lay quite still. She was trying to find words to soften the hurt, and could not.

"Oh, Jason . . ." There was a sob in her voice.

He said quietly, "Forgive me, Opal. Forgive me. And sleep now."

She moved his hand from her waist up to her breast, and held it there. Then she pulled away the shirt so that her naked flesh was under his touch again. He whispered, "Goodnight, dearest." She did not answer him. There was just the faintest circling of her hand over his. He held her firmly and closed his eyes.

He awoke once in the night, iron-hard again; but that stubborn streak in him would not allow him to move towards her as he so greatly wanted, even though he knew that, in her sleep, she was weeping silently.

They lay together side by side, and soon their arms were around each other again, as though to drive away all the demons of the night.

And restlessly, they slept.

CHAPTER FIVE

When Opal awoke in the morning, the sun, low in the sky, was a beautiful red-gold color, streaming into the cave that was their refuge.

She was conscious at first, although still half asleep, of a sweet smell that reminded her of holidays on the South Downs of her native England, of picnics in the green hills and the woods, where as a child she had picked great baskets of . . .

Wild strawberries!

She was suddenly wide awake. Jason was crouched over her, grinning broadly and dangling a bunch of them under her nose. He said, laughing, "Breakfast!"

"Strawberries, I don't believe it!"

"Yes, the mountain is full of them."

"And do we have clotted cream from Devonshire, and amber-colored sugar from Barbados as well?" She could not help laughing at his excitement.

"No, but there is water close by, a good clear mountain stream. But I have nothing to carry it in, so I must take you to it. If, indeed, there is any left. I drank so much that the whole river is surely dried up. And you must be dying of thirst."

"I am. But first . . ."

She reached up and pulled his head down to hers, and kissed him on the lips. She whispered, "Dear Jason . . . we were both very foolish last night, were we not?" It had been preying on her mind all through the long hours of the darkness.

He sighed. "I was, yes. Like a silly, sulking schoolboy, and I am deeply ashamed. But you . . . you were not."

"Oh, but I was! I had a good thought, but I expressed it so very carelessly. The thought was: *we have gone through so much together* . . ."

He interrupted her. "Ssshhh. Taste the fruit, it's delicious."

She sat up and nibbled at the berries. "Mmm . . ."

"I left you for a while just as the sun was coming up. We are very high on the mountain, but behind us it is higher still, and there are soldiers up there, on foot and on horseback. They are beating through the woods, but they are moving away from us, and this must mean that they passed us during the night. We were very lucky. Though there may still be others on this lower slope."

"Then we must stay here, hidden."

"Yes, of course. Now, far below us on the beach, there is a village, just a dozen huts or so, with some boats in the surf. But we cannot go there during daylight, so we will hide here for the rest of the day."

"Can we go to the stream? To drink and perhaps even *wash*? There is great pleasure in feeling . . . well, if not exactly clean, at least not quite so grubby." It seemed such a trivial matter!

But he said, smiling, "Then come." He helped her to her feet, took her to the cave's entrance, and pointed. "There, by the hazel trees. But we'll go this way, among the bushes, on our hands and knees, being very careful not to disturb the foliage. The soldiers are far above us, but the Berbers have eyes like hawks, and they must not see the slightest movement."

The stream ran under an overcrop of granite. It was icy cold. Opal lay on her stomach and scooped water gratefully into her mouth, drinking deeply. When she was satiated, she took off the cotton shirt, lowered the torn silk dress to her waist, and splashed herself lavishly. She saw him looking at her as though he were not quite sure whether she wanted privacy now. She said quietly, "I will not hide myself from you, Jason."

He replied steadily, "Nor will I turn away. You are so lovely, Opal! A dream come true!"

"It has not come true yet. But it will, for both of us."

"Yes. I am sure of it."

He knew that the Rubicon had been passed, that there would be no more awkwardness between them now. When she picked up the shirt again, he took it from her and dried her with it, then slipped it over her head, smoothing it down over her slender body, pulling her close and kissing her. Her hands roved over his bare and muscular torso. She touched the bandage around his waist and whispered, "And the pain is still there?"

"Very little now. In a day or two it will all be gone. Come, it is dangerous to remain here."

They crawled back to the cave. Jason carefully obliterated all traces of their presence there, scraping the sand to clear it of their footprints, even removing the tiny stalks and the leaves of the strawberries they had eaten. Then they chose one of the passages at random and entered it, crawling on their hands and knees to follow a tortuous path deep down under the mountain, sometimes lying on their stomachs to drag themselves under overhanging rock, deeper, deeper, always deeper. Once in a while a shaft of unexpected light streamed in from a crevice above them. At last light slanted down from a tiny bore-hole, illuminating, with a strange and ghostly light, a great cool cavern where water dripped from long stalactites that hung from the roof high above them. Opal gazed in awe, and she whispered, "It's beautiful."

Where the beam of light struck them, the stalagmites that rose up from the floor of the cavern were an iridescent amber color, streaked with shades of blue and gold and ivory. There was a great lake, shining with phosphorescence.

They clambered up the broken wall, hand over hand, to a high, wide shelf, and looked down on the shimmering spectacle below them breathlessly. Jason examined the area behind them, where a strange kind of moss was growing, very thick and smelling faintly of verbena, and dry to the touch. He whispered, "If they find the cave, as they might, then we will see them if they enter the cavern, though I do not think they will. The Berbers are fearless people, but very superstitious. They might think that demons live here, so they won't come inside. We will wait here for the rest of the day. The ray of light from the roof there will be our timepiece."

"And can we talk here safely?"

"In whispers, yes."

He laid his coat down on the moss for her to sit on, and sat beside her, an arm around her waist. They watched the slow drip of water from the stalactites splashing into the pool below with a tiny, musical sound. It was breathtakingly beautiful. Opal whispered, "I could spend days, even weeks here, just marvelling . . ."

"And are you cold?"

"No."

"Outside, the sun is searing the mountaintop now."

He lay down on his back and looked up at the lovely profile of her face. Her lustrous eyes shone in the blue light, which seemed to trace a delicate line over her high cheekbones. She turned to ease her position, and touched his chest with her fingertips, tracing idle little lines over his muscles. She leaned down and kissed him, sure of the course she was taking now, and he responded hungrily. The kiss lingered, and she felt a fierce determination. She said to herself, *This time, there will be no drawing back. I will not allow it*. She was resolved to take the initiative, and her fingers played with the buckle of his leather belt, unfastening it with slow and deliberate movements. She slid her hand down under it, to find his strong manhood, erect and pulsating wildly, and closed her fingers around it, savoring its heat. She began to moan softly with her desire for him, kissing his eyes, his cheeks, his lips.

In a few moments she sat up again and took off the heavy shirt, slipped her torn dress down to her waist, and lay down beside him, waiting for him to make the next move. His hand went to her breast, fervently, and then his lips were there, suckling on her as though trying to draw her very soul from her, while his fingers were molding the soft undersides and he was gasping, fast losing what little control he had left. She felt her skirt being raised up above her hips, a hand there exploring as she opened her thighs to his touch. She too could no longer control herself, and she gasped, "Now, now, now, my love!"

There was a dreadful moment of waiting as he struggled out of his breeches, but when he was naked he lay atop her and began the urgent probing at once, seeking her out and then thrusting fiercely into her, quite unable to hold himself back for the preliminaries he had always thought to be mandatory. But mandatory was a word that presupposed control, and his ardent desire for her had carried him far beyond the limits of control. She gasped at his power as he entered her, a young god with the strength of a lion, and she thrust her hips up to meet his impulses, welcoming them and feeling him flooding into her as the fierce spasm came on her. Her fingernails were raking his broad and powerful back, her long legs were wrapped around him, her ankles locked together as she sought to drive him deeper into her, containing him completely, refusing to let him go even after the sensation within her of the gentle softening, draining herself on him again and again till there was no life left in her.

They lay still at last, wrapped in each other's arms. She whispered, "My love, my love, my true love now."

"Yes, and for ever." He began to withdraw from her, but she held him tightly, and said, "No! You must lie still now. I want this moment to last and last." She began to work her hips against him, slowly and gently, and could not control her shuddering.

He had scarcely slept during the night, preferring to keep a close watch. But now he knew that there was safety for them in this ghostly hiding place, and he found utter contentment in the embracing warmth of her silken body. He slept for a while, relishing the close confinement, and awoke to love her again and then again.

They whispered endearments to each other, and Opal knew that something very strange was happening to her.

The realization came to her with a sense of shock, and she fell silent for a while, enjoying the touch of his gentle lips at her breast, and thinking to herself, *Have I spent so much time, and traveled so far, in a subconscious effort, never before fully realized, to put a broken life together? And have I at last succeeded?*

She knew that it was the truth.

The relief she felt in the strong arms of this good young man who had taken her not only from the evil clutches of the pirate Sinan but also out of herself was more than she could bear. She began to weep tears of great relief, and she murmured happily, "I love you so dearly, my Jason."

He smiled, his eyes on fire. "I am proud of your love! And mine for you . . . there are no words to describe it. Nothing shall ever part us, I promise you."

The only sound in the great cavern was the gentle, hollow insistence of water dripping into the phosphorescent blue grotto, as it had done for ages past.

The day passed all too quickly. She lost count of the times they loved. Gently, preparing her first with a skill and a thoughtfulness that both delighted and astonished her, he brought her undiminished passion almost to its climax before he slowly, gently entered her, bringing her again and again to the ultimate fulfillment.

When the slanting beam of light from the bore-hole in the roof told them that the sun was going down, they rose and embraced again, and climbed slowly, hand in hand, back up the trail they had followed to this haven. They waited at the cave's entrance for darkness to fall completely, and then made their cautious way down the mountainside, moving stealthily among the trees and the dense shrubbery until they reached the shoreline.

Here, they could not talk even in whispers. They crouched under a clump of gorse and waited, watching, examining every shadow. There were a few small huts at the water's edge, only a hundred feet or so away, dark and shuttered, with no sign of life save the faint glow of a tallow escaping through a chink in the shutters here and there. Half a dozen fishing boats were drawn up on the sand or bobbing at anchor, and there were rows of netting set out to dry or awaiting repairs.

Jason stared at one of the little craft, some twenty feet in length and sturdily built, with a single sail, lowered but not properly reefed. This was the boat he would steal, and he wondered how he could recompense its impoverished owner for his loss. He decided that time would find an answer to that question. It was in two feet of water and slightly on its side, and he was sure he could launch it quickly. He put his mouth to Opal's ear and whispered, "The dinghy on the left there. When we reach it, climb quickly and quietly aboard and lie down in the bottom. It will take me only a moment to free her, another moment to raise her sail. Come."

He took her arm, and they ran silently over the intervening sand. The night was dark, the moon behind a cloud, and the darkness was a great comfort to them.

But there was a watcher waiting.

The watcher was lying on the untidy thatch of one of the small huts, and he had been there, sent by his officer, ever since the sun had gone down. He watched Opal clamber into the boat, and saw Jason pick up the anchor and pull it quietly aboard. In accordance with his instructions, he sounded a shrill whistle.

At once, a score of men came running out of the house where they had been concealed. Some of them carried flares, and they all had their muskets or scimitars ready. They gathered around the two startled fugitives at the water's edge.

One of them, a lieutenant of the bey's armies, stepped forward. He was a tall and commanding figure in the clouded moonlight, bearded and wild-looking, with a patch over one eye. His naked sword was in one hand, a dagger in the other. He said harshly, in passable English: "You come with me now. If you resist, I kill you both. *Y'allah!*"

Resist? The odds were far too high. Jason's eyes went to the friendly forest, but the circle of guns and naked blades was too close about them for any attempt at escape. He could only look at Opal with a desperate pleading for forgiveness in his eyes. He had brought her into this trap, and there was no way out of it.

Rough hands separated them, bound them with ropes, and pushed them roughly towards a bullock cart. Then there was a long wait while the bullock was brought from its shed. Jason rolled over closer to Opal on the straw that lined the cart, and brought his hands, bound behind his back, close to hers, searching for the knots in a desperate, hopeless endeavor.

He heard a shout. One of the soldiers was standing over him. He saw the butt of the rifle coming up and down again on the side of his head, and with the blow, he lost consciousness.

The last thing he heard was Opal's terrified screaming.

In the summer palace, Karim Abdullah, the bey of Algiers, was holding a meeting.

As ruler of the most powerful of the Barbary States, it was his dubious privilege to try to hold this loose amalgam of volatile and jealous countries together. It was not an easy task.

He was in his fifties, a gross, cruel, ruthless potentate, with the power of life and death in his hands, to be used at his whim. He was a rich, venal barbarian, greatly feared by his subjects and by the European consular officials who had the unhappy duty of trying to deal with him. And his ruthlessness was backed by the largest pirate fleet the world had ever seen. Every inlet along the rocky coastline was infested with his ships, and the Mediterranean Sea was thick with them all the way from the Riff Mountains in Morocco, clear across more than two thousand miles of trade waters to Constantinople. American and European merchantmen used these routes, but only at the bey's pleasure, and only as long as tribute was paid promptly for a restraint that was not always kept.

Quite often, regardless of whatever treaties might be in force, the bey would send out his ships with the order:

Sink any foreign merchantman you may find, being careful first to seize its cargo. Let them know my strength and my hatred of them.

But Karim Abdullah Bey was in a good mood today. One of his frigates had just taken a Greek freighter in tow, with most of its crew dead and its cargo intact, and its cargo was three long tons of gold bars, a veritable fortune.

His guests at this meeting were three, all of them surrounded by sycophantic advisors.

Ismail Assada, the bashaw of Tunis, ruled his country by virtue of his deviousness. Mussa bin Senussi, the pasha of Tripoli, a tall and angry man in his late forties, was always spoiling for a fight. Abed Rashid, ambassador at large from Morocco, was a soldier, widely known as Abed the Bloodthirsty. He fancied that no woman could resist his brandishments.

They were all seated cross-legged on a luxurious carpet in the conference room of the palace, dressed in their most splendid robes. Slaves poured them interminable little cups of strong black tea and kept the trays of honey-dripping sweetmeats refilled.

The courtesies had long been dispensed with, the trivial matters all attended to, and it was time for a project that was very dear to the bey's heart. He sipped his tea and said, a little nonchalantly as though the matter were of no importance at all, "My very good friends, I have excellent news for you on the matter of the British tribute. As you know, I have been deeply concerned that the money England pays us has for so long remained at an insignificant level."

The bashaw of Tunis, a nervous man, grunted. He said glumly, "I have told you often, dear Karim, that if we demand another few pounds from the British, they'll opt for war against us. And they're the only people in the world with more fighting ships than we have. We can't risk a war with England. Prime Minister Pitt knows, as President Adams knows, that bribery is far cheaper than war; but push them too far, and they might well declare war again. And then where will we be?"

Karim Abdullah said smugly, "There will be no war. I have been trying for some time now to find ways of raising the tribute without that risk. And I have found it."

The bashaw did not want to listen; he hated the trend the discussion was taking. He said sharply, "Are you aware that Britain's Indian army under General Wellesley has just overthrown the last threat to British rule in India? And that England therefore now has a vast and well-trained army with no one to fight? An army that could be thrown against *us*? As well as the ships to put them ashore?"

Karim Abdullah popped a date and honey confection into his mouth, and held out his fingers for a slave to wipe. He said carelessly, "Oh yes, I have heard of Tipu Sahib's unfortunate defeat at Wellesley's hand. But in the European philosophy, my dear, *dear* Ismail, it is not soldiers who make war. It is their politicians who order out the troops."

"Ha!" Abed the Bloodthirsty was delighted. "Yes," he said, "it is the politicians who order the fighting to begin. Nincompoops who never wielded a sword in their miserable lives, and would be terrified if they ever saw one in the hand of an angry man!"

Mussa bin Senussi raised a didactic finger. "But Ismail is right, Karim Abdullah. We must be careful not to push the British beyond the point of their endurance. I too cannot afford a war."

The bey of Algiers was licking honey from his moustache and clapping his hands for more tea. As a slave poured it for him, he said slyly, "You cannot *afford* it? Then if you are so poor, can I count on your vote in a little scheme I have to raise England's tribute very considerably?"

The bashaw of Tunis said suspiciously, "What little scheme?"

"A new development, my dear Ismail. Allah has been kind to us, in his great wisdom."

"Allah is always kind and wise, Karim Abdullah."

The bey chuckled, pleased with himself. "He has sent to us an English milady," he said, "whose name is Opal

Grant. She is a young woman of quite ravishing beauty who is a member of the decadent English aristocracy. Now, her father is Sir Neville Grant, second secretary to the Foreign Ministry in London, the arm of government with which we deal in the matter of tribute. That is to say, my dear friends, that Miss Grant's father is a parliamentarian of tremendous authority. And his daughter is . . ." He broke off, relishing his good news. He went on, "His daughter is, in a manner of speaking, my prisoner."

Abed the Bloodthirsty, a step ahead of the others, said, "Ah . . ."

"As I think you all know," the bey continued, "my chief agent in London is a man named Horuc, a man of the most persuasive abilities, second only to those of his master, Admiral Sinan, who serves me very well indeed. Sinan has persuaded me that by apprehending this young woman we can hold her hostage against her father's good intentions on our behalf." He shrugged eloquently. "Really, such a powerful voice speaking for us! And it is merely a question of informing Sir Neville, who has the ear of the prime minister himself, I might add, of what might happen to his daughter if he does not add his strong voice to those of the few politicians we have already been able to bribe." They were all hanging on his words. "Do I make the situation clear, my good friends?"

Ismail Assada of Tunis was a very shrewd man. He said, worrying about it, "Your words, dear Karim Abdullah, were: my prisoner *in a manner of speaking.*"

The Bey replied cheerfully, "Yes, a manner of speaking, but a prisoner nonetheless. She was a captive aboard Admiral Sinan's ship. It seems that she escaped."

"What? How can that be?"

"Admiral Sinan," the bey said carefully, "is a man I would trust with my own very valuable life. Nonetheless . . ." He sighed. "Sinan keeps a score of homing pigeons aboard his ship, for instant communication. He does not know that two of those pigeons are mine, that one of his pigeon-masters is in my direct employ, to keep an eye, so to speak, on whatever machinations dear Sinan might have up his sleeve. And so, I have been informed that the lady in question escaped from the ship with the help of a sailor who is not a sailor at all but an American journalist and therefore quite possibly a spy."

"And how, in the name of Allah," Ismail Assada said, exploding, "can an escape be effected from a ship under sail?"

"With the assistance of an empty waterbarrel to carry them ashore. My men found the remains of the barrel here on Djidji Island itself."

"Then she is dead!"

"No. Together with her sailor-journalist, she was recaptured just a short while ago. And now, I am waiting for Sinan to contrive some way of bringing her to me himself, if only to assure me of his constant devotion to my interests."

There was a little silence. Abed the Bloodthirsty was chuckling to himself. Mussa bin Senussi was nodding wisely. Only Ismail Assada was still worried. He said nervously, "This can push the British, Karim Abdullah, into war."

The bey's voice was very hard. "No, I think not. I am sending instructions to my agent, Horuc, in London. He will inform Sir Neville Grant that if he does not speak up for us, and strongly, he will never see his daughter again. Are you all with me? Mussa bin Senussi? What does Tripoli say?"

"Tripoli says yes."

"Abed of Morocco?"

Abed the Bloodthirsty slapped his knee and laughed loudly. "Morocco says *double* their tribute, they'll pay it!"

"And Ismail of Tunis?" The bey's eyes were cold, knowing that there was opposition here, from a man who would not take risks however great the spoils. He said gently, "We decided long ago on the importance of unanimity in our deliberations with the European powers. I need your vote, friend Ismail."

The bashaw fidgeted. "I fear war."

"There will be no war."

"Then . . . if I may sleep on it, dear Karim?"

"Of course." He tried not to show his anger. "Important decisions such as this must indeed be carefully deliberated. Think only of the profit. Profit is all that matters. You will let me know tomorrow?"

"Yes, yes, tomorrow."

"Good." He wondered how he might dethrone this frightened, detestable man, and replace him with someone more to his liking. But he said amiably, "I truly do not like to see dissension in our ranks. Our aim, after all, is a mutual one: to get as much money from the hated foreigners as we can. A sensible endeavor, I think, and one that has long made us rich. And now, dear friends, since it is getting late, why don't we continue our wearisome business tomorrow? Let us sample the humble meal my cooks have prepared for us. A meal scarcely worthy of your nobility, but . . ." He laughed. "But satisfying, I promise you, to our stomachs. And first, perhaps a stroll through the gardens to take in the cool night air. The jasmine is particularly satisfying tonight. What do you say?"

Only a mile from the palace, high on a cliff overlooking the ocean, three signal fires were lit.

Half a mile out to sea, the flagship *Habou* saw them and turned into the wind to lower a boat. A furious Admiral Sinan leaped out as soon as it touched the shore, and strode through the surf to where the messenger was waiting. The messenger saluted, stood rigidly to attention, and shouted, "Sir! The three fires as ordered, sir!"

The admiral snapped, "I see them, fool! The prisoners?"

"They have been taken to the palace, sir."

Fury welled up inside him. "To the bey?"

The soldier, a simple man, hesitated. He himself was one of Sinan's spies against the bey, but he knew that his officer served the bey in like capacity against Sinan. He decided that discretion was the order of the day, and said, lying bravely, "No, sir. His Excellency does not yet know they have been captured."

Sinan could not be sure if it were the truth or not. He said evenly, "Where, then?"

"My orders are, sir, to say that they have been taken to the stables, to await you there."

"Good. A horse?"

"By the rocks there, sir."

"Well? Bring him, fool!"

"Yes, sir."

The messenger hurried off, and five minutes later Admiral Sinan was leaping from the saddle at the stables, and striding furiously towards the tallows that were burning there. The lieutenant with the patch over his eyes was hurrying to meet him—one of his own men, praise be to Allah—and he saluted and said, "Lieutenant Kabbagi, sir, to serve you. The prisoners are inside here, awaiting your attentions."

"Good. Take me to them."

Jason, his wrists and ankles bound, was tied to a post. Opal was lying in the straw at his feet, her wrists pulled up behind her back and tied there, one ankle tied to the same post.

For a moment Sinan stood there, arms akimbo, a fierce light of triumph in his eyes. He went to Jason, spat in his face, and said softly, "You, my friend, will learn what it means to make an enemy of a man like me."

He turned to the lieutenant. "Have him taken to the mill."

"At once, Excellency."

There were a dozen soldiers standing there, at attention in the presence of the admiral. On the lieutenant's orders three of them cut Jason down and took him away. He had been cruelly beaten, but he threw a look at Opal and was rewarded by the courage in her eyes. He wondered how courage might help her now.

Sinan stood above her with his feet widespread, his hands on his hips, his eyes burning with hate and lust. He said slowly, "So, dear lady, we meet again. Did you truly think you could escape from me?"

She would not answer him, nor even look at him. He

laughed, drew his dagger, sliced through the ropes that bound her, and pulled her to her feet. She swayed for a moment as the blood coursed through her veins again. Then she raised her hands and threw herself at him, her nails raking down his handsome, spoiled face as she shrieked, "Vile monster!"

The lieutenant's arms were around her instantly, pulling her back. Sinan struck her a light blow in the stomach, just enough to wind her. As she gasped and tried to catch her breath, he said savagely, "I do not like your seaman-lover's shirt on you."

He used the razor-sharp knife to cut it from her. The remnants of her silk dress—once so fine and beautiful—left her splendid breasts exposed, and he reached out and molded them heavily with both hands, his fingers digging into the gentle flesh. He said softly, "I will take you to the bey now, for his pleasures, if he will accept you the way you are, filthy, dishevelled, a wreck of what was once a beautiful woman. And why? Because it is my hope that he will look on you and reject you save for his political designs. In that case, perhaps, he will give you to me. And I know, as you do, that it will take little effort to make you beautiful again, with the attentions that only I know how to lavish on you."

He took her arm in a strong grip and led her away.

At the entrance to the stables he stopped and pulled her to him, slipping a hand down between her thighs and fondling her. He said hoarsely, "And even if he takes you himself, when he has finished with you . . . you will be mine. *Mine!*"

He marched her off to the palace.

CHAPTER SIX

There was fierce jubilation in Sinan's evil heart as he pushed Opal, stumbling, before him to the manicured garden of the palace. He found the bey and his guests there, taking their after-dinner tea and belching politely to show their appreciation of an excellent meal.

The beaten silver trays had been piled high with thick slabs of baked barracuda, mounds of tiny crabs that were eaten with their soft, succulent shells, clusters of sea-urchin casings filled with their coral, slices of lamb and goat braised in peppers and tomatoes, haunches of roast gazelle, whole quail, partridges, thrush, grouse and snipe turned on skewers over flaming coals. There were seven different kinds of melons, apricots, plums, apples, pears, raspberries and black currants, with sweetmeats made from sesame flour, dates, walnuts, raisins, pistachio nuts and honey.

Sinan was pleased to see that the bey was in a very good mood.

He bowed deeply and said, "Excellency, may I present Lady Opal Grant? I am mortified that there was a delay in my bringing her to you, but here she is at last, for whatever pleasures you may find in her."

The bey said, "A light."

Immediately, one of the slaves took down a flare from its fitting and held it high. The bey peered at Opal curiously. Her hair was dishevelled, her face and body smudged with dirt, her dress in shreds, and her satin slippers torn. He said, surprised, "This wretched creature is Opal Grant?"

Sinan thought, gloating, *Good, good, he does not want her.* He said offhandedly, "She has been living in the mountains for a while. But if she were suitably bathed and perfumed, there might perhaps be a limited satisfaction in her."

"Yes. She's a little thin, isn't she?" The bey muttered, "But I do detect a certain beauty, a very great beauty, under all that dirt." He held her by the chin, twisting her head this way and that, the better to examine her, as though she were a prize animal to be purchased. "Her eyes are quite splendid, though perhaps filled with too much pride. But that's a small disadvantage. A few strokes of a malacca cane judiciously applied will soon tame her."

Sinan's heart was sinking. He said quickly, "But if you should not want her, Excellency . . ."

"Wait, Sinan, wait," the bey said. "Control your impatience, my dear fellow." He placed his hands at her breasts, pressing his fingers deeply into them. "Small breasts, but very well shaped indeed, firm and high. A man could find great delight in them, I think."

He turned to Mussa bin Senussi of Tripoli: "What do you think, friend Mussa, is she worthy of my attentions? I need her for political advantage more than for anything else, but still in this harsh world of ours, we must take our pleasures where we can find them, is that not true?"

Mussa said mildly, "A woman worth a good fight, I would say, if she were suitably prepared. Her hips, for my taste, are far too small. Thin women are sometimes very passionate, of course, but were she mine, my first endeavor would be to fatten her up considerably." His hand was at her buttocks. He nodded and said, "Yes, a month or two of good fattening, at least." He pulled up the remnants of her skirt and felt her hipbone, and slipped a hand between her thighs as she tried to hold them tightly together.

Opal could hardly restrain her fury, but she kept her silence, suffering the humiliation because there was nothing she could do to prevent it.

But Abed the Bloodthirsty, a man who had taken more women than he could count, was eyeing her speculatively. He stepped into the little circle of yellow light. "By your leave, dear Karim Abdullah."

The bey, delighted, stepped aside. Abed Rashid took her breasts in his great hands and felt them, touching the nipples delicately with his fingertips. There was no feeling in his eyes at all, not the slightest trace of lust. He held up her chin and stared into her brightly defiant eyes, and then he laughed shortly. "This is no Englishwoman, Karim Abdullah."

"What?" The bey stared at him. Abed went on softly, "There is no Englishwoman alive with eyes like hers, nor with skin so cool to the touch, nor with breasts so widely spaced and upward pointing. I know these things, Karim Abdullah!"

The bey was stuttering. "But, but . . . she *must* be!"

Abed Rashid shrugged. "Perhaps by upbringing, who can tell. But *not* by the heritage the English prize so dearly. This woman has Negro blood in her veins. I'll stake my life on it."

The bey turned to her in astonishment. "Is it true? *Negro* blood? It cannot be!" And yet . . . For the first time, he noticed the trace of a slant to those lustrous eyes, the fullness of the enticing lips.

Opal's head was held high, and she returned his look with icy calm. She said quietly, "I am an Englishwoman, the scion of an ancient and honorable English family. My grandmother was a slave, a black woman who came from Brazil, perhaps of African extraction."

She could not stop the tears that came to her eyes and rolled unheeded down her lovely cheeks.

She had known it for a long time. She used to stand in front of the big mirror in the bedroom of the London house and peer at herself intently, studying the tilt of her nose, the shape of her full lips, and the almost imperceptible slant to her eyes, and knowing that she was somehow, subtly, *different*.

She had gone at last to her mother, the lovely, voluptuous Margherita, and had said to her, a little casually, "Mother, we're not really English, are we, you and I? I mean, not entirely?"

Margherita caught her breath.

She was a woman of stunning beauty, full-figured, with a narrow, hourglass waist and well-rounded hips, with white skin and very dark hair that shone like polished jet. Her breasts too were high and wide, firm even when she was forty years old. Seated at her dressing-table, she said quietly, smiling with genuine amusement, "How very perceptive of you, darling Opal. So, you found out at last?"

"Then it's true, Mother? Something in our blood?"

"It's true." Margherita took a long deep breath; what good was there in trying to hide it now?

"Your grandmother, dear Opal, was really quite dark. Your grandfather was white, a settler from Portugal, and your true father, as you know, was English and blonde." She laughed. "Does it bother you, darling, now that you know?"

"Of course not! Why should it? But I don't know why it should be such a secret."

"Because while England is a very tolerant country, not as tolerant as Brazil, of course, there is always a trace of uneasiness under that tolerance. And sometimes, underlying the humor, there is venom, there's no other word for it. An acute dislike of colored blood that sometimes borders on hatred. At the very least, it always invites a kind of contempt, sometimes politely concealed but nonetheless very strong. Hatred, venom, scorn . . . we must avoid these things at all costs, you and I."

"Why?"

"Why?" The innocent question startled her. She thought about it and said at last, frowning, "I don't really know why, darling. Perhaps it's because life is hard enough as it is. We should not *invite* calumny."

"Must I deny my grandmother, whom I never even knew, just because she was black?"

"No, you must not. She was a fine, fine woman whom I

have tried in many ways to emulate. She was once a slave, Opal. But she was a woman of gentility, and of quality. She was a kindly and very lovely woman."

Margherita looked at herself in the mirror, pulled down her peignoir to expose her body, and said, "Look at my breasts, Opal. This is what betrays us, always. Oh, not to the English, they have no knowledge of these subtleties. But in Brazil, where the races are all mixed together and no one cares a fig about color, a man will look at my breasts and know at once that I am *mestiza*, half-caste. It means little to him, save that he knows my skin will be cool to his touch even on the hottest nights, another little characteristic." She looked up at her daughter's reflection, and said gently, "One day, if you do not take pains to hide it, your secret will be discovered. I hope that it will not be at the hands of an Englishman. Will you make me a promise?"

"Yes, Mother, if I can."

"Do not mention it to your father."

"He doesn't know?"

"Of course not. I have kept it from him very carefully, because . . ." She hesitated. "Well, although I love him dearly, he's the kind of man who would brood about this. God alone knows how it would upset him. Promise?"

"Very well. If you wish it."

And now, this hateful Moroccan pirate was mauling her and saying, "There is Negro blood in her, black blood mixed in her veins. I can tell."

Admiral Sinan said, "Then if she is not truly—not a *thoroughbred*, excellency, she is not really good enough for you, so may I suggest that I myself take care of her till your political designs are satisfied? She will be in good and careful hands, and when the time comes, *if* it ever comes—"

"Not a *thoroughbred?*" the Bey said testily, interrupting him. "She's not a *horse*, dear Sinan, she's only a woman."

He had seen the interest in the tired old eyes of the bashaw of Tunis, and knew that he was holding a good card to play. He turned to him and said amiably, "But you have not given me your opinion of her, dear Ismail. What do you think? Do you find her captivating? Ravishing? Or at least meriting ravishment? Could you imagine yourself imprisoned between her quite delectable thighs?"

Ismail Assada was licking his dry lips. He had scarcely been able to take his eyes off Opal from the moment she had been brought in. His hands were twitching, and he nodded eagerly.

"Yes, dear Karim, indeed, I would say that my imagination in that respect is perhaps further advanced than your own."

"Ah," Karim Abdullah beamed. "Then as a token of my great affection for you, I give her to you."

"You do?" the bashaw's eyes were wide with anticipation. "For my bed tonight?"

"Well, not tonight. She must first be made presentable. I would not offend you by offering you the filthy animal she now appears to be. First, she must be bathed and perfumed, perhaps even trained."

"Tonight, tonight!" He was almost exploding with his urgent desire. Karim Abdullah decided that in spite of the demands of hospitality there was no need for the niceties with this despicable man, who still might thwart his ambitions, but he smiled and said carefully, as though he had dismissed the matter of Opal altogether, "Your vote on the London affair comes, I think, at tomorrow's resumption of our conference, is that not so?"

"Yes, yes, but . . ."

"It is as important to me as this young woman seems to be to you. Remember that we have ten more days of meetings, ten days and nights, enough for you to satisfy yourself on her fifty times, and that is a satisfaction not easily to be ignored, my dearest Ismail. Fifty times, my friend!"

"Tonight, I beg of you!" Ismail Assada was trembling, and the bey said firmly, sure that the battle was won, "Tomorrow night, and the nights that still remain to us."

He clapped his hands to summon a eunuch, and when he came—a large, muscular black man from the Fezzan—he said, "Take the girl to the harem. Bathe her, perfume her, oil her body well with oil of almonds. She is soon to be a present for my dear friend the bashaw of Tunis, and she must be worthy of him."

He turned to Sinan and said airily, "You may return to your ship, Admiral."

Sinan, masking his anger, bowed. "Your servant, Excellency." He threw a cold glance at Opal and stalked away.

The eunuch's hand, firm and yet gentle, was on her arm as he led her away. He took her into the palace, up a wooden staircase, and through the heavily bolted door that kept out all intruders from the quarters where the bey's women were kept. And in spite of her desperate condition, Opal could only gasp at the splendor that met her eyes.

There was scarlet and gilt everywhere, the sofas and divans upholstered in it, the colors repeated in the hanging drapes over wide windows, some of which were half-covered with wooden shutters, partly open now to let in the fine sea breezes that cooled the splendid room. A fountain was playing in one corner, the water spouting from the mouth of a ram, carved in stone, with fine curved horns. Nearby, there was a cauldron of beaten copper and brass under which a small fire of thorn twigs was smouldering. A gentle steam rose from the water, giving out the scent of lemon verbena. The floor was of mosaic tiles in beautiful, shimmering colors. Two ornate stone pillars supported the high ceiling, which was decorated with curlicues in darkly oiled walnut. There were repititions of the same design in carved stone around the windows, and more of the gleaming tiles in friezes around the walls.

Opal saw more than a dozen girls of varying ages, some who might have been in their late twenties and others who could not have been much more than ten years old. They were dressed in brightly colored gauze pantaloons, diaphanous blouses or waistcoats made of brilliant satin. Two of them were naked, one rubbing oil slowly and methodically into her immature breasts. Some were sipping tea or lemonade, and some were simply staring vacantly into space. They turned to watch her without emotion as she was ushered in.

The eunuch spoke in Arabic, and one of the women rose to her feet languidly. She was a little older than the others, perhaps almost thirty but still firm of body, her full breasts showing clearly under the gauze of her pale-blue blouse. She moved with animal ease as she went to an ornately carved cupboard and found a small bottle of opaque green glass. She poured the cloudy liquid into a silver goblet and held it out for Opal.

Opal shook her head. From behind her, the eunuch's skilled hand was at her cheeks, forcing her mouth open. The woman laughed as she pinched Opal's nostrils and tipped the fluid quickly down her throat.

It was a sedative, a very potent one, an extract of the *abira* shrub that grew profusely on the island. It burned the back of her throat as she tried to avoid swallowing it, without success. She heard the soft voice of the eunuch behind her. *B'taarifi Arabi, ya Sitt?*"

Opal shook her head desperately, only half-understanding the question. "No, no, I speak no Arabic."

"*Tayyib,* well then . . ." His English was limited and very labored. He said gently, "Is only medicine, you no worry, is good medicine, you feeling good now, you see."

Good medicine? Her head was reeling from its effects already.

The eunuch gave an order, and two of the younger girls stepped forward to help the woman who had given her the drug. They picked her up, laid her down on a marble, cloth-covered bench, and went to work on her body, to make it more acceptable to the bashaw of Tunis.

They washed her carefully from head to foot with soft sponges soaked in warm water and soap, turning her over like a roast in the oven when one side was done. The *abira* was not a dangerous drug, but it was very efficient, and all she wanted to do now was sleep. She did not even object when they used honey paste that was like beeswax, stripping off all her body hair so that she was smooth and naked as a baby in accordance with Moslem taste and custom. Once a moment of sanity came to her, and she closed her eyes and wept, but it was quickly gone again and there was only acceptance in its place.

She felt gentle hands rubbing oil into her flesh. They massaged her breasts with oil of myrrh, and she imagined that they were Jason's hands on her. Where was he now? Was he dead? She heard the eunuch's quiet voice speaking in Arabic, and she opened her eyes and saw them, their delicate hands all over her. She wondered why she did not object to the touch of other women.

The two very young girls moved away out of the periphery of her vision. The older girl was stepping out of her pantaloons and slipping off her blouse. Naked, she stood by the bench for a while, her hands at Opal's breasts, and then she leaned down and kissed them, teasing the nipples with her tongue, suckling on them and driving Opal, in spite of herself, to distraction. When a hand moved to her thighs she gasped. Her nipples were hardening. That lithe, firm body climbed up onto the bench, straddled her for a moment, and looked down on her with a kind of passionate adoration in large, dark-browed eyes. She stretched her body on Opal's, loin to loin and breast to breast, found her lips and feasted hungrily on them.

She was a handsome young woman, strong-bodied and muscular, and her name was Jamila. The bey had not summoned her to his bed for more than two months now, and she was starved for the only kind of love she knew. She had a terrible feeling that she was no longer acceptable to him, and that she would therefore be sent to the brothel the bey kept for his troops, or far worse!—to work in the fields of millet with a hoe, cutting down weeds for twelve hours a day, after which her duty would be to lie in her hut and await any of the servants who came to her.

She whispered words of endearment to Opal in Arabic; Opal only understood the import of that close contact, hips grinding into her own, and that womanly moaning of complete abandonment. She tried, half-heartedly, to resist the unaccustomed sense of euphoria, but the drug had left her completely acquiescent, ready to accept anything that might happen to her, and she let herself go, finding a vague and incomplete relish in the spasms that came to her so quickly.

She opened her thighs. There were other thighs entwining with hers, soft and enticing and heavily oiled, with a rhythmic cadence to their thrusting that sent her into delirium. The turbulence came to her again and again, and she knew that there could be no escape from it, knew too that she welcomed it; and so she let it take its hold on her. She was sure that there could be nothing in the world more wonderful.

The others were watching solemnly. Jamila lay beside her and whispered fiercely, "Soon I love you again. Your body is made of ice and fire, a body for a woman to drown in." But she spoke Arabic, and Opal did not know what she was talking about. She knew only that there were lips at her breasts, a hand between her moist thighs, and fingers still probing.

Watching, the eunuch whispered, "Enjoy her while you can. She is yours for a while."

Jamila was one of his favorites, and he felt personally hurt that the bey had neglected her for so long. Worse, he knew that she was shortly to be given to the slaves who ran the mill, as a reward for their good services, and it pained him deeply. For the bey, Jamila had outlived her usefulness. His harem was filled with girls half her age.

All night long, she loved a quiescent Opal, feasting on that slender, supple body in all of the ways that were so well known to her, insatiably, taking great pleasure in the close contact.

When morning came, the effects of the *abira* had quite worn off. Opal saw that her unwanted lover was still asleep beside her, exhausted by her efforts. The eunuch was sitting cross-legged in the corner, his head nodding. There was no one else in the spacious room. She wondered if she might find a way to creep silently out of the building to search for some kind of safety from the fate that was in store for her. She wondered where she could find something to cover her naked body. She looked at her depilated loins and gasped.

But then the eunuch raised his head and looked at her. He pushed the turban to the back of his head, scratched at his scalp, and yawned. He rose to his feet lazily, ambled up to the bench and smiled at her, a kindly man. He shook Jamila by the shoulder to awaken her, and spoke to her in Arabic. She too yawned and scratched herself. She clambered down with hardly a glance at Opal and went out. The Eunuch said, groping for the words, "She finding you dress now."

Opal swung her long legs off the bed and went to the cauldron in the corner. She tested the water and found it warm. She dunked her hands in it, and rubbed them over her face to drive the sleep from her eyes. She was surprised to see the black man beside her, holding out one of the towels from the bench. He dipped it in the water and wrung it out and handed it to her in silence. She took it from him gratefully and cleaned herself with it as he watched her. He reached out and laid his enormous hands on her breasts, with no hint of offensiveness at all. Nodding, he said, "Is very good, you making bashaw happy man, happy bashaw is good, good for you, for me, for bey, for all people." His hands were still molding her, with a kind of dispassionate interest. He said softly, "What you call in English? Am not knowing this word."

"Breasts. But please don't do that. This night has been . . . very trying for me."

Misunderstanding, he nodded. "Yes, is very good night. I am watching."

When Jamila returned with her new clothes, Opal looked at them and sighed. There were long, pale green pantaloons of some transparent material, a diaphanous blouse of a light old-rose color, a tiny waistcoat made from brilliant blue silk heavily embroidered in gold thread, and a small scarlet pillbox hat of velvet from which gold coins hung. A bright green silk sash had tiny silver bells hanging from it, and a pair of leather sandals, up-turned and decorated with gold thread, completed the ensemble.

When they had completed dressing her, with much fussing to make sure that everything was just right, Opal looked down at her body in dismay, and the image that came to her was of a houri from a book called *A Thousand and One Nights,* which all the girls at school had secretly read together, giggling, during a month of long nights in the candlelit dormitory.

But the eunuch, standing back to admire her, was delighted. His face was wreathed in smiles, and Opal was suddenly smitten with a great sorrow for him. He was not young. How long had he spent in this awful place? His testicles had been cut out as a child so that he could spend his life in the company of beautiful women and never enjoy them. She whispered, "You know that my name is Opal. If I may know yours?"

The smile had quickly gone. He was conscious of her distress and perhaps even guessed at the reason for it. His hand went to his plump cheek, stroking, and he said quietly, "My name, *ya Sitt*, is Zahair."

He walked to the door, opened it, and called out an order. Almost immediately, ten, twelve, fifteen young women streamed in and gathered around her, giggling and talking excitedly together, admiring her. Zahair spoke to them gravely, telling them who she was and whom she would soon be serving. The older girl, Jamila, was standing a little apart from the others, a veiled look in her solemn eyes.

Another of them was standing apart too, a girl of about twenty-two, slender and willowy, blonde and green-eyed, with fair, straw-colored hair that fell almost to her waist. She was dressed as the others were, in transparent trousers and waistcoat. Her skin was white and shining.

She went to Opal and said in English, her voice a trifle mocking, "Welcome, Mademoiselle, to this den of iniquity."

Her English was only lightly accented. Opal stared at her. "Mademoiselle?" she echoed. "You are French?"

"Yes, I am French. My name is Marie-France, and I cannot tell you how happy I am to see the addition to this harem of a cultivated woman. Zahair says you are being prepared for the bashaw of Tunis. I cannot help wondering if you know what is in store for you?"

"No, I do not. I can imagine it."

"Only if your imagination reaches beyond the bounds of the acceptable. I was given to him once. It took me a week to recover."

Opal said, uncertainly, "And will you tell me, Marie-France, how it is that a French lady finds herself in an Algerian harem? It is hard to understand."

The French girl said drily, "No more difficult to understand than your own presence here. And by the same means, I imagine. Twelve years ago, my parents were unfortunate enough to be on board a French schooner, and I was with them. We were attacked by an Algerian pirate ship, under the command of a man whose name I will never forget, a Captain Sinan."

Opal caught her breath. "Now . . . *Admiral* Sinan?"

"The same." Marie-France looked at her curiously, and not without sympathy. "You know him?"

"To my cost, I know him."

"Then you know the kind of man he is."

"I do indeed."

"Though no worse nor better than any other pirate. On that memorable day, twelve years ago, our ship was sunk, but not before a great many prisoners had been taken. My father, who was a colonel in the army, was killed in the fighting. My mother, who was young and very beautiful, was captured and taken aboard Sinan's ship, as I was." Her voice hardened. "He took me first, and then I watched him rape my mother."

Opal gasped. She whispered, "Twelve years ago?"

since." She laughed again, bitterly. "My time will soon come for the fields, to work among the grapevines with a hoe. Or perhaps, if I am lucky, in the officers' brothel."

Opal said, hushed, "And your mother?"

"My mother was carried off to some other harem, no doubt. She was really a very attractive woman. I have never seen or heard of her since." She shrugged. "I do not even know if she is still alive."

Opal could only moan for her.

CHAPTER SEVEN

The mill lay behind the palace kitchens, close to the stables in a pleasant little compound shaded by tall eucalyptus trees. Chickens and goats wandered among the bullock carts that had been left with their shafts upended, and in the air there was the sweet smell of the millet that was ground in the ramshackle building.

It was a round building, some thirty feet tall. There was only one door, of solid wood studded with iron bolts, and a single window high up in the wall, which had lost its shutter.

The millstones were enormous and very heavy. They were more than twelve feet across and two feet thick. The upper stone was turned laboriously by the animals harnessed to four long spokes on iron-bound beams. Sometimes there would be four oxen, or camels, or mules, and sometimes there were men mixed in with them as well.

Now, there was a bullock, a camel, a condemned Libyan bandit whose hands had been cut off at the wrists, and Jason.

Turning the wheel was backbreaking work, and the two men were sweating heavily, their half-naked bodies caked with the fine flour-dust that hung in the air. Straps went around their shoulders and were fastened to the spokes, just like the harness of the animals that accompanied them as they slowly pulled the monstrous wheel round under the watchful eyes of the mill guard.

The guard was a big, powerfully built man from beyond the Atlas mountains, half Berber and half Sudanese, and though his skin was black his whole body was white with the dust. He seldom left this little domain where he was king, though he was only a slave. He carried a long whip, which he used relentlessly on man and beast alike, and there was a long dagger in his belt. He could not speak; long ago, his tongue had been cut out for some forgotten offence. He strode around the circle growling his guttural *rrhhhs* whenever he thought not enough effort was being put into the work, slashing out savagely to assert his authority and taking pleasure in the use of the whip.

The Libyan bandit was tall and very thin, and the muscles at his shoulders were like steel cables. His beard and moustache were thick and black, his eyes shrewd and alert, with a bright intelligence in them. He had been working in the mill for more than six months, ever since he had been captured in one of the caves high on the mountain. He spent eighteen hours of every day at the wheel, being released twice a day—at the whim of the guard—to eat and sleep for a few short hours before being kicked awake again. Since he had no hands, a loaf of bread was tossed on the ground for him, with sometimes a piece of cheese or goat's meat, which he ate like a dog, lapping up water from the trough to wash it down.

And in all this time, his spirit had never been broken.

On the next spoke, ahead of the bandit, Jason labored, forcing his shoulders into the shaft, his feet slipping constantly on the chaff that lay on the floor. He had discovered that he could talk in low monosyllables, when he could find the breath and the strength, without inviting more retribution than an occasional cut of the whip. He contrived to turn his head so that he could study the Libyan from time to time. He saw the fiery light in those angry eyes and knew that he had an ally here.

He said quietly, "Your name, *ya habibi?*"

"My name is Osman. And yours?"

"Jason." He waited a while before speaking again, and then, "There is no way out of here."

"There is. In a wooden box."

"Maybe."

The guard articulated a horrible noise of censure and struck out at them with his whip. For a turn or two they fell silent.

The bullock ahead of Jason stopped to defecate, and the camel screamed its anger as the wheel stopped and broke its steady rhythm. It knew that once the wheel stopped it was very hard to start again. The bullock was taking its time, and they rested on their spokes till it was ready to move again, grateful for the brief respite. At last, the ox began to move, forcing its great weight forward with a sudden lunge. The furious camel was prancing, lashing out at the Libyan ahead of it with flailing forelegs, and the bandit turned and shouted obscenities at it. The guard was laughing as they slipped in the slime. He unwrapped a piece of meat from a rag at his waist and began chewing on it.

Jason said quietly, "I will leave here. Are you with me?"

There was no hesitation at all. "*W'Allahi,* by God . . ."

The guard growled. Jason threw him a look, wondering if he had heard, but it was only that he had dropped his piece of meat to the floor and was searching for it angrily. He found it at last in the dirt and popped it into his mouth.

A moment later, Jason said quietly, "When the time comes, you will see."

"I will be ready. It is good to have a man with me."

When the spoke came round again to where the guard was, Jason straightened up, no longer thrusting his shoulder forward but letting the others do all the work. The guard saw at once and screamed at him. He raised the whip and brought it down hard across Jason's back. On the second stroke, the long lash curled around Jason's body, and he was ready. He seized it with both hands and pulled it sharply towards him. In a fury, the guard, held on tightly to the handle, and the Libyan shot out a foot and kicked his ankles from under him. When he fell Jason slipped the strap around his neck and tightened it, dragging him down into the circle with them, holding on firmly as the man thrashed out in panic.

Behind him, the Libyan shot a strong foot forward, aiming for the lower chest. He said sharply, "The knife, get the knife!"

"In a moment!" After two more revolutions of the wheel Jason could drop the guard's body and slip the long dagger from its sheath. The blade was sharp. He sliced rapidly through his harness with it and turned to free his friend. The wheel was slowing down and finally it stopped altogether, the camel screaming out its anger again.

The Libyan said urgently, "A piece of cord, quickly! Tie the knife to my wrist."

Jason found a length of rope and bound the dagger's handle to the stub of the arm. The bandit hissed, "Ah, a fighting man again. Quick, the window!"

He was already clambering up the timbers, using the crooks of his elbows to pull himself up, squeezing through the aperture. Jason followed him. They found themselves on a low thatched roof that abutted onto the main building, and dropped to their bellies at its edge, staring down into the compound. It was dark. The moon was half-hidden by scudding, threatening clouds. Jason tried not to cough the dust out of his lungs in the silence. The bandit whispered, "Not here, the other side."

They crawled across the roof and found that the compound wall met the building there. Osman nodded furiously. They dropped quickly to the ground and ran fast for the forest over soft sand, and they did not stop till they were nearly a mile away, deep in the friendly shelter of the trees.

They fell to the ground, exhausted. Osman rolled over onto his back and looked up at the stars, and said quietly, "My first sight of the sky in many months. I thank you, friend. It is hard for a man with no hands to escape from such a place. I will never forget what you have done for me."

Jason turned to look at him. "How long have you been there?"

"I lost count a long time ago, it seems like eternity. You are English, I think?"

"American."

"Join me in the mountains, American, you will find a good life there, much fighting. And my people are good people."

"Your people?"

"We are rebels, though they call us bandits. Rebels against the rule of that Karim Abdullah, who had my hands cut off and thrown to feed the crabs. We live in caves on the other side of the island, at the very top where the soldiers find it hard to climb."

Osman's voice was very quiet as he told of the terrible depredations his people suffered; of the savage oppression, the constant raping of the women, the murderous beatings if they dared raise their voices in the hope of a little freedom. He said urgently, "Join forces with me, Jason! You will be welcomed as a hero by my people, because you have saved their leader from certain death. A man can only last so long in the mill. Another month, and I would have been dead. Listen."

They strained their ears in the darkness, and heard the distant sound of running water, a very friendly sound. Osman whispered, "This way."

They moved off through heavy shrubbery and found the stream, only a few inches deep but running fast over shining pebbles. Lying on their bellies, they drank their fill, and then rolled over and over in the water to wash away the caked dust on their bodies. Gasping, they lay on the mossy bank to dry, and Osman said, "Well, will you come with me?"

Jason shook his head. "I cannot, though I thank you, good friend. There is work that I must do. I must return to the palace."

"What? They will kill you on sight!"

"It is not my intention to be seen," Jason said drily. "Do you know where the palace harem is?"

"Ha! At a time like this you look for a woman?"

"One particular woman. I do not even know if she will be in the harem, but it's the logical place to start looking."

"Madness! I will give you one of our own women instead, a dozen if you like! No woman is worth such risks."

Jason shook his head. "I *must* find her. And I will!"

Osman sighed. "Well" he said, "if you insist on inviting your own death . . . The harem will be on the second floor of the palace and overlooking the sea, without a doubt. Look for heavily latticed windows with tallows flaring brightly behind the shutters. There will be a balcony, perhaps climbing plants. It should not be too hard to find. But getting in there is a very different problem."

"I'll never know until I try. And you, Osman? How will you manage now?"

The Libyan shrugged, and raised the stump of his arm with the dagger bound to it. "This is all I need. You think I am useless because I have no hands? By daylight I will be among my own people again. Will you do something more for me?"

"Of course!"

"You know this island well?"

"No, I do not."

"Very well. To the west of the palace there are three small fishing villages. The second of them is called Bir Birein. Look for my daughter there. Her name is Helua. Will you do that for me?"

"I will find her."

"Helua, my daughter. She too is a rebel, like all of my family, though this is not known to the soldiers. It is certain that she thinks I am dead. She knows that I was captured, that I lost my hands, and knows too that there are not many who live for long after capture. Tell her that I am alive, that I am free, and tell her to come to the cave on the rock of the eagles. But not at once, in two days' time. Will you do that for me?"

Jason nodded. "I will be glad to. But first, I must find the harem and do what has to be done. Even the time we waste here is important."

"I understand. And will you tell Helua that my first words were for her? It will please her greatly."

"Yes, I will do so."

Jason began to reach out for a handshake, but caught himself in time, and said, "I will go now."

The bandit-rebel was grinning at him in the moonlight, and shaking his head slowly. "No," he said quietly, "not yet, my friend."

"Oh? And why not?"

"Learn from an old professional rogue, Jason! In a very little while now, they will discover that we have escaped."

"If they have not done so already."

"No, we would have heard their shouting. Their voices will carry well on the night air, and we are above them and downwind. With a moon like this, we will even see them. When the moment of discovery comes they will turn out the guard in a fury to search for us. There was soft sand down there by the palace, and they will quickly discover that we have taken to the forest to hide, merely by following our footprints, which they will lose the moment they come to the trees."

"Ah, yes . . ."

"They will be spread out in a long line, searching for signs of our movements. And the more there are of them, the fewer there will be left at the palace, the easier it will be for what you have to do. When you hear them coming, conceal yourself carefully and wait until their line has passed you by. Then and only then will it be safe for you to move down the mountainside."

"You are a good man, Osman."

Osman laughed quietly. "Not a good man at all, but skilled in such matters through long experience."

Jason grimaced. "It will be hard to wait. Every minute that passes means more danger for the lady I must find."

"A dead man will leave her in greater danger, with no hope of rescue at all. You must wait!" He sighed. "Tell me about her."

Jason said dreamily, "The most beautiful of women, *ya habibi*. And she loves me as much as I love her. I cannot bear the thought of the pains she may be suffering."

He broke off. Below them there was a vociferous shouting, the voices carried to them with surprising clarity on the sea breeze. At first it was nothing but a babble of sound, and then more definite orders.

"Two trackers at once, on the double!"

"All ranks in extended order!"

Osman said nonchalantly, "You must come with me now, away from the stream, four hundred paces at least. They know that the stream is here and that we may have used it."

Jason was quite content to let the expert take command. They climbed a little higher, walking carefully on rocks that would not show their footprints. Osman whispered, "Beware the trackers, Jason, they are highly skilled."

They turned back at the edge of a thick clump of shrubbery, and could make out the shadows below them that were the searchers, moving slowly up towards them. Osman said quietly, "I will leave you now. They will be here in a little while, so hide yourself well under the bushes. Make no sound, no movement as you hear them approaching, and wait in patience till they have passed you by and gone on their way. You must not disclose yourself too soon in your eagerness to help your woman, or there will be no hope for her at all. You are young and impetuous, but this is a time for patience. And then you move like a thief in the night, in absolute silence." He said gruffly, "And I thank you for my life, dear friend. You remember the name of my daughter?"

"Helua, in the village of Bir Birein, the second of the three that lie to the west of the palace."

The bandit's eyes in the darkness were on fire, and he was laughing softly. He whispered, "My daughter is not beautiful, friend Jason, but if you do not find your own woman, then take her. She is yours with my consent." He chuckled, enjoying a huge, secret joke.

"I took her myself once, only a year ago when I still had my hands. She fought me like a mountain lion until I was deep inside her, no virgin, though she has never been married. There is warmth in her thighs, and they are very strong, as a mountain woman's thighs should be."

Jason said courteously, "I thank you, friend Osman, for your . . . understanding, and your help."

"And I thank you for my life. I leave you now. Allah go with you, and if he wishes it, we will meet again."

"If Allah wishes it, as I do."

The bandit was gone, running quickly and effortlessly up the steep mountainside, soon lost among the trees. Jason, stepping carefully on hard rock, found a place where the bushes were so dense he could hardly find a way into them. He eased himself carefully under them till he was well hidden, and waited. It was a long time before he heard them crashing carelessly through the undergrowth, and when they came nearer, he held his breath and did not move a muscle.

Two of them stopped so close to his hiding place that he could have reached out and touched them. He heard one of them say, growling, "We will never find them, they are too far ahead of us. Once we lost their tracks . . ."

The other answered him gruffly, "Tell that to the sergeant. Come, we are dropping behind." The pair of them moved on, and in spite of his intentions Jason waited a short time before crawling from his cover and moving slowly and soundlessly down the mountainside again, keeping all the time to the trees in which lay his safety.

He came at last to the compound wall and skirted it, finding his way around it to the front of the palace, slipping in utter silence from shadow to shadow. He drew deeper into the shadows as a patrolling sentry passed him, and studied the lines of the building. There was a high turret up there, a man on it no doubt, and therefore to be avoided. There were heavily barred windows, with either no chinks in their shutters or no flares behind them. On the second story there were six latticed windows in a row with a balcony outside them. They were all well lit with tallows, and curtains were billowing out on the breeze through those that were open. He was sure that he had found the harem.

He examined the rest of the building's front: a two-story

room, also well lit, with wide doors leading into the garden, next to it, four small barred and darkened windows. A guardroom, perhaps? He turned his attention back to the balcony and the latticed windows. There were heavy vines climbing up the wooden supports. He took a long, deep breath and knew that the time had come.

He raced across the intervening space and hid himself in the shadow of the portico, waiting for a shout from the tower that would mean he had been seen, but none came. He began climbing carefully up the thick, twisted trunks of a creeper that bore bright, heavily scented yellow flowers. It was not easy to find safe handholds on it, but at last he threw himself over the veranda railing and crouched in silence by the wall, listening, watching, waiting.

The windows were embrasures in the thick walls. He moved stealthily from one to another, peering through half-opened shutters into the rooms. In the first, two eunuchs in their scarlet robes were playing backgammon at a little table of inlaid rosewood. In another, a pleasant and comfortable room decorated in blues and greens, a naked black girl, slim and young, was lying on a bench, being massaged with oil by another eunuch. At a third room, much larger than the others and furnished in scarlet and gold, he saw eight or ten young women lounging on divans; one of them was idly making a cat's-cradle from colored thread, and two others were rolling dice and moving little chips around on a board.

He moved on to a window that was set higher in the wall than the others, its jalousies fully opened. It was much like the others, heavily tiled and furnished in blue and gold, with beautiful tapestries hanging on the walls and a lion's-head fountain in one corner, and two doors, both of them closed. He looked carefully, but could see no one there at all. There was only a single tallow candle burning, though light came from another, brighter one immediately below him and out of his vision.

What should he do now? The awful impossibility of what he was attempting came to him and made him shudder. Once inside, where could he take cover if one of those ominous doors opened? Some of the divans were covered with silk sheets. Could he hide under one of them? And what then? Could he casually go from room to room searching for her?

One step at a time. And the first step was to find her. After that, he would turn whatever fortune came his way to advantage.

He gritted his teeth, aware of the dreadful danger he was in, and pulled himself up to the sill. The window was small, hardly enough to admit him. He thrust his upper body through, and pulled up short in utter consternation. Below him, close against the wall and hidden from his previous vision, there was another divan. Stretched out on it, an opened book in her hands, a young woman was staring up at him in shock.

There was only one thing he could do now. He dropped quickly inside the room, and as she opened her mouth to scream he covered it with his hand, holding her tightly, and whispered urgently, in Arabic, "I have not come to harm you, I swear it! Please, will you listen to me? I promise you, no harm . . ."

Her green eyes on his were terrified, and he whispered again, "I beg of you, you *must* hear me out! I am not a robber, as you might suppose, but an American, a gentleman."

The fear in her eyes had turned to a kind of astonishment, and she nodded slowly. Carefully, ready to replace it instantly, he took his hand away from her mouth. On his knees beside the divan, he whispered, "Will you listen to me for one moment?"

He was very conscious that her full breasts under the tiny waistcoat were lightly overlaid with glorious straw-colored hair that reached almost to her waist. He said swiftly, "I have come here to find an Englishwoman who is being kept here against her will. I *must* find her! And if I am discovered here, they will kill me, as you must know."

She spoke at last, very low, with a strange kind of excitement. She whispered in English, "An American, you say, and a gentleman? It is not often that we see a gentleman in the harem, M'sieur."

"You are French?"

"Yes. And I speak English well."

"Then will you hear me out?"

"Yes, I will listen."

Jason said quickly, "I too was a prisoner of the bey until a short while ago. I escaped—"

"From the mill?"

He said, surprised, "You know?"

"Not everything. But there is little excitement in a harem, and news of this kind travels fast. We heard that a prisoner escaped from the mill. It has never happened before."

He threw an anxious glance at the closed doors. "And can we talk here?"

"Yes. This is the resting room. I have been prepared for the bey or for one of his guests, I do not know which. No one will come here till I am called. It will be a little while yet, I think, though I cannot be sure."

There was great excitement in her eyes, almost the color of emeralds, as she looked at him. She saw a very handsome young man with a fierce and determined look, dressed in tattered breeches, with the marks of the whip on powerful, muscular shoulders. She could not credit his coming here in the face of such terrible danger.

He sat back on his heels, staring at her as he wondered where to begin. Her long pantaloons were of the flimsiest amber-colored gauze, fastened at the ankles with green ribbon. The waistcoat that did not hide her body was purple silk bound with gold wire. She smelled strongly of cinnamon oil. She whispered, "It is the English girl you have come for, I think? Opal?"

He felt the beat of his heart quickening. "Yes, for Opal! You know her? And is she truly here? I was afraid that she might not be."

"Yes, we all know her, and she is here."

"And will you help me?"

She said fiercely, "Yes, I will help you!" There was a

moment of hesitation, and then she said gently, "And I am sure you would wish to know . . . she has not been taken yet. Prepared, yes, bathed by the eunuchs, all the hair removed from her body as mine is, as you see, oiled and perfumed—but not yet taken."

"And you know where she is?"

"No, I do not. But I will find out. But first . . ."

She took his hand and laid it on her breast, moving it slowly back and forth over her erect nipples for a moment. Her eyes were glazed, and she whispered, "To feel the caress of a man who is not an animal . . . A sensitive woman needs the touch of a man." To his consternation, she slid his hand down over her body and placed it between her smooth thighs. She whispered, tears in her lovely eyes, "A moment only, I beg of you. It is so long since, since . . ." Her hand left his wrist and reached up to his head, pulling it down to kiss him full on the lips. He found that of their own volition his fingers were working on her, and almost at once she shuddered uncontrollably and gripped his wrist again, pulling his hand away from the intimacy.

Her eyes were wide as she looked up at him, and then the heavy eyelids covered them as she swung her long legs off the divan and moved to the door.

She looked back at Jason and whispered, "Will you forgive me, m'sieur?"

Jason said steadily, "There is nothing to forgive, mademoiselle."

"It is just that . . . There are only forty-seven women in this harem, but young virgins are brought to the bey from all over the Barbary States. It means that we are serviced only once every three, four, or even five or six months. It is not enough for a woman. And the servicing is sometimes very cruel, and without pleasure for us. I wish that there were more time, so that I could feel you within me, but there is not. And now I will find your Opal for you. May I know your name?"

"It is Jason Farn, mademoiselle. If I may know yours too?"

"I am Marie-France. I will not tell you my family name,

for I do not wish to disgrace it. Indeed, I have almost forgotten it, in the long years I have been here. I too was taken prisoner, from a French ship that was sunk by these pirates. I was very young, and innocent, and perhaps attractive to the depraved tastes of a man whose name I will remember till the day I die. His name was Sinan, Captain Sinan, now the bey's admiral."

Jason said harshly, "I know him. A monster."

"Yes, a monster. As a child, I learned from him in one night all the—the intricacies of what the Arabs call love. And now, I will find your Opal for you."

Marie-France opened the door and called out a few words in fluent Arabic. She stood aside as more than a dozen startled young women moved into the room, all of them staring at Jason in shock. She closed the door and then opened it again, and said, "Sari, wait in the other room, close by the door. If someone comes, slip quickly in here and close the door behind you. We will know what it means."

Sari was shining black, a tall Sudanese girl with a slim, high-breasted body, clad only in a veil. She nodded silently and returned to the other room, closing the door behind her. In a few words Marie-France explained the situation. She said, "Does anyone know where Opal is now?"

A plump child with masses of dark hair and very bright eyes, a round face with a cupid's bow mouth, narrow of waist and full of hip, said, "She is in the preparation room, being oiled. She is to go to the bashaw of Tunis tonight, a mean old man. I hate him."

She advanced on Jason and laid her hands on his chest, stroking. She whispered, "Such a beautiful man. And he has come here for Opal?"

"Yes. He has come to take Opal away."

"And do you know what they will do if they find him here? A man in the harem?"

Marie-France nodded and said fiercely, "Yes! They will kill him!"

"But not quickly. First they will cut out his balls and make him swallow them. And then they will take him to the bey to find out how he should die." Her hand was at Jason's loins. She found his manhood and grasped it, and whispered, "So long since a man lay between my thighs. I am starved. I think the bey does not like me any more."

Marie-France said angrily, "No! We are all starved, but there is no time!"

He had to trust them. Marie-France said, speaking Arabic so that they would all understand, "We must hide him. If Opal is being prepared, then she will be brought here soon to rest. We must find a place!" She dragged the divan a little away from the wall and said to Jason, "There, when the time comes, behind it."

The young girls began to gather round him, their childish eyes alight with interest. A man in the harem! It had never happened before in all of their experience. One of them, older than the others, was hanging back. Marie-France said to her evenly, "Are you with us, Jamila?"

Jamila nodded solemnly. "I am with you. What Opal wishes, I wish for her too."

The young girl with the cupid's bow mouth was fondling him, reaching up with her other hand to pull down his head and kiss him on the lips. She was grinding her hips into his, thrilling to the close contact of his strong manhood, uncontrollably erect as she brushed her gossamer-covered nipples against his bare chest. Some of the others were giggling in nervous apprehension as they watched. Some of them, scared out of their wits, were wondering what would happen to them if he should be discovered.

Marie-France was furiously angry as the young girl dropped to her knees and fumbled with the buttons of Jason's breeches, but before she could speak, the door opened and closed quickly, and the Sudanese girl, Sari, was there, a slim finger at her lips. Someone was coming. Marie-France reached for him, but he did not wait. He threw himself behind the divan and made himself as small as possible, lying absolutely still.

From under the divan's hanging, tasseled silk he saw the door opening and saw the splayed feet of a eunuch and next to them a pair of tiny feet in ornate leather slippers trimmed in scarlet and gold. He heard a deep voice roaring in anger, "What are you all doing here, have you taken leave of your senses? This is the resting room, not a gathering place! Back, all of you, to your quarters!" He saw the little crowd of slippered feet running quickly to the door, and heard the voice again, softer now. "Rest here till I come for you, child. Sleep if you will. You will need all of your strength. The Bashaw is a very demanding man. Please him, or it will go hard with you." And then, "Marie-France, come with me. Abed Rashid of Morocco awaits you."

He heard the French girl's voice. "Yes, of course. I am rested."

"Good. He is strong tonight. Later, Sari will join you, dressed in the tatters of a beggarman. You will love her. It pleases him to watch."

"Of course, anything he wishes."

The door closed behind them, and the room was suddenly very empty. Jason held his breath, knowing that there was no one there now—except the young woman he loved to the point of folly.

CHAPTER EIGHT

Opal was in despair.

She could not forget the awful feeling of that woman lying atop her, the naked thighs between her own, loving her, bringing her to a kind of drug-induced fulfillment time after time. And she could not dismiss from her mind the memory of the hatred in Sinan's cruel eyes as he had said, in the stables, "Have him taken to the mill, a fitting punishment." Her beloved Jason . . .

What, in God's name, was the mill? And what dreadful pains was he suffering? She wept at the remembrance of him, bruised and beaten, being dragged away from her to God alone knew what frightful tribulations.

And then, at a sound beside her, she found herself staring, bewildered and utterly unbelieving, into Jason's darkly handsome eyes as he rose up from behind the divan, a finger to his lips that stifled her sharp intake of breath. *This could not be!* But there he was, close beside her, rising to his feet like a vision from the past, his arms around her, clutching her to his chest in a kind of desperation.

He whispered, "No time now, my beloved, for explanations. Come quickly, make no sound."

Even before she could recover from her shock he was urging her to the window. He helped her through it, her heart beating wildly, and they ran along the balcony to the strong vines at the corner. He whispered, "Hand over hand. I will go first to show you how."

It was a strange and fearsome situation for her, and her

mind was full of unanswered questions, but she knew that those questions had to wait. Her faithful and beloved Jason was there once again when she needed him the most.

Fearfully she clambered down the vine after him, and they ran together across the broad, moonlit gardens and climbed over the low wall. No one challenged them. They ran on hand in hand over the hard wet sand. When he felt her lagging, he pulled her into a tiny gully where the cool seawater lapped at their feet. He lay down beside her and embraced her fiercely. He whispered, "Opal, Opal my love, are you truly here, are you safe again? Are you truly safe?"

"Yes! In your arms I am safe, but I understand nothing! I am thunderstruck! How did you find me?"

"I will tell you later. Have they harmed you, my love?"

"No, they have not . . ."

"Will you swear it to me?"

"I swear it! A few indignities that I can bear, no more than that!"

Jason was trembling. "Oh, God! I was so worried for you!"

"And I was sure that they must have killed you! And so I was resigned to whatever awful fate was in store for me. My heart, my mind, my soul, they were all numbed, because I was sure that you were dead!"

He clutched at her, forcing their bodies into closer contact. "I do not die so easily," he murmured, "when the woman I love so dearly needs me."

Her arms were around him. She felt the weals on his back. "And you have been so cruelly treated . . ."

"It is all behind us now."

"Yes, please God, for ever." He was kissing her passionately, her eyes, her cheeks, her lips. She whispered, "And now? How shall we leave this accursed island?"

"When you are rested, there is a little way more to go along the beach, and we will come to a fishing village named Bir Birein. We will find help there."

"I am ready when you are, Jason, my love. In your hands, as always."

"I love you so dearly."

"My love, my love for ever . . ."

"Come," Jason whispered. "We must find the village. It will not be far."

Hand and hand, they hurried down the beach, and passed the first of the little fishing villages in silence, the thatch and adobe huts well shuttered against the demons of the night.

They came to the second village. Jason whispered, "Here, somewhere, the help we need now." They found a shack where a chink of light was showing. Jason hammered on the door and waited.

In a few moments a frightened voice came to them, the voice of an old woman. "*Min?* Who is it?"

He said clearly, "My name is Jason, and I look for the woman Helua, whose father Osman is my friend."

There was a very long silence. Then the tired voice again, "I know no one named Osman. Go away."

She would not open the door. It was perhaps a sign that there was no man there to tell her to. Without a man's permission, the door to the house could not be opened. And at night it was doubly dangerous.

Jason said urgently, "Osman is my friend! Though no man is there, open! No harm will come to you."

There was another long silence. But then at last, a hushed voice, "Osman is dead. Go away."

"Osman is not dead. I spoke with him but a few hours ago. He is alive and well. He has escaped from the mill." The silence was even longer now, though he fancied he could hear muted whisperings. And then the tired old voice said, "Wait there."

They waited.

The door did not open, but at the back there was a shadow streaking away from the hut. It was a young boy, running fast to the center of the little village. They waited, and in a little while four very old men moved out of the shadows behind them, fearful of the intrusion but determined to do whatever might have to be done. One of them had an ancient flint-lock musket. Trembling, he said, "Strangers, who are you?"

The old man stared at them in the moonlight, not believing what he saw: a handsome youth who was obviously a foreigner, a damned European, no doubt, and a young woman dressed in the disgusting clothes of a houri, her body almost naked; he was glad to know that his ancient crone of a wife was not there to see his hungry eyes devouring her. He said again, "Who are you? What do you want with us? You spoke of a man named Osman. We know no one of that name."

Jason said angrily, "Old man, you are a fool! What, you think I am a spy for the bey? You see that I am a foreigner, an American. And the lady with me, look at the clothes she wears! I have rescued her from the bey's harem, where she was a prisoner of that hateful man! Would a spy come to you like this? We came for help, the help that only you can give us. And with a message of the greatest importance for the woman Helua."

The old man shuffled his feet and looked to the others for support. They were nodding their heads wisely, and he mumbled, "Very well, we know a man named Osman. But he is dead, killed by the soldiers."

"No. I left his company a few hours ago. He was a prisoner of the bey, as I was, and we escaped together. And now he is returning to his people on the mountain, with a dagger strapped to the stump of his arm."

One of the others murmured, "Osman indeed, the leader," and the old man went on, still uncertain, "And the name of the woman you look for?"

"I told you!" Jason said angrily. "Her name is Helua, and she is Osman's daughter."

The waves made a gentle sound behind them, but the breeze was bringing them another sound, a rhythmic splashing in the surf. Jason swung around.

A woman was walking up out of the breakers. She was thickset and darkly handsome, with long, raggedy hair carelessly bound with a rag around her forehead. She wore a long black dress, drawn up between her thighs and tucked into the length of rope that served her as a belt, and her bare legs were heavy and powerful. It was unusual for an Arab woman, even a fisherwoman, to display her legs so blatantly. She stopped at the edge of the surf, with her hands on her hips and her bare feet widely spaced in defiance of all accepted decorum, as they stared at her.

Her dress was cut high at the throat in the modest Berber fashion, but it was wet, and clung to her body. Her full breasts were strong and aggressive, the nipples large and prominent, straining against the wet black cotton. She moved like an animal of overpowering sensuality. Her every movement seemed to say: *I will take you, hold you in my inescapable embrace, suck the life out of you till you are an empty corpse.* There was a look in her angry eyes that said all of this and a great deal more. Carnality seemed to flow from her in great waves.

Her voice was a surprise. It was almost the voice of a man, deep and strong but with a melody all its own.

"I am Helua, the daughter of Osman. And you say that my father is still alive?"

Jason said steadily, "He is alive, Helua. He sent me to you with a message."

For a moment she held his look, her proud head tilted back a little. And then she said harshly, "Come. I will take you to my house."

Without waiting for an answer, Helua strode off into the darkness. They followed her to a modest little shack, consisting of a single whitewashed room with mud walls, a thatched roof, and a lean-to as a kitchen. A large, rumpled bed occupied most of the room, but there was a small table, a bench, and a shelf on one wall for a few plates and dishes. A tallow was burning in a small clay pot of oil. The patchwork quilt on the bed was in brilliant colors, and Helua smoothed it over mechanically as they went in. She sat them down on the bench and said, her face creased with anxiety, "Forgive me if I talk of other things before the courtesies, but I *must* know! You say my father Osman is alive?" They could almost hear her heart beat.

Jason nodded gravely. "Yes, Helua, he is alive. And in

surprisingly good health, if we consider what he has been through."

"You swear it to me? It is not a trick?"

"I swear it to you."

A low, shuddering moan escaped her, and there were sudden tears in her eyes. She put a hand to her face to wipe them away, and turned her back so that they should not see her deep emotion. "We will talk of this in a moment," she said, "but I will not neglect my duties. First, are you hungry?"

This was a poor house, and the news he had brought was shattering; but Jason knew the rigid demands of Arab hospitality, and he answered courteously, "You are most kind. We are not hungry, though a small piece of bread would be welcome. We thank you, as we thank God."

Helua turned back to him, aware of his hesitation, and she said somberly, "This is a poor village, but we are fisherfolk. And fisherfolk never go hungry. The sea is rich, and we are part of it." She clapped her hands, and a very young girl, barefoot and dressed in rags, came and stood hesitantly at the door of the lean-to. "Food," Helua said. "Fish and bread, and while it is cooking, make tea."

The child disappeared, and Helua sat on the edge of the bed and began the mandatory courtesies. "Please God, you are well?"

"Thank God, we are well," Jason answered. "And you?"

"Thank God. And your house prospers?"

"If yours does, so does ours. Thank God."

The formalities were of vital importance, but Helua could not control herself, and Jason said quietly, seeing the moisture in her eyes, "And your father, too, is well."

She shuddered. "I was sure that they had killed him. And where is he?"

"He wants you to go to him in two days, at the cave in the rock of the eagles. That is the message he sent with me."

Her voice was anguished. "Two days? How can I wait so long?"

He smiled. "It is possible that he wants to change his

appearance as much as he can before you see him. To change his rags for good clothes, to put food into his belly, above all, to sleep off the exhaustion that must be on him, even if he would not admit it. He was on the millstone for a long, long time."

She stared at him. "All these months on the millstone?"

"Yes."

"It kills a man in a few weeks!"

"Not a man like your father, Helua." She was sobbing unashamedly now, and she brushed at the tears and mumbled, "I am not a weak woman . . ."

"I am sure of it."

She took hold of herself with a visible effort. "And your name, you said, is Jason?"

"Jason. And my woman's name is Opal." Opal looked up at the mention of her name, and touched his hand affectionately. Helua said, "She does not like to talk. It is good in a woman."

He smiled. "Oh, she talks a great deal! But she speaks no Arabic."

Soon the child came in with a large enamel washbasin filled to the brim with tiny red mullet and a pile of round, flat loaves. "Eat with good appetite," Helua said, "and be filled by the grace of Allah, who gives us fish when we are hungry." He answered with the formal phrase, "We thank you, as we thank God."

They ate with their fingers, delicately pulling the crisp, succulent fillets away from the spinal bones, wrapping them in the hot bread, and wolfing them down hungrily. Helua said, a little shyly, "And will you tell me more of my father?"

He told her in great detail of their escape, and she listened avidly, her eyes shining with pleasure. Turning to Opal, he laid a gentle hand on her arm and said, "Forgive me, my love, that all this talk must be in Arabic. One day soon, I will tell you all that I am telling her, how I escaped with her father and found the woman I love. But she speaks no English, and so . . ."

Opal nodded eagerly. "Of course, I understand. And

isn't the fish delicious?" She was ravenous. She could not remember when last she had eaten. Jason laughed and turned back to Helua.

"So now your father is free, my woman is free, and I am free. It is a matter of great comfort for all of us. Could we perhaps find a gown for her in the village? She is understandably deeply embarrassed to wear the clothes of a houri."

"Yes, it is easy. I will arrange it."

"And then, could we find a boat here, a fishing boat that I could sail to Gibraltar? I would recompense the owner, though it might take a little time." He broke off, puzzled by the look in Helua's eyes, and said, "Yes, it is not an easy journey in a small boat, but I am skilled in these matters."

Helua was shaking her head. "No, it is not that at all." Jason waited patiently, seeing that she was thinking hard and not wanting to press her. He saw to his surprise that the huge bowl of fish was almost empty, and he remembered his manners and belched loudly to show his appreciation. Opal stared at him with her eyebrows raised, but he only smiled, and said nothing even when she murmured, "Well, really!"

Helua said at last, frowning, "Do you know, Jason, about the rebels on the mountain?"

He nodded. "Your father spoke of them, yes. I have also heard that there are as many as a thousand of them up there."

"No longer. Yes, once we were more than a thousand strong, but a year or so ago the bey decided to wipe them out, and brought a great number of troops over from Algiers. And since that time, we have been reduced to less than a hundred. Have you heard of a man named Admiral Sinan?"

Jason threw Opal a look and said harshly, "I know him, to my cost."

"Since we were reduced by massacre to only the strongest of the men, who are still holding out up by the rock of the eagles, Sinan has started sending his spies into the villages here. That is why we were so careful when you came looking for me. His intention is to discover the relatives of the men on the mountain. We caught one of these spies and beat him, and before he died he told us. All of those women are to be arrested and imprisoned under torture, and the bey will offer to exchange them for any of the rebels who will give themselves up, which means that they will at once be killed. Another of Sinan's spies is secretly working for us, and we know all about this terrible plan." She hesitated. "But I am not like other women, Jason. I have spent long years with the mountain people, using a gun and a sword. A year ago, I even had my own company, fifty men under my command. I can take care of myself. The others cannot."

Helua was an anomaly in the Arab world, a woman who had somehow escaped from the confines imposed on her by her sex. She was physically very strong, having worked on the heavy nets since the age of seven, helping to haul the day's catch from the sea, and later she had been well trained as a guerrilla by her father. She was shrewd, determined, and ruthless. Once, on the mountain, finding herself pregnant, she had aborted herself with her dagger, and then had gone on to fight a major battle, killing three soldiers with the same blade. She was a woman of steel, and a very dangerous creature. In Arabic, the name Helua meant *sweet*; it was not an apt description of her.

She went on, "So now, we have been rounding up those poor women in the hope of sending them somewhere where they can be safe from the bey's depredations. There is no such place in the whole of the Barbary States. It must be Gibraltar, where you wish to go."

Jason was excited, knowing that they could help each other.

"There are no men among us who can safely make this journey. I myself was ready to command the vessel, but now I must go to my father. You are skilled with a boat, you say?"

"Yes, yes!"

"The tides are treacherous in these waters. It is not easy."

"I know it. And I know how to counter them."

"Then is it decided?"

"Yes, yes!" He explained what they were discussing to Opal. Aware of his excitement, she was watching him. She whispered, "I knew you would find a way."

"But there is a difficulty," Helua said, worried. "We have learned that the authorities in Gibraltar will not accept us readily."

"I'm sure that can't be true."

Helua sighed. "There were refugees there once before, and they were turned away. Oh yes, they were given supplies of food and water, but not allowed to land. They turned south again, beyond the Rock, and were driven ashore by high tides. They landed in Morocco, hundreds of miles from their homes where they could perhaps find help. And this may happen again."

"Well," Jason said tartly, "we'll see about that! This time, they will have to argue with me, not with a helpless group of refugees!"

"Good. You give me great comfort."

"But we must be careful," Jason said. "I have no wish to navigate a strange boat in darkness, yet we must be out of sight of the shore before it is light. It means that we must leave shortly before dawn and head north to get as far away as possible before we turn west, as soon as there are the first signs of daylight in the sky."

"Yes, you are right. And it will take me a few hours to round up the women. Some of them are in the other villages."

"I would like to see the boat as soon as possible."

"Very well. It is the largest we have, and the best. Come, I will show you."

They went out together down the beach. She showed him the craft with pride. It was about twenty feet long, solidly built, and carried a single mast with a broad, square sail, reefed now. He checked the ropes, the fittings, the spare sail, the bailing cans, found that they were all adequate, and asked, "How many passengers will there be? We have room enough for twelve or even fifteen, but no more. We'll meet with very heavy seas at this time of the year."

Helua said evasively, "There will not be too many, I think."

"Good. The lighter we are, the faster we can travel, and we must remember that these are pirate waters. There are watchtowers along the coast?"

"Three on this side of the island."

"And since we will be passing through the reef in darkness, I will need to be guided through it."

Helua pointed. "There, where the coral is high, there is room enough."

In the dim light of the moon, the opening seemed very small. He turned to Opal and said cheerfully, "I must leave you for a few minutes, my love. Stay here with Helua and wait for me."

She nodded as he stepped into the water and swam strongly out to the reef. He found that the gap between the outcrops of coral was nearly thirty feet across. He dived deeply around it, and found that there was plenty of water.

When he returned he found that the two women were sitting on the sand and trying hopelessly to talk with each other. He laughed. He said, "Then all we have to do now is wait for one hour before dawn while you gather our passengers together."

"First," Helua said, "we will drink tea to salute our new friendship, as is fitting. And then, while I search for the women, you will sleep in my house till the time comes. It is a humble house, but it is yours."

"It is a fine house," Jason said courteously, "and you are very kind."

They went back and drank the mandatory three cups of sweet tea together. Helua smoothed the bed over for them again and said, "I will go about my work now. The servant sleeps on the floor of the kitchen. Her name is Binta. If you need anything in the night, call her."

"Only a gown of some sort for Opal. A simple shift will

do, just to cover her body. And I thank you again for your help."

"A small thing for the man who brought my father back to me." They stood at the door for a moment, staring up at the dark clouds that drifted from time to time across the moon, and Helua said carefully, "You will be safe here, but it is always possible that the bey's soldiers will come searching, and so . . . on the roof there is a guard, a very young boy who keeps watch. His eyes are strong in the dark, his ears like the ears of a jackal. If anyone comes, he will know in good time and will warn you. If that happens, go with him into the water and hide behind one of the boats, as I did when you approached. Bar the door after I am gone."

A few moments later, the little room, warm in the friendly yellow light of the tallow, was theirs alone.

They lay together on the comfortable bed, their arms around each other, sharing their unspoken thoughts, each knowing exactly what the other was dreaming of . . . times gone by, the hazards they had overcome, the future that one day, without a doubt, would be theirs together. But they knew so little of each other. And when Opal whispered, "Tell me about yourself, Jason my love," he laughed in sudden surprise and answered, "My dearest, I was about to ask you the same thing. Do we read each other's thoughts? Are we indeed so close?"

"Even closer." She snuggled up to him.

"Then let us bare our souls to each other."

"Yes," she whispered. "I would like that so much. There are so many things I want to know! First, were you once a soldier?"

"A soldier, no, but a marine. How did you guess?"

"Well, I have seen you four times in a—a kind of battle. First, you rescued me from those awful men in the Casbah. Then, you fought against Sinan's men in the hotel room. And then in the cabin on board ship, when you put that foul monster Sinan out of action before he could even realize what was happening. Then the escape from the harem.

I was sure that you must have once been at least a general in the American army!"

He said, laughing, "Not even a humble lieutenant. Just a marine."

"And where were you born?"

"In a place called Suffolk, in Virginia, twenty-seven years ago. It was a year in which almost nothing of importance happened, save for two things."

Catching his joyous mood she said, "Your birth, and . . . ?"

"And the emptying of three hundred and forty-two chests of tea into Boston Harbor."

"Ah yes, the celebrated Tea Party. They still tell us in school what dreadful people the Americans are! Have you brothers and sisters?"

"None. I am an only child, and therefore horribly spoiled. A brat."

"And your parents?"

"My mother died very young, quite soon after I was born, and my father . . ." He hesitated. "He was a tobacco farmer. When I was six years old, the British came, and they burned Suffolk to the ground. He was killed."

"Oh, Jason . . ." She fell silent for a moment, holding him tightly. And then, "Is one generation enough to wipe out all those old scars?"

He answered her fiercely, "It *must* be enough! Fathers who fought each other have children who meet and fall in love."

"Yes, yes, you are right."

He sighed. "And in the course of time I became a fighting man myself, a marine. But four years ago I was involved in an unpleasant enterprise. We seized a place called Providence, in the Bahamas, and it was not an operation I was proud of, for reasons I will not bother you with. So I did what I am afraid I quite often do."

"And that is?"

"On occasion, when a moral dilemma comes my way, I avoid both its horns by evasive action that may sometimes be thought of as reprehensible."

Opal took a long, deep breath. "Well now," she said. "I am convinced that you just made a very brilliant observation of the most profound social significance. And I will admit that I haven't the slightest idea what you are talking about."

"I ran away," Jason said glumly. "It means that rather than take part in what I considered to be barbarities, or get myself hanged for mutiny, I took the coward's path and deserted."

"What coward's path?" Opal said indignantly. "I have seen your bravery so often!"

He still felt a little uneasy about it. "I simply left my ship, and she was a good ship too, named after my home state, the *Virginia*. I had so many good friends aboard, and I left them." His hand was at her breast, caressing, and it was strange to feel her soft flesh under that strange gossamer material that was neither gauze nor silk but something in between. He said quietly, "Will you condemn me for it?"

"Condemn you? Good heavens, no! Why should I?"

"It is not considered very honorable to desert."

"If reason demands it, it cannot be reduced to such simple terms. As for honor itself . . ." She was suddenly very sad. "There is sometimes a kind of dishonor that we must learn to accept. I too have had my share of it."

"No, this I will never believe!"

"Yes, one day I will tell you of it. Indeed, I *must* tell you, we will have no secrets, you and I." She bit her lip with the memory of her stepfather's assault. Jason sensed the change in her mood, and sought to change it back again. He was desperately weary, trying to keep the insistent need for sleep away, and with the surf so close outside their hut there was only one way to fight the drowsiness. He said happily, raising himself up on one elbow and kissing her, "Come, a great delight is in store for you. We will go down to the water and lie in the surf together."

"Do what?"

"Lie in the surf, have you never done that? Have you never felt the gentle waves wash back and forth over your naked body?"

"Jason! Mercy, no!"

"Then you shall tonight!"

He leaped to his feet and slipped out of his breeches, kicking them aside in a sudden burst of enthusiasm. "The blouse first," he whispered, and pulled it up over her head. He dropped to his knees and untied the ribbon at her waist, and pulled the fragile pantaloons down to her ankles. Then he clutched her tightly to him for a moment and kissed her. He rose to his feet and pulled their warm bodies close together. She whispered, "Jason, we *cannot* go naked outside of this room! There are people there!"

"Nonsense! We can, and we will! They are all asleep in their shuttered houses. And the moon is almost down now. Come!"

He took her hand, and she whispered again, "Jason, my love, if anyone should see us . . ."

She welcomed the caress of the breeze as they ran together over the sand to the whispering surf. They splashed ankle-deep in the water. It was still warm from the heat of the day. He pulled her down in the shallows. The tiny waves rolled up from her feet to her thighs, to her waist and her breasts, and then receded with a caress that was unlike anything she had ever experienced. Jason's hands were as light as the surf itself as he gently parted her thighs to receive the stroking of the tiny waves. They splashed over her as though they had a sensuous mind of their own, seeking her out and exciting her beyond endurance.

In a few moments, she was gasping. She reached out and found his manhood, as hard as iron, and moaned softly as she pulled him onto her. He thrust into her at once and held himself there for a moment. And then, with the rhythm of the waves, he began a slow and deliberate lunging, driving into her as the surf climbed up her body, pulling back as it receeded with him, then filling her again as the waters returned, matching his motions precisely to their cadence.

She could not count the spasms that came over her, engulfing her completely, nor could she count the time that slipped by in her delirium. She felt him flooding into her when he could no longer restrain himself. She could hardly breathe.

She stared up at the dark sky over his shoulder, and gently touched the savage lacerations on his back. In a little while he eased himself from her and lay beside her, an arm around her shoulder, a hand over her breast. He whispered, "I love you so dearly, Opal. Nothing must ever separate us again."

"Nothing ever will, my beloved."

"To be together, always . . ."

"Yes, forever." She stroked him gently. He was still fighting sleep, but he knew that his strength would soon return. He murmured, "Shall we sleep now for a while, my love? The sand is a good bed for lovers."

"Here? In the water?"

"Yes."

"The tide will come in, Jason dear, and drown us both if we sleep."

"The tide is going out now, not coming in. Talk to me while I fall asleep. I long for the comfort of your voice."

"And what shall I tell you? How much I love you? There are not the words."

"Tell me who you are, Opal Grant."

"You know who I am. I am the woman who loves you so dearly."

"Yes. The Arabs would say: *Insh'Allah*, may it please God."

"I will tell you . . ." She hesitated, and fell silent for a while. He rolled over and threw a thigh across her own, and rested his head on her breast. He murmured, "Tell me about your family."

"My family? I too am an only child. My mother was a very beautiful woman, she died a long time ago. Her name was Margherita, and she came from Brazil." She did not hesitate. "There was Negro blood in her veins, as there is in mine."

"Yes, I was sure of it." His eyes were closed.

"You were?"

"Since the day we first met, my love."

"Does it disturb you, Jason?"

"Disturb me? Why should it disturb me?" He was murmuring, in that void between wakefulness and sleep. "It should disturb no intelligent man. You are so warm, dear Opal. I could sleep like this for ever. And your father?"

For a little while, she did not answer.

"The man who brought me up in his house is not my true father, but he is the only one I know. He is Sir Neville Grant. You may have heard of him, a very famous man."

"Uh-huh . . ."

Should she tell him? *Bare our souls*, he had said, and she had agreed, *There must be no secrets between us.*

"He is a brilliant man," she whispered. "But he is not—not a very nice man." She took a deep breath and whispered, "One night, when I was seventeen years old, he raped me, Jason. He threw me to the floor in our library and he raped me, do you understand what I am saying? I left home at once, and since then I have traveled the world, searching for . . . for you, I think. Jason? Jason?"

Jason was fast asleep, his lips still touching her breast. Opal sobbed, and soon fell into a deep sleep too, conscious of the cool breeze playing over her naked body, conscious that in his sleep he was growing strong again under the touch of her light fingers.

The water was lapping at her ankles now.

CHAPTER NINE

Helua carried a dagger and a revolver in the rope around her waist when she returned three hours later with the refugee women.

She found the door unbarred and open, and drew her gun before she went inside. She whistled shrilly when she found the bed empty. The small boy came clambering down from the rafter where he had been on watch. She slapped him hard across the face for no reason at all and said, "Well? Where are they? Where are they, child?"

He said happily, "They are in the water, sleeping now."

"In the *water*? The soldiers came?"

"No. They went there for another purpose." Grinning, he made a vulgar gesture with his fist, moving it up and down, and she slapped his face again. "Where are they?"

"In the water," he repeated. "I told you! Making love. I watched them. Four times, *w'allahi*, I counted. I have good eyes in the darkness. Four times! He is a very strong man."

"Imbecile!"

She hurried out of the shack and found Jason and Opal fast asleep, lying close together on the sand. She stared at them for a moment in the darkness. Then she grunted, and crouched down on the sand to tap Jason on the shoulder. He awoke at once from a deep sleep of utter exhaustion. He stared up at her in shock, acutely aware of his nakedness and wondering in panic what he could cover himself with. He reached out and found a mass of seaweed and dragged it over their hips, and said, "Oh God . . ." He saw that Opal had awakened too, and was trying to pull the slippery weeds over herself.

Helua looked down at him and laughed shortly, ignoring Opal completely. "Have no fear," she said. "I have seen naked men before, more than I can count. But you must come now, the refugees are here. And soon it will be dawn."

He stood up and clutched at his vegetable protection, feeling very foolish. Helua held out a black gown that was slung over her shoulder and said curtly, "A robe for your woman, as you wanted."

Opal took it from her gratefully and pulled it over her head. She looked at her beloved Jason and tried not to giggle; he was so embarrassed!

Helua strode away, and they followed her back to the hut. Jason slipped quickly into the breeches he had cast aside, as Helua studied him calmly, appraising him, relishing the looks of him. When he was decent again, he said, "And where are the refugees?"

"At the edge of the woods," she answered. "It is better that they hide until they go aboard."

"Good. How many are there?"

"Not too many." Her voice was deceptively casual, and he threw her a sharp look. But he said only, "I'd better have a word with them. Will you take me to them?"

"Yes, when you are ready."

"I am ready now."

He took Opal's hand and they followed her out into the cool dark night. When they reached the trees, Helua called softly and the refugees began streaming out from under cover. There were very old women, hobbling on sticks, mothers clutching babies to their breasts, and very young girls. They were all staring at him with a hope in their eyes that touched his heart. But when they were all gathered round him, waiting expectantly for him to speak, he said to Helua, "In God's name! How many are they?"

She answered calmly, "Thirty-two women and children."

He was aghast. "Thirty-two people in a twenty-foot boat?

I was hoping for no more than fifteen, which is already too many!"

Helua said quietly, "Then you will leave half of them behind, if you insist. And perhaps you yourself should select the ones you sacrifice to the tender mercies of the bey. The very old ones, I would say, who have little left to live for."

He was furious. He muttered, "You know I can't do that!"

"Yes, I know it. And so you will make room for all of them."

By the fragile light of the stars, he looked at their faces, the old and ravaged, the bright, desperate eyes of the younger girls, the tranquility of the unsuspecting babies. He made a little speech to them in Arabic, trying to comfort them.

"My friends, there is a hard and perhaps perilous voyage ahead of us. The boat will be greatly overloaded, so you must listen to me carefully or we will never reach our destination. You must all lie or sit as low down in the boat as possible, even though we will undoubtedly spend much of our time carrying a great deal of unwanted water. I will expect all the younger women to bail constantly. Our great danger—" He broke off. One of the very old women was grinning toothlessly at him, and she said, cackling, "The *younger* women? I can bail faster than any of them. I have been doing it for forty years." She laughed happily. "The children cannot say this!"

"Well, good." He turned to Helua. "There are only two bailing cans aboard. I must have more. Ten, twelve, fifteen if you can find them."

Helua nodded. "I will find them." She singled out three of the young girls and told them to go from boat to boat, from house to house, and find every receptacle they could, and as they ran off he said to the others, "Our great danger lies in being swamped. Our boat was made to carry eight or nine people, not thirty-two. But I ask you not to be afraid. I am a skilled sailor, and I promise you that I will bring you safely to Gibraltar. I promise you too that when we arrive there we will not be turned away. My life on it."

To his acute embarrassment, they began to clap, and some of the older women were even making that strange ululation with their tongues that they reserved for occasions of great emotional import. He was deeply moved. He felt Opal's hand in his, clutching at him involuntarily. She did not understand what he had been saying, but she understood their reaction to his words, and felt his deep concern for them all.

He turned to her then and said quietly, "The boat will be heavily overloaded, my love, and I have told them not to be afraid. I tell you the same thing—"

"With you, how could I be afraid?"

He wanted to take her in his arms instantly, but he contented himself with squeezing her hands tightly to give her a sign of his great love for her. Then, to his consternation, Helua came close to him, ignoring Opal, reaching up to pull his head down and kiss him. She said fiercely, "You are a strong man, Jason, perhaps even as strong as my father. And if you did not have your woman with you, who speaks no Arabic, then I would take you to my bed before you sail to show you what it is to be loved by an equally strong woman. But it may not be, so go now. Take my people with you to safety. And know that there is one woman on the island of Djidji who will never forget you."

He swallowed hard. Her hand had slipped down between their close bodies to find his manhood, and she was gripping it firmly. He said, stammering a little, "It may be that . . . that I will never forget you either, Helua. When you go to your father, will you give him my *sala'ams*?"

"I will. Go now. Very soon, there will be light in the sky."

"There is one more thing you must do for me."

"Anything!"

"Can you swim well?"

"Of course! That is a foolish question. I am a fisherwoman!"

"I marked carefully in my mind exactly where the opening in the reef is. But we will be very deep in the water."

"Very well, I will guide you in the darkness. Come, it is time to leave." She raised her voice and said to the women, "Remember one thing. You must do instantly whatever the foreigner tells you! His name is Jason. He is not only your captain, he is my friend and the friend of my father Osman, whom you all know."

She led them down to the boat. They splashed through the gentle surf, and piled untidily into the little vessel as Jason stood waist-deep in the sea and steadied it for them. He looked back to the shore. Three young women were splashing towards them, carrying old cans and a few metal cooking pots, tossing them into the boat. Soon they were all aboard. He turned to Opal and said, "Now, my love, you must help me. Helua will swim ahead of us to find the opening in the reef and guide me to it. We are very low in the water and I cannot see her. So you will please lie down in the bow, and watch her, and guide me."

She had understood nothing of their talk, but she nodded eagerly. "Yes, of course. Port is left, I think?"

"Port is left, yes. The opening is quite narrow, so precision is the order of the day."

"I will be precise." She forced her way through the water and dragged herself aboard in the bow, and looked back to see Jason hauling himself over the stern. He raised the sail to the quarter-mark, and she heard the thud of the sail as the boom swung over. The boat began to move slowly forward. Helua was already ahead of them, swimming strongly, and as they followed her Opal called back, "Ah . . . port the helm a little!" Jason answered her happily, delighted with her eagerness, "Just tell me left or right, my darling!"

"Left then, but only a little! Ah, two points."

"Thank you!" He swung the tiller over a trifle and called out, "Are we overtaking her?"

"No! Falling behind a little, I think."

"You *think*? There is no place in this operation for 'I think,' my dearest!"

"Yes, we are falling behind!"

He hauled on the sheet and raised the sail a little. Opal

shouted, "Good! A little to the right . . . Steady as she goes."

He held his course. In a moment the reef was looming up on him, perilously close. He called out anxiously, "Opal! Are we all right?"

"Steady as she goes . . ."

They swept through the opening, and he saw Helua clambering up onto the reef. She stood there with her feet widespread, the black dress clinging to her body, her arm raised in a salute. He heard her strong voice calling, "Farewell, Jason! *Ruh ma sala'am,* go in peace!"

"Wa aleikum sala'am kaman, ya habibti! Peace to you too, my friend!" On an impulse, he swung the boat into the wind and circled skillfully only a few feet from the reef. She gasped; they were only a few feet from the coral. He shouted, "Do not worry, the boat handles well!"

"My thanks to you, Jason! Do not forget me!"

"I never will! Tell your father, when you meet with him, that I found my woman, that with your good help we sail now to safety! Tell him from me: God go with you always, friend Osman! Please God, we will meet again one day!"

"Farewell, dear Jason!" Was there a catch in her voice? "Be happy with your woman!"

They were in open water as the wind filled the sail, and Jason knew that the time had come to take full advantage of the elements, though the waves were alarming. He shouted, "Opal! Back to me, quickly!" She stumbled over a score of wet bodies, struggling her way back to him. He said, "Take the tiller, lean your body into it, we cannot lose the wind now or we'll be swamped!"

She took the smooth oak bar from him and was amazed at the resistance it offered her. She shouted, "Over, over, get back, damn you!" and forced it back where it was supposed to be, as Jason hauled on the sheet and raised the sail fully. He shrieked, "Harder, harder, force your body into it!"

She fought it as though it were a living thing. One of the young women was suddenly beside her, helping her to control it, speaking to her in rapid Arabic of which she understood not a word. She saw the sail billowing out as Jason raised it and fastened the sheet. He was beside her instantly, taking the tiller and correcting the course by a trifle, turning the boat head on into pounding waves that towered more than ten feet over them, tossing them savagely. The young woman who had helped Opal moved away. She was young, and though muscular she was very slender and not unattractive. He said, "Wait!" and she turned, her bold eyes on him. He said quietly, "The course was very correct there. Was it by chance? Or from knowledge?"

There was a mocking smile on her face. "From knowledge, American!"

He was surprised. "You know me for an American?" Helua had used the word *frangi*, foreigner.

Her voice was mocking. "I was not always just the daughter of a bandit. For more than a year I was a whore in the Casbah, working to earn my dowry. It was after the war, and many of my customers were Americans. I know Americans when I see them. I can *smell* them. I even speak your damned language!" She switched to English and said, scornfully, "Hello, Johnny, you want love me, Johnny?"

The waves were pounding at them rhythmically. Jason said quietly, "And yet you know about boats?"

She answered, with that peculiar Berber arrogance, "Yes. I know about boats! Before he became a rebel, my father was the best fisherman on the coast. At the age of ten I was helping him, and by the time I was fifteen I was a better helmsman than he was. That was when I went to the Casbah, because we had no money, you understand? After a year, I had earned enough money for my dowry, but my betrothed, whom I had never seen of course, had been killed in a brawl." She shrugged. "And so I went back to the sea again. And I am a better sailor even than Helua, who took such a fancy to you."

"And your name, child?"

"My name is Andara."

"Then stay close by me, Andara. I do not like the turn of the wind. I may need help."

She said, mocking, "Perhaps we will all drown, American!"

As though to echo her thoughts, a wave caught them broadsides and almost capsized them. Some of the women screamed out their fear at the sudden, unexpected motion, and Jason shouted, "*Kulshi tamam*, all is well!"

They were head on into the seas again. The little boat rose and fell as they crested the heavy waves. He looked over the side, and saw that they had alarmingly little freeboard. The water was only a few inches below the toe-rail, and it was beginning to pour in with little rushing sounds that were very ominous.

He called out, "Begin bailing now, please! As fast as the water comes in, it must be bailed out." Some of the women instantly took up the cans and the cooking pots and began fighting the onrush of the dreadful sea. A few of them were moaning, squatting on their haunches and swaying back and forth, sure that they were about to die. And the journey had only just begun!

Jason looked at Opal, close beside him, and saw the apprehension in her lovely eyes. He said quietly, "There is nothing to fear, my love. The boat is good, it responds very well. And though we are shipping water, we have hands enough to bail it out. In two days' time, we will be in Gibraltar . . . safe again."

They were settling into a steady course and holding their own very well. Her arm was around him, searching for the comfort of his presence. He said softly, "Not only safe again, but . . . also we will have thwarted the evil ambitions the bey had for you, a pawn in the dreadful game of Berber diplomacy."

"Diplomacy?" Opal was puzzled. "What the bey had in store for me hardly merits the term *diplomacy*! Unless you mean that I was to be his present to the bashaw of Tunis."

"You did not know?"

"Know what, my dearest Jason?"

"About your father."

She felt the blood draining from her face. She whispered, "My father? No! What has my father to do with this? I have not seen him or heard from him in three long years!"

He knew that it would pain her, but he had to tell her. He said quietly, "The bey was planning to hold you hostage, to bolster his demands for more tribute from England. You did not know that?"

She understood immediately. Her hand was at her throat. "A hostage? Oh God . . ." She whispered hoarsely, "We are not very close, my father and I. But if I understand you correctly . . . The tribute, you say?"

"Yes. With you as hostage, the bey thinks he can persuade your father to raise it. If he does not . . ."

"No man in power should have to face such a choice!" Her voice was hollow. "And even if he were to agree, it would not change my position, am I right?"

Jason said gravely, "Yes, you are right. The Arabs take, they do not give. It is part of their philosophy. And what they have, even when the price is paid, they will not easily give up. Sir Neville, by all acounts, is not a fool. He will know that whatever he does, you will not be returned to him. Even if he were to persuade the prime minister to increase the tribute. Once this has been done, they will have won their battle. And why should they honorably reciprocate with your release? They are not honorable people, the Arabs. And so, if we can get news to him fast enough of your safety, perhaps we can save him from the awful problem he has to face."

She could not really believe the extent of the disaster. She whispered, "You are telling me . . . my father *knows* what has happened to me?"

"Without a doubt he knows. Or soon will."

"Oh lord . . ."

Opal fell into a deep, brooding silence as their boat ploughed heavily into the waves. The water was still pouring in, and the women were bailing furiously.

The letter from the bey had arrived in London by pigeon.

This exotic means of communication had first been established six and a half centuries ago by the sultan of Baghdad, who was a fancier of homing pigeons. It was very popular with the Barbary pirates, since wherever their ships might be, these strange birds would find their way back to their lofts, the messages tied to their legs in tiny cotton cylinders.

This particular pigeon found its way to the loft on the roof of a house in Chelsea, a little village three miles outside London. It was lovingly fondled by a man named Huroc, Admiral Sinan's chief of intelligence in England. He clutched it closely, holding it to his cheek and hearing the beating of that powerful heart, whispering to it, "Ah, my beloved Andusa, the most beautiful of all birds, and what have you brought to me on this fine day?"

He unwrapped the cotton sheath and took out the tiny roll of paper, and found his magnifying glass to read the fine Arabic script. It was brief and to the point:

> Horuc from Karim Bey Abdullah. Sir Neville Grant, Second Secretary at the Foreign Ministry. We hold his daughter Opal hostage. There is the matter of increased tribute. It is in your hands, Horuc, and we rely upon your own initiative and your known persuasive powers. Act quickly. Remember that you are our son, our brother, and our father.
>
> Karim Bey Abdullah.

Act quickly? Horuc was not the kind of man who acted quickly on anything. He went to his study and unlocked the cupboard where he kept his secret files, written in the *nahwi* Arabic of classical scholars that few could understand, and leafed through them: Garland, Gillman, Giser-Browne, Grant . . . He extracted the sheaf of papers and took them to his desk by the window. In the fading light of the evening he read:

> GRANT, Sir Neville Harvey Price Edward . . . perhaps one of the most powerful speakers in the House, he has been heard referring to the Berbers as

"pirates and barbarians," and he regards them as England's implacable enemies. Prime Minister Pitt considers him an ally and a staunch defender of British claims to supremacy in the Mediterranean . . . has been considered by the Tories as a possible future prime minister, a possibility that has been somewhat eroded by his addiction to alcohol. It is seldom possible to be sure whether Sir Neville is drunk or sober, a condition known in English parlance as "holding your drink like a gentleman" . . . a womaniser of very liberal tastes. He has bedded half the most desirable ladies of London's society, and has frequently been seen at brothels and stews. In his own opinion he is rigidly honest, and all attempts to bribe him have failed, although our women spies, after being in his company, have often reported to us many closely guarded secrets. . . . A widower, living well. His late wife Margherita, who was born in Brazil, had a daughter, Opal, by a previous marriage. For the last three years she has been on the so-called Grand Tour of the Mediterranean countries.

Huroc leaned back in his leather chair, stretched out his long legs, and ruminated.

He was tall and thin and very elegant, a young man in his early thirties, good-looking, with darkly flashing eyes and full lips, a hawk nose, neat beard and moustache, and a taste for the finest clothes that London's tailors could provide. He boasted an English-French education, spoke seven languages fluently, and prided himself on his blunt, down-to-earth approach to the most complex problems. He was very, very rich; it gave him pleasure to reflect that his high standard of living was paid for by his enemies the British out of their blackmailed tribute.

He had come from very humble stock. His father was a Bedouin, and his tribe still lived in some remote fastness of the Saharan Atlas mountains. But he had risen fast in the bey's employ, and now he flaunted his fine clothes, his sophistication, and his ease of language, and he thought of himself as a gentleman.

He stood at the high window of his study and looked at the darkening sky for a while. Then he called for his carriage. Half an hour later he was raising the heavy brass knocker on the door of his quarry's house. He said pleasantly to the butler, "Please give Sir Neville my apologies for disturbing him, but the matter is of some importance. My name is Huroc, and I am an ambassador from the Barbary States. Tell him that I crave a few moments of his time."

The butler inclined his head. "If you will kindly wait in the library, sir?"

The library was lined with family portraits, and Huroc studied them as he waited.

Soon Sir Neville entered, his hand out politely but a look on his face that seemed to indicate suspicion. Huroc summed him up: a powerfully built man in good physical condition, with no sign of alcohol's ravages, and with an air of authority about him.

And what, Huroc thought, could be the reason for that evident distrust? Sir Neville enlightened him at once. "My man told me only the name Huroc," he said, "but I assume it is Huroc Bey?"

Huroc took the proffered hand and shook it; the grip was very strong, but there was no warmth in it at all. "A bey indeed," Huroc murmured, "though I seldom use my title, Sir Neville. This is a great honor for me. I feel that we should have met before, and it is to my chagrin that we have not."

"An ambassador from the Barbary States, my man said. Not *the* ambassador, whom I know personally, but *an* ambassador. If, of course, he reported you correctly."

So *that* was the reason for the wariness! Huroc smiled. "Correctly indeed, sir. In your parlance I might be called a minister without portfolio. I am a confidante of Karim Bey Abdullah, and of the other rulers. And their servant, as I am yours."

"Well. Be that as it may." Sir Neville turned away and

said, "I won't offend you, Horuc Bey, by offering you a drink. But you won't mind if I take a small glass of brandy in your presence?"

Huroc bowed and said affably, "Ah, those Moslem prohibitions! I have long since discarded them, Sir Neville, as being far too inhibiting for a gentleman of sophisticated tastes."

A gentleman indeed, Sir Neville was thinking. *The man's an overdressed bloody Berber!* But he said, "Then you'll join me?"

"You are most kind, sir, and I thank you."

Sir Neville poured the drinks and handed him one. He asked, "And to what do I owe the honor of this visit, Huroc Bey?"

Huroc raised his glass and said piously, "May Allah grant that your house always prosper. The matter I must acquaint you with is both political . . . and personal."

Sir Neville frowned. "Personal? I find that quite extraordinary, sir."

"Yes, I fear so. And may I compliment you on the excellence of your brandy."

Sir Neville said coldly, "I flatter myself that everything in my house is excellent."

"Excellent indeed. A fine library, a fine house . . . it is hard to believe that your daughter could ever bring herself to leave such excellent surroundings."

There was a tiny, frigid silence. Sir Neville put his unfinished drink down and said coldly, "My daughter, sir, cannot possibly concern you in the least."

Huroc smiled. He said quietly, "She concerns us both very closely, Sir Neville. She is our prisoner, sir."

Sir Neville felt the blood draining from his face. He whispered, "I think I do not fully understand you, Huroc Bey."

"Our prisoner," Huroc said again. "You are aware, I believe, that we Berbers are—what is the phrase you like to use? Ah yes, 'pirates and barbarians.' Well, your daughter Opal is in our barbaric hands, and she will stay there till you agree to our terms for her release."

Sir Neville was in shock, and could find no words. Huroc went on smoothly, "Those terms, simply stated, are that you persuade the Prime Minister to double the tribute England pays to my master and yours, the bey. The bey's demand will shortly be made officially, and at that time, we will expect you to persuade the Prime Minister that compliance is far cheaper than war. When you do so, then your daughter will be returned to you, less harmed than she will be if you procrastinate."

Sir Neville said harshly, "*Less* harmed? In God's name, Huroc, what is happening to her now?"

Huroc shrugged. "If you will accept a guess," he said blandly, "the bey is probably making sport of her. He enjoys English women. And when he has finished with her, it is probable that he will pass her on to the ruler of Tripoli, or perhaps Tunis, as a gesture of his friendship to them. But one thing is certain. In the course of time, unless you come to her rescue, she will eventually be handed over to the soldiers. It is customary with the bey's discarded women. Has it ever occurred to you in how many ways a woman may be enjoyed?"

Sir Neville was trying desperately to control his trembling. His glazed eyes were on the heavy poker that stood by the open fireplace.

He knew that no matter what he did, Opal would never be returned to him. There was nothing he could do now to help her. He had dealt, at the official level, with these people for many years, and he knew that honoring bargains was no part of the Berber philosophy. They would kill her before they would release her to tell the world of their malevolence. He knew it.

He said quietly, "You will return her to me, if I agree to your demands?"

Huroc said, smiling, sure that the battle was won, "My word on it."

"The word of a barbarian? Scum that you are, you expect me to believe such a travesty of the truth?"

Huroc's face tightened. He said softly, "The word of a gentleman."

Sir Neville could no longer control himself. "Scum!" he roared. "What, is she already dead? Savage! Swine!" It was a bellow of livid fury. He picked up the poker and swung it furiously. In alarm, Huroc threw up his arm to avoid the blow, but the weapon was in the hand of a man obsessed by maniacal rage. The poker crashed through and split the self-styled gentleman's head wide open.

Huroc lay dead at his feet. Sir Neville swayed above him, trying to convince himself that there was triumph in what he had done, the triumph of revenge for a dead daughter. He dropped the bloodied poker to the floor and turned away, finished his brandy and poured himself another. He sat down in his favorite chair with the bottle beside him, and drank one glass after another, staring at Huroc's body and thinking of the lovely lost daughter he had ravished and driven from her home to degradation and death.

An hour had gone by before he staggered to his feet, the bottle empty. He grabbed the body by the throat and shook it like a rag doll, and screamed, "May you rot in hell, Huroc!"

He found his feet again and clambered laboriously up the long staircase. On the fourth landing, he took down a portrait of Opal as a child that was hanging there. Clutching it to his chest, sobbing, he went on up to the roof.

The night sky was bright with a beautiful moon. He walked to the low wall that surrounded the roof and climbed up onto it, and looked over the rooftops of a city he had always loved. He held the painting tightly. The moonlight was very cold.

He screamed at the top of his voice, "Opal! Forgive me!" And then he stepped forward into the void.

Four stories below, he smashed into the pavement and lay still. Sir Neville Grant, scion of an ancient and honorable family, the last male of his line, was dead.

CHAPTER TEN

The sea was pounding the fragile craft with a ferocity dreamed up by the demons of hell.

The wind had changed, and was blowing against the currents. The waves were built up to monstrous proportions, rising more than twenty feet above them, erratic in their direction.

Jason had hauled on the sheet for a close tack with the sail half reefed, and he forced the bow into the waves. There were great walls of water ahead of them, followed by terrifying valleys into which they dropped with ferocious speed, then up the next wall of water again. This was a well-built Berber boat, but there was precious little freeboard, and the waves were swamping in.

And a new danger approached. It was still dark and they were heading as closely to the north as they could. There were red-gold streaks in the distant sky to their right. Against these were framed the tall sails of a three-masted ship, fully rigged and bearing down on them fast. Jason said urgently, "Everyone quiet now, no sound at all."

Opal whispered, "A pirate?"

He nodded. "Yes, an Algerian frigate, by the looks of her."

"And can they see us?"

"No, I think not. We can only see her because of the light behind her. Behind us, there is still darkness. Ssshhh."

In silence, they waited as Jason held his course. Even the

bailing had stopped. But he whispered, "No, keep bailing. No other sounds."

The frigate was a fine ship, her sails billowing splendidly, and she was moving very fast, her tall prow biting into the sea. She passed them by no more than a hundred yards off their beam. They could clearly see more than a dozen cannon in their ports on the lower deck. They all held their breaths as she swept by. Opal whispered, "So close, and they could not see us?"

"They saw us. They must have."

Then, as though to prove the truth, one of the frigate's rear cannons roared, and then another. Two balls dropped into the sea a hundred feet ahead of them. One of the women screamed. But Jason said calmly, "We are in no danger. We are too small a target, the seas are too heavy, and she is moving away from us too fast."

Opal whispered, "But if they stop?"

Jason shook his head. "They will not."

"Can you be so sure?"

He laughed. "They don't know who we are, they know only that this small boat is too full to be an innocent fisherman, so they fire at it on principle. More important, no frigate skipper will stop his ship when she's running so well. A ship is not like a horse that can be reined in and spurred on again immediately. If he stops now, it will be half a day before he can be under way again."

He tried to speak convincingly, but he was not at all sure that he was right. Their escape was certainly known, and soldiers would be scouring the island for them. It was possible that ships had been warned to be on the lookout for any strange vessels. And the soldiers might have come to Bir Birein and found someone there to beat the truth out of. It was a possibility, and it worried him.

Then a final shot was fired at them, and the frigate was disappearing, well out of range, not changing her course.

They were lucky. On board the frigate, the captain had said, growling, "Refugees, by the looks of them. Though in seas like this they won't get far in a fishing boat. Give the rear gunners some practice, Gunner-Master, while they're still in our range. There's little chance of hitting so small a target, but we may as well take it."

He had been out of touch with Algiers for more than a week, and knew nothing of Opal and Jason, or he would indeed have stopped his ship for so worthy a prize.

So the little boat sailed on. The frigate's strong wash was tossing them about like a cork. Jason ordered, "Bail, bail, never stop bailing!" The waves were lapping over the sides as they crested one huge wave after another.

But now their difficulties were increased.

The Berbers were some of the greatest sailors the world had ever known. They could maneuver large frigates in and out of tiny coves scarcely large enough to hold a rowboat, and their knowledge of sails, winds, currents was formidable. They could judge the movement of the waves and the consequent rise and fall of their decks with an astonishing precision that permitted them to fire their cannon with deadly accuracy, most of the time. And yet, in the important matter of detail, they were careless to the point of stupidity. Maintenance was a word they hardly knew, because in their philosophy if something worked it would go on working for ever.

The caulking of the fishing boat's timbers had not been attended to in a very long time. Jason realized what was happening when he saw that the water was rising in the boat faster than the women could bail it out. They were redoubling their efforts, but it was not enough.

He saw the young woman he had spoken with before, Andara, staring up at him with that mocking look still in her eyes. As though reading his thoughts, she shouted over the wind, "A leak, American! Perhaps many leaks! We will all die now!" The thought did not seem to disturb her in the least, and he thought of the Arab reasoning that said *kulshi min Allah*, everything is from God and therefore to be accepted and even welcomed, whatever it might be. But he said to her angrily, "No! We will not sink! Bring me the spare sail, and ropes, quickly!"

She was laughing suddenly, full of spirit. "You are mad, *majnoon*! You think we can stop in seas like this?" But she dragged out the sail and a coil of rope, crawled back to him, and said fiercely, "A knife. I need a knife, I do not have one!"

Someone produced a dagger for her, and she began cutting the rope into lengths as she said, "I know what has to be done now, but it is dangerous, very dangerous. We cannot turn into the wind, or the waves will capsize us instantly." She was fastening the ropes to the grommets of the sail. "But you have to fother now, or we will surely sink. You know, I hope, that it cannot be done while we are under way?"

"It can, and that is what we must do. But fothering is not easy at the best of times, and we have no oakum aboard."

"We Berbers do not use oakum in fothering. It means that the sail must be drawn very tight. And one man cannot do it alone. I will go down with you."

He hesitated. For a man alone, it would be next to impossible in such a sea. But he knew there was no other solution to the problem. He asked, "Have you done it before?"

"Many times."

"In such seas as these?"

"Once, yes."

"While the boat is still under way?"

"Never."

"You know the dangers?"

"I can imagine them. We will need a safety rope."

"Of course." He said, worried, "I do not like it, Andara. One man alone cannot do it, it is quite impossible. But a woman down there—"

Her dark eyes flashed. "What, a woman?" she said angrily. "I am as strong as you are, American! And I am sure that I swim better. I am a Berber!"

"You know the power of the water down there?"

"I know it! I can fight it! I can fight *you* if I must, and win!"

Jason sighed. "Very well. I will be close beside you if you have any difficulty."

Andara said scornfully, "*I* will be close beside *you.*" Her voice was heavy with sarcasm. "If you are drowning, reach for me. I will drag you to safety and then finish the work myself."

He watched her long fingers flying expertly with the ropes, fastening the rapid clove-hitches with a speed that would have done credit to a marine. They were holding their own with the bailing now as the women worked furiously, some of them exhausted, dropping back and handing the bailing cans to others. He said quietly to Andara, "You are not lacking in courage, child."

Her shining eyes were on him momentarily, but her fingers did not stop working. "Stop calling me *child,*" she said angrily. "I am not a child, not even a virgin. I am a woman, as I will show you if we have the chance."

He sighed. "How many ropes have we?"

"What, you cannot count? We have six. It is enough. Three each."

"I will take four of them."

"We will take one each, the foremost first, you on the left and I on the right. And then we will dive for the others. Two for you and two for me."

"As you wish. Tell the women what we are doing."

"Very well." As she called out, explaining in detail what was happening, Jason turned to Opal and said, "And now, my dearest, my life is in your hands. I am going over the side with this young woman here."

"You are doing *what*?"

"The boat is leaking badly. We have to drag the spare sail under our hull and fasten it there, and it is a job that requires more than two hands. In the marines it was never done with less than six men. We call it fothering, and it calls for a certain expertise. It calls for strength and speed underwater too, but Andara tells me she has done it before. So, you must handle the tiller for me, and keep us headed into the waves, holding the same steady course unless a heavy wave comes to us on our beam, at our side, when you will instantly turn into it—Oh God! How can I teach you seamanship in one quick lesson?"

"Tell me!" Opal said furiously. "Tell me what has to be done, and I will do it!"

"Yes, I am sure of it. The danger will come from a wave on our beam, and you must watch for this and head into it at once. It is essential to keep the bow headed into the heaviest wave at all times. The bow, that's the front of the boat—"

"Jason! I am beginning to hate you!"

"Watch for rogue waves all the time. If one comes at us from the side, that is to say on the beam—"

"I know, I know! You told me."

"Good." He gave her the tiller and said to Andara, "Someone else to handle the sail. If it spills . . ."

"Of course." She called, "Nasira! *Ta'ali*, come!" A sturdy young woman raised herself up from the bottom of the boat and Andara told her what had to be done. She said to Jason scornfully, "She is a woman of no quality at all, but she knows a little about sailing."

"Then we are ready."

Jason fastened the guideline and tossed it overboard. "Be sure to seize it at once."

"I know what has to be done."

They fastened the ends of the foremost ropes to the post, and took the corners of the sail on their hands. As they stood together in the bow, Jason said, "The force of the water will drive the canvas back where we need it. Hold onto it, find the safety line, hold onto that too."

"I know what to do!"

"Then haul yourself forward for the second rope on the port side. I will take the starboard. Are we ready?"

"Ready!"

"Then . . . *Fi'l ba'hr*! Into the sea!"

They dropped into the water in precise coordination. It caught them and drove them aft with its monstrous fury. Jason found the safety line instantly and let go his corner of the canvas, reached for Andara and was reassured to discover that she had found it too. But the force of the water, the surge of the waves, and the speed of the boat—all these things thrust him onto the wrong side of the hull, and he was entangled in the billowing canvas, reaching out for something to grab to save himself from being swept away and lost in the limitless ocean. He collided with Andara, his lungs bursting. She was kicking out furiously with powerful, naked legs. He could not get under the boat. He came up gasping for air and found that she was ahead of him, gasping too but still with strength enough to shout, "Yours is the starboard side, you said!"

She was already throwing her end of the rope aboard, and yelling to the women to fasten it there. He shouted, "We crossed the ropes!" and she shouted back, furiously, "No! *You* crossed them! You have no strength in your arms! If your loins are as weak, you will father only chickens!"

He dove deeply under the boat again, uncrossed the ropes and came up on the correct side, and when he went down again for rope number three on the starboard side he found that the strong current was thrashing it around like a snake. He gripped it at last and dragged it up, and shouted across the beam of the boat, "Andara! Where are you?" He waited, holding on to the inwale, and shouted again, "Andara! *Fain?* Where?" One of the women answered him. "She is not here."

He dove deeply again in alarm, found the safety line and put a turn around his waist so that he could use both hands. He was dragged from side to side, flailing, as he thrashed out with arms and legs, looking for her. Then his foot found resilient flesh, and he doubled up his body and wrapped his legs around her waist, his hands exploring her limbs. He found one of the ropes tangled around her thigh as the boat dragged them along. He fumbled with it, and could not free it, and his lungs were exploding. At last he loosened the knot and as she was swept away from him he threw an arm around her body, his hand at her firm, naked breast. He pulled her tight and surfaced with her. He held her there for a moment, both of them gulping in great quantities of welcome air, and heard Opal's voice. "Jason! Jason, my love! Are you all right?"

He shouted back, "Yes! All is well!"

Beside him, Andara was coughing the water out of her lungs. He said, "Two more ropes to go. Stay there, I will get them."

He went down again swiftly and grabbed at the trailing canvas for security. And at that moment one of the dreaded beam waves caught the boat. As Opal swung the tiller over desperately to head into it, the rudder caught him a fearful blow on the side of the head. He gasped involuntarily and filled his body with water. Consciousness was fast slipping away from him. He lost his grip on the canvas that was his lifeline, and was swept away. He saw the boat rising high on the crest of a wave. It was more than fifty feet away from him and dropping down into a distant trough. He fought the coma and tried to swim. Then there was suddenly a hand under his chin, holding his head up out of the water, and Andara was there, kicking out furiously as she supported him. She screamed, "I cannot speak English! Tell your woman to turn into the wind, quickly!"

Jason gasped, "I cannot! They will be swamped!"

"And can they sail without you? No, they cannot! Tell her!"

He raised his voice and shouted, "Opal! Opal! Let go of everything!"

Opal let go of the tiller. It swung over and knocked her violently into the bottom of the boat, but the bow swung around and the sail started flapping with that strangely ominous cracking of spilled wind.

Andara was on her back in the water, swimming strongly with Jason's head in her hands. He was recovering fast. He turned over onto his stomach and began swimming, and shouted, "I am all right now. Thank you!"

"Then swim, Jason! Swim for your life!"

She was pacing him as he swam, with a strange kind of sidestroke. A wave picked them up and dropped them down into its trough, and picked them up again. There was the little boat, only twenty feet away, slipping down a wall of water to meet them. It slammed into them, and they grabbed at the stern-post and held on. A dozen pairs of hands helped them aboard. Andara's dress was pushed up under her armpits, her body shining.

Jason threw himself quickly at the tiller and pushed it over. He watched a gust of wind fill the sail, and then they were heading into the waves once more. Blood was streaming out of a gash at the back of his head. Opal tore a strip of cloth from the hem of her gown and made a bandage for his head. He kissed her quickly, and said gravely, "The fothering is done, we won't sink now. And now that it's all over, I will confess . . . I was not at all sure that we could do it."

Opal's eyes found Andara's, and saw the jealousy in them. She turned back to Jason and whispered, "And you are safe with us again. It is all that matters."

Safe? Jason looked to the west. It was light now; the early morning sun streamed down on them, drying them out. But there were dark and angry clouds on the horizon; another violent storm was gathering, and they were heading directly into it. But he could not allow his anxiety to show itself. He embraced Opal and whispered, "And with my loved one again . . ." He shuddered, knowing that had not Andara come to his rescue at a critical moment, he would have surely drowned.

Andara crawled over to him, a strange light in her lovely eyes, her bedraggled hair hanging down. She laid a hand on his thigh, giving Opal only a cursory glance. She said, "I was tangled in the ropes, American, and I would have drowned. You saved my life."

He answered gently, "But you saved mine, Andara."

"Yes. It means I belong to you now." She threw a quick look at Opal, and then her solemn eyes were on his again. "It means that you must take me into your harem. I will love you in ways your English watermelon has never even imagined."

He was smiling at her. "In my country, Andara, we do not have harems."

She was startled. "No harems?"

"No. A pity, perhaps, but . . . no harems."

It was a shock to her. "But that means . . . one woman only!"

"Yes. That is exactly what it means."

"But this is insanity! How can a strong man be satisfied by only one woman? It makes no sense at all."

"That," Jason said drily, "is a question I sometimes ask myself. But that is our custom, Andara."

"What foolishness! Take me too! And my sister also. She works in the Casbah as I once did. She is fourteen years old and very expert already, with thighs of alabaster that melt under a strong man's caress. We will both serve you, with delight, which you will share! Because you are a beautiful man, to gladden the heart of any woman."

Jason said gently, "Thank you, Andara. But I cannot."

Her eyes held his. "Even though you wish it? I *know* that you wish it!"

"I cannot, Andara."

She said steadily, "Under a terrible sea, your hand found my breast. And even though I was at the point of death, I felt the passion, the longing, in the touch of your hand."

"I have a woman I love dearly. There can be no other."

For a moment, she held his look. Then she laughed, mischief in her dark eyes, and she said, "Then when you tire of her, as you will, search for me, in Gibraltar or in Bir Birein, or anywhere on the face of the earth. It will be worth your effort, I assure you! My sister and I will bring you delights you cannot even dream of!"

"I am sure of it. But I must refuse. But we have a more pressing problem. We are heading directly into a very bad storm. Take the sheet for me, and watch the sail. I do not want to jibe, but I may have to."

Andara looked up at the sail, and at the approaching storm. She said flatly, "Like it or not, you will have to."

"Yes, I fear so. But I will hold this tack as long as I can."

"Jibe before it hits us."

"Yes, of course."

"And perhaps you should reef a little more?"

"No, I don't want to do that. The boat is sturdy."

"Very well, as you order." She took over the sheet and hauled it in a little.

Opal said, "And would you mind telling me, Jason dearest, what all that was about? There was a look in that young woman's eyes . . ."

Jason said offhandedly, "She wants me to take her into my harem."

"Your *harem*?"

"Yes. Together with her fourteen-year-old sister, who is a whore in the Casbah." He said, musing, "I have lived for so long with the Moslems, perhaps I should adopt their ways."

"Jason! I hate you!"

"No. You love me dearly, as I love you, to the exclusion of all others." He was suddenly very serious. "There is no greater love, my dearest Opal, than ours."

"For no one else?"

"No one! The two of us, together, for all of eternity! I do not come to you as a saint, Opal. But my past is behind me, if you will accept me."

"I accept you. You are my love, forever!"

"For longer than eternity."

The storm hit them with all of its fury.

Some of the women, the ones who had lost husbands, fathers, sons, to these Mediterranean furies, knew of its danger. They were terrified. They began those awful ululations, their tongues vibrating rapidly as they screamed out the high-pitched sound of their terror. It spread from one to another, until the sound echoed over the water, Jason shouted over the bluster of the approaching wind, "Enough! Save your energies for bailing! We are still alive, the boat is strong, and we are headed for Gibralter."

They renewed their efforts, but listlessly, as though they were accepting, as coming from their God, the inevitability of their destruction.

The wind came down on them, and the little boat was tossed in a frenzy as Jason strove with the tiller. Andara screamed, "Reef in, reef in, we carry too much sail now!"

He shouted back, "No, I will not." He was driving the boat to its maximum performance. He looked at Opal, close beside him, trying to hide her anxiety, and he muttered, "If there were something I could do to encourage them . . ."

Opal nodded. "If we were to sing? A hymn, perhaps?"

Jason laughed. "Yes, a song! But I fear they don't know any of our hymns. But there is a famous Arab ballad they will all know."

He called out, "Andara! A song!" and without waiting for her he raised his voice and sang lustily: *"Baladiya ba'ida, ehna bidna aru'h na baladiya* . . . A distant town, a distant town, we all want to go to a distant town . . ." Andara joined him at once, laughing, and the ancient faces of the old women were lighting up too as they all began to join in. It was a song about tribesmen visiting a city for the first time, and the first of the lyrics were innocent enough; but soon the tone changed as the simple hillmen found what delights were awaiting them, and indelicacy crept in, tinged with the dry humor that turned to outright vulgarity and bawdy licentiousness.

Some of the women doubled up with laughter as they sang. Opal picked up the simple melody and a few of the words that were repeated over and over again, singing them in a fine soft contralto. Jason said mildly, "I take great comfort, my love, in the knowledge that you do not understand the meaning of the words you are using."

They bailed and sang, sang and bailed, and it seemed they were holding their own as they rode the furious waves. The sky was bright behind them, but in the west, where they were heading, lightning was splitting the clouds open.

And in the distance, there was a ship under full sail. They all stared at it, and as it came closer they saw the Union Jack flying proudly from its masthead.

Jason said triumphantly, "An English merchantman! We are saved!" He shouted to the women, "An English ship, an English ship!" They stopped their bailing at once, and waved and cheered, and screamed and clapped. Andara told them angrily to get back to work, and he echoed her words. "Even faster now, we cannot sink at this last minute!"

The ship was less than a mile distant. He saw that the sails were coming down. They had been seen, and she was shortening sail. He held his course and waited.

She came in close. There was a bull-chested man in the starboard rigging of the foresail. They were close enough now to see the insignia on his uniform: he was the bo'sun. In a moment, his powerful voice came to them as the two vessels crossed only yards apart.

"We are turning! Nets at the stern!"

The rest of his words were lost on the wind. Jason saw the bold gilt lettering at the stern: the *Astride*. She made the difficult turn, sweeping in a wide circle more than two miles across. He watched the maneuver breathlessly, grateful that there were skilled men aboard her, glad too that he had not shortened his own sail as he had been tempted to do, so that now he could hold a reasonable speed of his own; it still would not be easy.

The turn was complete, and the *Astride* was bearing down on them again from the east. Jason shouted, "Andara! Go forward! A rope around our stem, quickly, before it drags you overboard!"

She was very excited, and she screamed back, "I know! I know what to do!"

Then the great ship was plunging at them, so close that it seemed they could reach out and touch her. There were trailing lines from her everywhere, but they were gone before Andara could grab one of them. But the net behind her was a great wide swathe of safety, and there were more than a dozen men on it, most of them in the water, being dragged along. One of them threw a rope aboard as she swept past them. Andara had a hitch over the stem post in seconds.

Jason yelled "Hold tight now!" He let down the sail as their boat lunged forward suddenly like a living thing, and in a moment of panic he was sure that the stem-post would be dragged out by the force of the sudden hauling. But it held, and the *Astride*'s sailors on the net were reaching out helping hands. He heard one of them shout in a voice of authority, "No more than three men aboard, she's mighty low in the water! Jenkins! Smith! Martin! Up you get, give the poor critters a hand!" Jason shouted in Arabic, "The older women first, the younger ones help them up the net!"

Their little boat was being dragged so fast that it seemed to be riding on air, clear out of the water. But then the net was around them and a dozen skilled hands were helping the women to climb it.

Jason said to Opal, "Careful now, I can't lose you at this stage." There were men reaching for her, grinning broadly, and one of them shouted cheerfully, "Careful, ma'am, the water's mighty wet around here." She fell into the net and began climbing, and looked back to see that Andara was close behind her. Only Jason was left aboard the fishing boat. He was watching carefully to see that they all made it to the deck. He found the knife that Andara had used, and clambered onto the rope that led from the *Astride* to their stem. Slicing the line behind him, he found his footing on the net.

Five minutes later, wet bedraggled, excited, they were all on board the *Astride*. The women were laughing and shouting and clapping their hands, and Opal, the exhaustion of relief suddenly sweeping over her, threw her arms around Jason's neck and rested her head on his chest. Full of emotion, she could not speak. He held her close and said quietly, "It is all over now, my love. And soon we will be safe in Gibraltar."

He heard a pleasant, quiet, educated voice behind him say, "Not Gibraltar, sir, but Algiers. We will take you to Algiers."

Jason swung around in consternation.

CHAPTER ELEVEN

The skipper of the *Astride* was Captain Augustus Charles Hays-Fox, a dry old stick of a man, deceptively fragile-looking, gentle in manner, and highly skilled at his trade. He had fought with great distinction at San Juan de Nicaragua with the young Horatio Nelson, and had learned much from that naval genius. His hair, his moustache, and his neatly trimmed beard were white against a ruddy complexion, and his eyes were light blue. He was a good-looking man, and there was always a touch of humor in his voice. Retired from the navy, he was a merchant skipper now.

He sat in his cabin with Jason and Opal and poured liberal quantities of good naval rum for them, saying to Opal when she demurred, "Drink it, ma'am. Any lady who can survive the high seas in a small fishing boat—a little rum will cause her no damage at all, my word on it. And it will bring a blush, if you will permit me to say so in the presence of your husband, to lovely cheeks that are pale with anxiety. The anxiety is over, Mrs. Farn."

Jason had introduced her as his wife, thinking it simpler. The captain had responded by bowing over Opal's hand and saying, "Your servant, ma'am. I am honored to welcome a lady aboard my ship, particularly an American lady."

"Not American, sir," Opal said, "though my—my husband is. But I am English. My father is Sir Neville Grant of the Foreign Office. You may, perhaps, have heard of him."

"Sir Neville Grant?" There was almost no change of expression in those pale eyes. "Yes of course," he said. "A famous name, and, ah, highly respected. Would it be presumptuous of me, ma'am, to ask how long you have been away from home?"

Opal sighed. "A long time, Captain, I fear. Three years now."

"And no communication at all? *Recent* communication, that is?" His eyes were worried, and he went on, "My question, ma'am, is not prompted by vulgar curiosity, I assure you."

She knew at once that something was dreadfully wrong. Her hand went to her cheek. "No communication, sir, for reasons with which I will not trouble you. But do you have news of him?"

The captain muttered, ill at ease, "No, of course, how could you have learned in so short a time? It is my painful duty, ma'am, to be the bearer of sad news. It grieves me deeply to tell you that Sir Neville died but a few days since."

"Oh, God in heaven!"

Opal dropped her glass and seemed about to swoon, but Jason was at her side instantly, his arm around her, comforting her with murmured words of sympathy. She could not stem the flow of tears that flooded into her lovely eyes. Her mind began to whirl insanely, the memories, till now half-forgotten, coming back to her in a kaleidoscope of rapidly changing images. Her father. Not her true father but the man who had raised her—and the man who had abused her.

The kindly captain's eyes were on her, and Jason was holding her tightly. The twin images were strong in her mind, one of the benevolent father she had once known and the other of the drunken maniac who had raped her as she lay on the library carpet screaming, "No! No! I am your daughter!"

The captain said quietly, "It pains me, ma'am, to be the bearer of such bad news." He picked up her dropped glass and poured her another tot of rum. "Drink it, ma'am, it will ease the pain a little."

She took the glass and whispered, "He was a very strange man. Will you tell me how he died?"

"A fall, ma'am," Captain Hays-Fox said, "from an upper story or perhaps from the roof, it seems. An uncertain step . . ." It had been reported that Opal's portrait was clutched in her father's arms when he died, but the captain chose not to mention it; it smacked of suicide, and this was not the time for her to know. He said instead: "He was a parliamentarian of great worth in the House, ma'am. We will all miss him. England will be the poorer for his untimely death."

"Yes. Thank you, Captain, for your sympathy."

Jason was sure that it was best to take her mind off the dreadful subject, and said, "I suffer with you, my love. But we must return to the urgent matter of our destination."

Opal's eyes were glazed and distant, her mind still in torment. She murmured absently, "Yes, yes of course. We cannot return to Algiers."

Jason said carefully, "I have not explained, Captain, why a landfall anywhere in the Barbary States would be such a torment for both of us, but especially for my wife. The fate that awaits her in Algiers is . . . far worse than death. The bey himself is her enemy."

Hays-Fox stared. "I do not entirely understand you, sir."

Jason told him. He explained almost everything that had happened to her since Sinan's first attempt to abduct her. The captain listened attentively, his old eyes wide with shock and filled with deep sympathy. He said at last, harshly, "The bey's harem, you say? An *English* lady? It's monstrous!"

"The bey's tastes seem to be quite catholic. There was a Frenchwoman there too, who helped us escape."

"A Frenchwoman too? Good God! Of course, the

French, it's not quite the same thing, is it? But even so . . . And were you in time to save her from, ah, the ultimate degradation? I pray God that you were."

"Thank God, sir, I was."

"And you yourself, sir, were at the mill? I have heard of this terrible punishment. I have been told that the victims seldom last for more than a few weeks."

Jason said urgently, "This, Captain, is why I ask you now: can you turn about and take us to Gibraltar before you go to Algiers? Algiers is not a safe place for us now, nor is it for the thirty-two poor refugees aboard your ship."

The captain rose to his feet and started pacing back and forth. He was wrapped in deep thought. At last he said, "I am aware of your concern, Mr. Farn, and I understand the valid reasons for it. And may I say that I greatly admire the fortitude you both show after such fearful adventures. But in Algiers we will be at anchor in the harbor, and no one need know of your presence aboard. I will see to it that the refugees are kept below decks. I will fulfill my mission, and then, on our return journey, I will take you all to Gibraltar."

Jason said tightly, "You know, sir, of a man named Admiral Sinan?"

"I know him. A scoundrel."

"Sinan's spies will be swarming over your decks the moment you tie up at the wharf."

"Perhaps not." Hays-Fox said thoughtfully. "I will tell you, Mr. Farn, what my mission is, though it is greatly to my shame. I am bringing England's yearly tribute to the bey—a man I detest as much as you do—a wooden coffer filled with gold bars. It is not an assignment that I relish, but I am a sailor and under orders, and what can I do? Mr. Pitt himself has sent me here. I cannot change my course now and head for Gibraltar, it would invite disaster."

Jason said hotly, "And is there no disaster if you put into Algiers with an English lady who is wanted by the bey for his personal pleasures, hidden below decks but subject to instant discovery? To say nothing of thirty-two women refugees who will be killed the moment they are dragged ashore? Not the younger ones, of course; they will be kept for worse infamy, as you must know!"

The captain was greatly perturbed, but he said helplessly, "Your argument is very persuasive, Mr. Farn, and under normal conditions I would accede to your request without the slightest hesitation. But unfortunately, for a day and a half now there have been two Algerian frigates skulking over the horizon and following me at a distance. It does not bode well for any change of course."

Opal said, "If we *beg* you, Captain?"

The pleading in her voice cut him to the heart. But he shook his head stubbornly and said firmly, "No, ma'am, I cannot. I would be prepared, under the present circumstances, to disobey my orders and change course, save for one thing. Those Algerian pirates over the horizon are not there by happenstance. They are there, I am convinced, to see that no rambunctious Tripolitanian, Moroccan, or Tunisian pirate attacks me, not knowing that I carry a chest of gold to the bey of Algiers. The Algerians are shadowing me to make sure that I reach port safely. If I were to turn about and sail west again, they will close in on me, and I cannot afford to fight them. But when we arrive in Algiers, I will see to it that all the refugees are battened down in our deepest hold, and you yourselves will stay in the cabin I will put at your disposal. And no one will learn of your presence on board." He emphasized, "You will be safe. You have my promise."

Jason asked, "Do you have any Berber sailors aboard, sir?"

"Two or three, I think. I will see to it that they are also below decks when we dock."

"It would be wise, Captain. Admiral Sinan's spies are everywhere."

"I know it. But you must trust me to guard you with all the means at my disposal. After all, I am an officer of His Majesty's Merchant Marine." He said heavily, "It is a fact that the bey must recognize."

Jason said quietly, "I came here, sir, on the American ship *Virginia*. You may have heard of her."

"Yes. A fine ship, I know her well. Captain Bainbridge in command, a splendid sailor and a credit to your navy."

"And I left his ship, sir, because of the same kind of revulsion against this humiliating bribery. Captain Bainbridge was also delivering tribute to the bey. He was ordered to Constantinople with routine dispatches as if he were a messenger-boy, under threat of sequestration of his ship and imprisonment of his crew—an insult he was forced to swallow."

Hays-Fox said tightly, "Yes, I heard of it. The whole seagoing community heard of it."

" 'My slave,' the bey said."

"Yes, I heard that too. I cannot change course, Mr. Farn."

Jason sighed heavily. The captain said, "Trust me, sir. And meanwhile, one of my officers has vacated his cabin for you. It is small but adequately comfortable, I hope. You will need rest after your commendable efforts to keep a sinking fishing boat afloat in such seas."

"I thank you, captain, for your consideration."

The captain himself escorted them to their cabin, muttering, "No danger in Algiers, you have my word on it."

He left them alone. Jason said, "He is not convinced one way or the other. And yet, from his own point of view he is right. If he is indeed being followed by pirate ships, then a change of course is impossible. But also it is not possible that we can dock in Algiers and not be discovered. Every dock rat there will be one of Sinan's spies! The image of that scoundrel hangs over us like a cloud. I propose giving the good captain time to reflect on what he has already learned. And then I will try once more to convince him. He is the kind of man who will not act without a great deal of reflection, but also the kind of man who knows right from wrong."

"And are you sure that Sinan will find out we are on board?"

"There are no secrets in Algiers. Our only hope is that I may persuade the captain to change his mind and his course."

He took her in his arms, very gently. "And I have not told you, my love, how sorry I am to learn of your father's death."

Her eyes were moist with suppressed tears as she held him tightly.

"When I was a child," she whispered, "he was a kind and gentle man, and I worshipped him. When I was older, a change came over him, brought on by too much strong drink, perhaps. For the last years we were not very close. And at the very last, I hated him for what—" She caught her breath, and whispered, "I grew to fear him."

She hesitated, but then said steadily, "I told you while . . . while we were loving each other in the surf at Bir Birein, but exhaustion had overcome you and you were sleeping, and you did not hear me. It is something you must know, Jason, if there is ever to be love between us, a love more than just . . . just physical attraction."

He whispered, "Oh, my darling! What nonsense is this?"

She laid a finger on his lips and went on, "When I was eighteen, I went searching in my father's library for a book. I crouched down to find it on the lower shelves. He was sitting there and staring at me, a glass of brandy in his hand. He said, his voice a little slurred though he held his drink very well, 'Your lips are beginning to thicken, child.' It was an accusation, because my dear mother's blood was in me. I will never forget the look of loathing on his face as he said it. From that moment on, as far as he was concerned, I was no longer his daughter, not even a member of his family, but an outcast living under his roof. I had long known of my colored blood, my mother told me of it, but the realization of it was more than he could bear. I was a stranger to him, to the man I had once worshipped and had called 'father' for all these years! He called me 'nigger.' "

Jason's strong arms were like steel band around her, forcing on her a kind of peace of mind. She went on, "He said he could detect a slight thickening of my lips, and it was enough."

"Your lips are rubies, jewels of priceless value." His mouth was on hers, but she turned her head away. "No, you must hear all of it! After all those years of devotion, a change came over him. He saw that I was not truly the English daughter on whom he had lavished so much of his affection. Instead, I was someone quite foreign whom he could not accept. It was the brandy, Jason, I am sure of it, I know it! But he reached for me, and ripped my gown open, and threw me to the ground."

The tears streamed unheeded down her face. He kissed them gently as they fell, knowing her pain. She whispered, "He threw me to the ground, and there is the memory only of his heavy weight on me, his knee forcing my thighs apart. He raped me, Jason. He raped me."

His arms were about her, holding her close. "Oh, my love, what can I say? Except that you must not think of it, you must thrust it behind you, with the strength of will I know you have. There are no words I can find to comfort you, other than these."

"No, no words. There are none that can erase the shame."

"There is no shame! You were the victim, not the perpetrator."

"There *is* shame. I was despoiled. I was a virgin till that terrible evening!"

"I love you so dearly, Opal."

"Even so?"

"More so, because of what you have suffered."

"And now he is dead. With never the chance to say what I am sure was in his mind after I left him."

"To say what?"

She whispered, "To say, 'Opal, forgive me.' Had I not left home . . . one day, he would have said it."

"And you would have forgiven him, even for this?"

She said fiercely, "Yes, yes, yes!"

"Oh, my darling! Our love is so strong, dear Opal! What is behind us matters little now, in your past or mine. It is only the present and the future that concern us, and they are filled with our love. A binding love for each other, forever."

"My revelation has not . . . stifled your love?"

"How could it? It is stronger than ever, even though I thought it could never be greater."

"Oh, my Jason."

"And will you love me now, my love?"

"My darling."

His hands had dropped to her hips to press their loins together, and she could feel his rampant manhood, erect and demanding, throbbing against her. He whispered, "Touch me, please. Hold me in your hand." She eased her hand down between their bodies and found him.

"I need you now, so badly."

"Yes, I know it."

He said hoarsely, "There are urgent matters we should discuss, but I can think only of the softness of your thighs."

One hand was at her breast, stroking, molding, pressing, and the other was drawing the Arab gown up to her waist, finding her slender loins and delighting in their soft coolness. He pressed himself to her, relishing her touch, and then he picked her up and laid her down on the narrow bunk. Future dangers had left his mind, and he could think only that the woman he loved so dearly was in his arms again. But as he began to pull the dress over her head, fumbling in his urgency, he became aware of a change in the ship's motion. There was a creaking of heavy timbers, flapping of sails, an assault on the hull from waves that were coming from a different direction. He stared up at the cabin's ceiling as though his eyes might penetrate the woodwork and discover what was happening. Then he whispered, "We are circling . . ." And then, "We're changing course! A complete turn!

The ship was heeling over alarmingly. Jason shouted, "A turn of a hundred and eighty degrees! Either there is some unexpected danger ahead of us, or—we have a new course, for Gibraltar!"

To Opal's frustration, he slipped off the bunk, leaving her lying there half-naked, and said quickly, "I must see the captain at once! We must know what is happening, and if it is what I think it is, there will be peace of mind for us at last!"

He hurried out and went to find the captain.

The skipper was on the bridge, and he was not in a good mood. There was a distant look in his blue eyes. He said slowly, "As you have perceived, Mr. Farn, I have changed course and am now heading for Gibraltar, on two hundred and ninety-seven degrees. And my reasons, sir? I will tell you. I gave further consideration to the problems you told me of, and I came to the conclusion that you were right, that Admiral Sinan will indeed learn of your presence aboard the *Astride*, whatever pains I take to conceal you. Therefore, we cannot yet dock in Algiers. I will take you all to Gibraltar first."

"I am grateful to you, Captain! We are all grateful."

Hays-Fox raised a warning hand. "You may have cause, young man, to regret my decision. I spoke to you, I believe, of two Algerian frigates?"

" 'Skulking over the horizon,' you said, sir."

"Yes. Well, one of them has changed to a course of interception." Alarmed, Jason stared out at the wide sea, but the captain shook his head. "You cannot see her, unless you climb to the crow's nest. Her mainmast is very high, and it seems that their lookout has spotted our maneuver. It is highly probable that he saw me circling to pick you up, and though he would not be able to discern the reason, he must be wondering what we were up to and will want to find out. In either event, from the hight of her masts I suspect she may be the *Habou*, Admiral Sinan's own ship, as you have sad cause to know. She is a formidable warship, Mr. Farn, and the *Astride* is only a lightly armed merchantman."

Jason said steadily, "It means all available sail, Captain. I make no suggestions, of course."

Hays-Fox nodded. "Yes, our hope lies in outrunning her, and perhaps we can do that. We are running with the wind, while she is on a difficult tack, she's too far to the north of us. And they have a lot of water to make up. If we can reach the protection of Gibraltar's guns before they shorten that distance to cannon range, we shall be safe. If not . . . it is a contingency that I will contemplate with the greatest anxiety. A gamble, Mr. Farn, with very high stakes. Well, I have fought against heavy odds before, and won. And as a man of honor, I cannot permit an English lady to fall into the hands of a man like Sinan. I will not allow it."

"I thank you, sir."

"Do not thank me," the captain answered drily, "until we have come out of this encounter afloat, which we may not do. Ah, there she is now . . ." There was the tiniest black speck on the horizon. The captain took his glass and peered through it intently for a long time. "Yes, the *Habou*, I think," he said at last.

There was a call from the crow's nest, almost lost on the wind: "Twenty points east, a Tunisian!" The captain swung the telescope around and studied the second tiny speck. He said heavily, "The other of our two watchdogs. And if she is indeed a Tunisian, she will do her damndest to stay out of our range. The Tunisians do not make good fighting men. Our problem will be with the *Habou*. She carries twenty-two guns, and I have only eight small demi-cannon with which to defend myself. Moreover, Mr. Farn, the *Habou* is fitted with charcoal grates which we, as a merchantman, do not carry. I will confess that I do not like the charcoal grates."

They constituted a fearsome threat indeed.

They were a kind of secret weapon, which had been invented by the British on Gibraltar only a few years previously. They were great braziers, more than twenty feet long, filled with flaming charcoal and bearing on their fiery beds the cannonballs to be used in battle.

A single iron shot could make a hole below the waterline or even, skillfully aimed, break a mast. But most of the balls would do minimal damage, rolling into the scuppers if they landed on the deck, there to be collected by the enemy to enlarge his own supply of ammunition. But not the red-hot balls. Wherever they landed, they would burn their way through the decks one after the other, causing several fires in quick succession, even though seamen who could not be spared from other duties poured bucket after bucket of water over them. In a very short time they could reduce a fine wooden ship to a flaming wreck. It was a weapon of great potential, and the Barbary pirates, many of whose ships had been destroyed by them, were quick to learn its value, and had fitted out their larger ships with the iron grates.

On the bridge of the *Habou*, Admiral Sinan was watching the distant *Astride* through his glass, his captain by his side. He asked, "The calculated point of interception, Mustafa?"

"Three hours and a half from Gibraltar, Admiral."

"I would not like to come under Gibraltar's batteries before we catch them."

"We will not."

"Our speed?"

"Fourteen knots."

"The wind is changing."

"I know it. The wind has been inconstant all day."

The skipper, Mustafa Ajou, was a thickset man in his forties, with an unkempt beard and very long moustaches, and a livid knife scar down one side of his face. It was his boast that he could outrace, in the splendid *Habou*, any vessel afloat on the Mediterranean. He hated having his admiral aboard; he was convinced that he himself was a better man in every respect, and why should he have to suffer this loathsome dandy breathing over his shoulder? But he did not stand in fear of him, as so many other captains did; Mustafa Ajou feared no one.

Sinan said, "The fires?"

"Alight and flaming, as you can see."

The admiral contained his anger. "As I see indeed," he answered. "What I do not see is the men at the bellows."

"They will be there when the time comes."

"And the shot, how many shot?"

Mustafa Ajou sighed. "One hundred and eighty for the demi-cannon, one hundred and twenty for the whole cannon, and sixty-five for the royals. A total of three hundred and sixty-five shot."

The admiral's narrowed eyes were gleaming. Three hundred and sixty-five balls of red-hot iron, ranging in weight from twenty-eight to sixty-three pounds. Forty would be enough to sink the *Astride*. What in the name of Allah was this rash and arrogant man thinking of? He said carefully, forcing a smile, "Mustafa, my brother and my dear friend, the *Astride*, as you know, carries a very valuable cargo, a chest of gold for your master and mine, the bey."

"I know it."

"And yet you plan to hurl so much shot at her?"

"I do not. Twenty or thirty will be enough to disable her. But I like to have all my shot ready. What if we should be interrupted by a British man-of-war, with only a score of balls on the grates?"

He was right, and Sinan was angered to know that he could not pursue the argument. He said instead, "We must come alongside and board her the moment she begins to burn."

"The boarding nets are ready."

"And a search-party to find the gold?"

Mustafa Ajou could feel his wrath mounting. He was being questioned like an incompetent child who had not yet learned to fight. He said stolidly, "Thirty men have been detailed to search the *Astride* for that chest. Six of those men have been detailed to interrogate the *Astride*'s officers, with duress, to facilitate the search. I am not a fool, Admiral Sinan."

"Ah no, my dear friend!" Sinan said in mock horror. "I have always known this! And when the operation is over, I will have the opportunity once again to commend you to His Excellency the Bey. As I have done so often in the past."

He hated this presumptuous upstart of a captain, and he was making a mental note to find a new captain for his flagship, and have this insolent peasant thrown to the crabs. But he said, smiling suavely, "It is upon men of your mettle, my dearest Mustafa, that the might of the Berber navies has been built."

"I know that too."

More insolence! Sinan controlled himself and said, "Bring me, with the chest of gold, also that *Astride*'s captain, Hays-Fox. I wish to know why he changed his course."

"It shall be done. Other prisoners?"

"None. Put them all to the sword."

He strode off, descended to the lower deck, and found the bo'sun, who was one of his personal spies and a man in whom he had the greatest confidence. His name was Munir. The admiral took him aside and asked, "You will be leading one of the boarding parties, I assume?"

"Aye, Admiral. The second of them." He was a small and wiry man who scratched constantly at the lice on his body.

"Good. While you are aboard the *Astride*, I want a chance bullet to strike Captain Mustafa Ajou in the heart."

Munir's eyes were gleaming. "Ah . . ."

"The shot must come from the enemy's vessel, you understand? So that we may carry his dead body to Algiers with full naval honors, a martyr to our cause. But a dead martyr, is it understood?"

Munir scratched furiously, a wide grin on his face. "It is understood, Admiral. It shall be done."

"There will be a purse of gold for you."

"Your slave, Admiral, as always. Your grateful slave."

Sinan went back to the bridge and took the telescope from the captain. He saw that the distance to his quarry was considerably less now. He snapped the telescope shut and handed it back, and said amiably, "Mustafa, we are closing faster than I could possibly have hoped. I must congratulate you on your superb seamanship. Truly, our Barbary States need men of your caliber! And I am honored to count you as my friend!"

The ships were drawing closer and closer together. The Tunisian frigate accompanied the *Habou* was coming in on the beam, cutting swiftly through the water to be in at the kill. She was the *Jamara*, sixteen guns, lightweight and fast, and she was flying the personal pennant of the bashaw of Tunis, which meant that he was aboard.

All three of the ships were on the same parallel course, all under full sail, with the *Astride* far ahead and racing for her life, and the two pirates behind her, one on either side, in hot pursuit.

And all three captains knew that the chase could not last much longer.

CHAPTER TWELVE

The battle was joined at three o'clock in the afternoon, when the valiant *Astride* was only fifty miles from the safety of Gibraltar.

Over Jason's strong protests, Captain Hays-Fox had insisted that he remain with Opal in the captain's own cabin, which was on the port side and less likely to be damaged by cannon fire.

"I can better serve her," Jason said hotly, "by fighting with you, sir! I am a skilled marksman. Put me in the rigging with a gun!"

But Hays-Fox was a stubborn man. "No, sir, a gentleman's place in time of stress is at his wife's side."

The captain was standing now on the bridge and watching the *Habou* close in fast. She was already beginning to take the *Astride*'s wind. A mile away, the second Algerian pirate ship was ploughing towards them on the port beam. She was identified now as the *Jamara*, flying the Tunisian flag and the personal pennant of the bashaw himself, which meant that he was aboard.

Hays-Fox looked up at his sails. He called down, "Bo-'sun! Your topgallants are spilling!" He heard the angry voice shouting back, "I know it, sir! I must have ten more degrees of wind!"

"I give you five!" He turned to the helmsman with the order: "Right rudder five degrees." The helmsman swung the wheel. The uppermost sails were filling again, but the *Habou* was still gaining on them apace, and to the south the lighter *Jamara* was less than half a mile away now, close enough to see the men manning the guns.

The first mate shouted, "The *Habou* is signaling, sir, to the *Jamara*," and the captain watched the pennants going up, a blue-white followed by a green-white and a solid red. He murmured, "The *Jamara* is being ordered to hold her fire," and the mate answered him stolidly, "He wants the pleasure of sinking us himself, and to the devil with our chest of gold."

The captain laughed shortly. "No Berber will ever send bars of good gold to the bottom, Mr. Mate. It means that he wants the controlled fire of a single ship."

"He?"

"The bashaw of Tunis is flying his own pennant at the *Jamara* masthead. And there is only one man in the navy who can give him orders. It means that Admiral Sinan himself is aboard the *Habou*. He is a skilled fighting man, Mr. Mate. He will hole us, burn us, and board us. We must expect his boarding parties as soon as he comes alongside."

"The sharpshooters have been detailed to pick off the men with the nets the moment they start preparing them."

"Good. Our own cannon?"

"All at the port embrasures, Captain."

"Demi-cannon will not hole a ship as solid as the *Habou*, Mr. Mate. Have the master-gunner sweep their decks instead."

"He's been told, sir."

"Good. Our cutlasses?"

"Forty-two men, sir."

The captain's heart was heavy. Only forty-two brave men against perhaps two hundred screaming Berbers, armed to the teeth and lusting for blood? He said grimly, "But we won't make it easy for them, Mr. Mate." He turned to the grizzled old man at the wheel. "When she closes to fifty yards, helmsman, she'll take what little wind we have left. At that moment, give me sixty degrees left rudder. Don't wait for my order, turn when the time comes."

"Aye, aye, sir." He was chuckling to himself, a veteran

of a great many naval battles. "Sixty degrees it is. It will take us directly into the path of the *Jamara*, Captain."

"I prefer to think it will bring the *Jamara* directly into *our* path. We will try to ram her. She's a light and fragile ship."

"Aye, aye, sir!"

Everyone on board the *Astride* was watching the fast approach of the *Habou*, and they could clearly see the black snub noses of the cannon in their embrasures. Four of them were the dreaded royal cannon, which fired massive iron balls weighing sixty-three pounds each. She was correcting her course very slightly with each vagary of the wind, lining up her hull with remarkable precision. The captain murmured, "I do not much like the Berbers, Mr. Mate, as you know. But I will confess to a great admiration of their seamanship."

The guns were speaking now on both sides. As the *Astride*'s sails began to lose their wind, the helmsman spun the wheel and set his ship on a collision course with the *Jamara*. But the Tunisian, as the captain had noted, was very light and maneuverable, and she made a quick turn to the north and swept past them, her guns blazing in spite of Sinan's orders. None of her shot struck home, but dropped harmlessly into the water around them. They were close enough to hear the admiral's furious bellow in Arabic: "Hold your fire, *Jamara*! The *Astride* is mine!"

The cannon were firing fast, the twenty-eight-pound balls of the *Astride*'s demi-cannon sweeping the *Habou*'s deck, the *Habou*'s red-hot shot starting fires already as men ran to pour buckets of seawater over them. The Berber admiral's vessel was a magnificent ship, towering high above them at this range, and fifty men aboard her were dragging the heavy boarding nets and the grappling irons into position. Hays-Fox looked down onto his main deck and saw the sharpshooters waiting with their rifles poised and ready. Hendricks, Bell, White, Whitmore, Saunders and Gregg, some of the finest marksmen in the British merchant marine. Whitmore, a scarred old veteran who was also ex-Navy and had been with the captain at San

Juan, looked up at him and grinned broadly. Seeing the look in his beloved skipper's eyes, he shouted, "The odds against us were as high in Nicaragua, Captain!" The bo'sun was there too, and he shouted angrily, "Keep your eyes on the enemy, Whitmore!"

The two hulls scraped as the ships passed each other. Cannon and muskets were firing furiously at point-blank range. Men were dying. Spars were crashing down tangled with their lines, and on board the *Astride* fires were burning, too. The two ships, held together by grappling irons, were riding side by side now as though they were one. The pirates were struggling with the nets, and the musketeers were firing and reloading as fast as they could, chewing furiously with broken teeth on their lead bullets to round them before ramming them down their barrels on top of the explosive charges, clicking their triggers repeatedly till the sparks fired. Each of them could fire no more than a single round a minute, and six, eight, a dozen grappling irons were already embedded in the *Astride*'s woodwork as the pirates hauled on the lines and fastened the two ships together.

There were more than twenty holes below the *Astride*'s waterline, six or seven fires burning on her deck quite out of control, and three boarding nets in place, with a hundred savage, jubilant pirates swarming across them, using their scimitars and their knives to deadly advantage. There was chaos and mayhem everywhere.

Below decks, Jason heard and felt the shuddering as the two hulls ground together in the heavy seas. He was in a dilemma. He held Opal tightly and said, "They are boarding us now, and I do not even have a sword!"

All her fears returned to her; she was trembling in spite of her resolve. Had they come so far, and escaped so much for nothing? She whispered, "Do not leave me, Jason!"

"I must! But only for a moment. I need a weapon, any kind of weapon. I will come back instantly. Bolt the door behind me and open it only when you hear my voice."

He was gone, and she shuddered, sure that the end of the world had come for them both.

He ran up to the deck and was appalled at the intensity of the fighting. He saw an English seaman lying dead, his head shattered by a Berber musket-ball, and took the cutlass from the frozen hand. He found a wounded Berber and took his dagger from him, and thrust it up to the hilt in the chest of a fiercely bearded pirate who was lunging at him, then swung the cutlass at another who was crouched over the fallen first mate, slashing his throat open. He saw Captain Hays-Fox, down from his burning bridge, using his sword with practiced efficiency against three Berbers who were slicing at him with their curved, deadly scimitars. He ran to help him, but a swung musket caught him across the chest and drove all the wind out of him. He fell to the deck, gasping in pain and trying to gulp in air. As he looked up, he saw that one of the men standing over him, a look of acute astonishment on his face, was Admiral Sinan. Then Hays-Fox fell, almost decapitated by a furious sword-cut, and there was a foot at Jason's throat, forcing his head down into the decking, and he heard the admiral say calmly, "*W'Allahii*, by God! Mr. Jason Farn! And does that mean that *she* is aboard too? I'll warrant it does."

He tried to struggle to his feet from under that fearful pressure on his throat. But the admiral drew back a booted foot and kicked him savagely in the side of the head. As he lost consciousness, his last thought was for Opal. He knew that there was no hope for her now, and he thought, "If only we could have died together!" Then the coma swept over him, and everything was black.

There was indeed little hope for Opal. Six men, detailed to search for the oaken chest that contained the treasure, had gone immediately below decks to the captain's cabin, battering down the door.

One of them seized her, ripping her gown open and laughing as he fondled her. She screamed, struggling with him furiously in an overpowering rage, and he called out to his companions, "A wildcat, but a prize, an unexpected and very welcome prize!"

Their leader was a young man named Yussef. He eyed

her hungrily and said, "She fights like a Berber woman. Hold her arms."

Her captor swung her around and pinioned her arms at her back, one arm around her neck, pressing cruelly against her throat. Yussef stood for a moment with his coarse hands at her breasts, savoring them; young women of this remarkable quality were usually far removed from him. He said, "Put her on the bunk. Two of you hold her down and spread her legs for me. I will be the first, as is my right."

They carried her, struggling mightily, to the bunk and threw her down. She kicked out savagely and caught one of them in the groin. He screamed, and Yussef shouted, "Tie her!" Someone ripped at her gown and tore off strips of cloth, and they bound her wrists together, fastening them to the rail at the top of the bed. A rag was stuffed into her mouth. They dragged her legs apart, tying her ankles to the lower rail. Then they stood back, laughing at her.

There was a dagger in Yussef's hand. He touched it gently to her face, laying the flat of the cold blade on one cheek and then the other. She stopped struggling and lay still, unable to control her trembling, trying desperately to detach her mind from the physical horror in store for her. He spoke to her in Arabic, not caring that she could not understand him, saying hoarsely, "A dove, a desert gazelle, to be enjoyed by all of us. Allah has no greater gift than the body of a beautiful woman, to be used as a man desires."

One of the men, far older than the others, turned away and said, chuckling, "Go on, enjoy her. Perhaps the sound of your pleasures on her will arouse even an old, broken man, and then I will take my turn too." He sighed and began searching the room for the tribute chest. He dragged it out from under the bunk and fingered the heavy padlocks on it. But for Yussef, the gold was for the admiral, while here on the bunk was a prize of his own. He stared at her half-naked body in wide-eyed delight, and said triumphantly, "Now you will learn the strength of a Berber!"

He raised his long gown, exposing himself to her, laughing at the anger in her eyes. He knelt on the bed between her spread thighs. She fought desperately against the bindings, but suddenly she saw her assailant look back over his shoulder in surprise and alarm.

She had not heard the door open. Admiral Sinan was there, striding furiously towards them. He seized Yussef by his unruly hair and his chin, and swung him savagely away with a rapid twist that broke his neck. The others stood still in fright. Sinan shouted angrily, "Out, out, all of you!"

They ran, all except the old man. Fawning, he said, "The tribute chest, Excellency. I found it as you instructed."

"I see it! Out with you!"

"Of course, Excellency, your servant, Excellency . . ." He scuttled out and closed the door behind him, grateful for his escape.

The admiral turned back to Opal, and looked at her for a long time, saying nothing. In silence, he reached out to touch her, running his hands over the curve of her breast, her hips and thighs, lingering with a surprising delicacy. He said at last, smiling in the friendliest possible manner, "It seems, dear lady, that Allah cannot find enough blessings to shower on me today. The ship is mine, what is left of it. The tribute is mine, for delivery to my grateful master, the bey. And now a greater satisfaction even than these—*you* are mine too. But once again I must regretfully postpone the pleasures that await us together. The poor *Astride* is sinking fast."

The ship was burning. She could smell the acrid smoke. But the admiral seemed quite unconcerned. He dropped to his knees beside her and rested his head on her naked breast, cupping it with his hand, stroking, molding. He whispered, "Not even amoung our own young girls have I seen anyone so beautiful."

There was a discreet knock at the door. Sinan rose and went to open it. The corridor outside was rapidly filling with blue smoke, yet he seemed unconcerned. The bo'sun was standing there, looking past the admiral at Opal. Sinan said shortly, "What is it, Munir?"

"A matter of prisoners, Excellency."

Sinan interrupted him sharply. "I have already given instructions! No prisoners save the captain. And the American, of course."

"The captain is dead," Munir said flatly, "but there are thirty-two Berber women you should know about."

"What?"

Munir grinned. "Thirty-two of our women below decks. But not whores for the English sailors. They are the women of the bandits on the mountain, Excellency. The very same women the bey wished to imprison."

"Ah . . . Then this is a fortunate day for us indeed, Munir."

"I have ordered that their throats not be cut, unless you wish it."

"By no means," Sinan said easily. "The bey has other plans for them. Have them taken aboard the *Habou* and secured below."

"Aye, aye, sir. And we have little time left afloat now."

"Send six men for the tribute chest. Have it taken to my cabin."

"Your servant, Excellency."

The bo'sun left. The admiral went back to the bunk and said, laughing, "You see, dear lady? There is never any time for what pleases us the most. But do not despair, it will not be long now." He drew his dagger and cut the strips of cotton that bound her. As soon as she was free she slashed out at his face with both hands, raking her nails for his eyes. But he fended her off easily with one arm and grabbed at her hair to yank her head back. He said mildly, "And we have no time, either, for disputing my authority. So by your leave, ma'am . . ." He laughed at her mockingly as he drew back his arm and hit her, with careful precision, just behind the pink shell of her ear.

Opal fell back as the darkness swept over her. She was unconscious when he picked her up in his muscular arms. He strode with her into the smoke-filled corridor as the bo'sun and six men ran past him to retrieve the tribute chest. He took her up the companionway to the open air.

The flames were crackling all around them. A broad plank had been thrown across the gap between the two vessels and lashed down, with men standing by to cut it loose when the time came. Some of the pirates were pumping water up through wooden sluices, to wet down the *Habou*'s deck and prevent the flames from spreading. The decks of the British merchantman were slippery with blood and littered with dead bodies. A score of Berbers were moving among them, cutting the throats of those not yet dead and slipping rings off their fingers.

Sinan carried her across to his flagship, and said to the junior officer there, "The bo'sun's party is still to come. The Berber women?"

"In the hold, Excellency."

"Our casualties?"

The officer shrugged. "Very few, perhaps forty men killed, twice as many wounded. But I have to report, sir, that Captain Mustafa Ajou is himself a casualty. He was killed by a musketball from the *Astride*'s deck."

The admiral nodded and said nothing. Ten minutes later Opal's unconscious body lay on his bunk, covered with a sheet against the prying eyes of the men who were stowing the tribute chest away.

When they had gone, Sinan removed the sheet and sat on the bunk beside her, fondling her as he waited for her to recover consciousness. He lost patience in a little while, took a jar of water and splashed some of it onto her head.

Her eyes opened, and she stared up at him with deep loathing. She whispered, "Why did you not leave me there? I would rather have died aboard the *Astride*."

Sinan shook his head. "No," he said softly. "Now nothing will stand between me and my pleasure with your delectable body." Laughing, he went on, "The bey chose to give you to the bashaw of Tunis, for political reasons. The bashaw allowed you to escape because he is a fool. They both had their chance, and they threw it away. Now you are mine. And you will find that I am stronger than both of them."

Her plight was worse than it had been before. Then, she

had thought only of her own imminent peril, but now her danger meant nothing at all when she thought of the man she loved so dearly.

Was he already dead?

Her heart was breaking for him. She thought: *If my Jason is dead, nothing that happens to me now can have any importance at all.* It came to her with a shock that this meant a kind of surrender, and she fought against it, steeling herself to a pretense that her body was not really her own, that someone else was lying there, that only the mind was Opal Grant's, that the mind would *never* surrender. She said to herself over and over again: *"Jason, Jason, Jason . . ."*

But Jason was not yet dead. Like Osman the bandit, he was not a man to die easily.

When he recovered consciousness, he was being unceremoniously dragged by his ankles down the *Habou*'s companionway, and his head was banging mercilessly on the steps. He suffered the rhythmic pounding, feigning unconsciousness and opening his eyes just to slits to study his captors. The two men who dragged him along a corridor were both young Negroes from the Fezzan, their hair frizzled, their chests bare, dressed in tight-fitting breeches of blue ship's canvas, with desert sandals of camel leather upturned at the toes. They wore scimitars and daggers in their belts, and their muscles gleamed as though they had been oiled.

Since he had not been killed, it meant that they wanted him a prisoner, for a slower death no doubt, and that meant the brig with its iron-barred gate that would defy any attempt at escape. He was bounced down another companionway and yet another. The third deck, then, and the brig would be in the hold, one level lower. But there would be no stairs here, only a ladder. He was ready.

When they reached it, one of the men hoisted Jason onto his shoulder and grunted, "*W'Allahi,* he is heavy." The accent was thick with the gutturals of the southern Sahara Desert. The descent down the ladder was slow and uncertain, and when they reached the bottom, Jason went into action.

He twisted his body around quickly, broke free, and slammed a fist into the chest of the man who had been carrying him, knowing from the feel of the tight muscles that it was not enough. The man fell nonetheless, and the second man dropped down from his foothold on the ladder and made the mistake of trying to draw his scimitar, thereby wasting a precious moment. Jason drove his fist into him with all the considerable strength he could muster, and as the man went down he turned and ran, stumbling in the semidarkness of the hold among the barrels and packing cases. He moved into a narrow passageway, tightly packed with stores, and found an opening among them, scarcely larger than a dog kennel. He rolled over into it, doubling himself up, to lie still and await the next step, whatever it might be.

Their sandalled feet ran swiftly past him, and then there was a long silence.

The feet padded back, and two rumps descended into his vision, squatting by a box that was part of his shelter. They began to discuss this new calamity. Jason held his breath, not moving a muscle. Their voices were very low.

"He is still in the hold, my brother."

"Yes, without a doubt, my uncle. There is only one way out of it."

"We must find him! If the admiral learns he has escaped from us, it will mean our lives."

"What, escape?" The second voice was very confident. "He cannot escape! Go to the ladder, climb out, batten down the hatch and I will find him. Open it only when I call you."

"So be it."

In a moment, Jason heard the hatch closing. There was only one way to batten it down—from the outside. He waited for the second man to move off on his search, and crawled out of his hiding place. The heavy packing-cases were piled high around him, forming narrow passages everywhere. He climbed cautiously to the top of one of the piles, in absolute silence, moving like a cat. He rolled onto his stomach to look down on the little corridor below. Sooner or later, his adversary would be sure to pass this way.

He lay still and thought of his beloved Opal, his wife without benefit of clergy.

Where was she now? A prisoner too, surely, and no doubt suffering at the hands of that hateful scoundrel Sinan. He felt desperate as he thought of her and the fate that must be awaiting her. He knew that her fragility was deceptive, that she was in truth a woman of very strong character. Yet how could she defend herself against such a man as Sinan? He whispered to himself over and over, "Opal, my love, my love . . ."

There was the slightest sound below him, and he tensed. He moved his head cautiously and saw his pursuer, bent double as he peered into what had recently been Jason's hiding place.

There was no time for thought. Jason dropped to the ground, landing squarely on the back of the man's neck. He picked him up like a rag doll and drove his fists, one after the other, into the muscular chest, with enormous force. As the man swayed and began to fall, Jason hit him so hard on the point of the jaw that he felt the bone break.

One of them out of commission now. He did not wait, but ran quickly to the ladder and climbed it. Tapping on the underside of the hatch, he whispered, *"Iftah, y'akhui,* open, my brother." He tried very hard for the guttural accent of the Fezzan, but was not sure that he had found it correctly.

He heard the muffled voice above. "You have found him?" and he answered fiercely, "I found him."

To his great relief, he heard the bolt being thrown. When the heavy hatch opened, he reached up quickly to seize a fistful of frizzy hair and yank on it hard. The body came tumbling down in a rush to smash into the timbers of the floor. Jason did not wait. He slipped through the hatch, battened it down, and ran. There was only one thought in his mind now: *find Opal.*

He heard footsteps as he turned a corner, and froze. There was a half-open door close by, a closet filled with mops, brooms, buckets. He slipped inside and closed the door, and waited in the darkness for the footsteps to pass by. But they did not. Instead, the door was opened. But he was ready.

He shot out a hand and gripped a scraggly throat under a pale and undernourished face—a face he had seen before. He stared, and whispered, "Clayton? Is it not Clayton?"

The strangled voice was hoarse. "The Yankee!" he gasped. He seized Jason's wrist with one hand and said fiercely, "Leave me be, Yankee! I've suffered enough on your behalf already!" He held up his left arm, and to Jason's shock there was no hand on it, just a filthy, bloodied rag over a stub of wrist.

Jason stared at it, and lessened the pressure at Clayton's throat. He whispered, "On *my* behalf?"

Clayton was not even struggling. It was as if all the fight had gone out of him. "Aye," he said, "on your damned account, Yankee. When the admiral learned I'd allowed his lady-love to escape, he had my left hand cut off."

It was not the time for pity. Jason said, "The English lady is aboard again, did you know that?"

"Aye, I know it, the whole ship knows it."

"Where?"

"In the captain's cabin, where else?"

Jason was trembling as he thought of her. He restrained his emotions and said steadily, "The last time our paths crossed, Clayton, I came close to killing you, but I spared your life. Will you admit the truth of that?"

"Aye."

"And now, after such a terrible mutilation, I do not imagine you have any great love for Admiral Sinan."

"I want to see him dead for what he done to me."

"Then will you help me now?"

Clayton shuddered. "I'm afraid . . ," He stared down at the floor, but then he looked up and held Jason's gaze, and whispered, "I make no promises, but . . . tell me how."

"First, a weapon. A gun, a knife, a sword, anything."

There was a dagger in Clayton's hand instantly, pulled up from his boot with remarkable speed. He held it out by its blade. "Take it, it's sharp. There's an edge on it to cut a Berber's throat if he even looks at it. What else?"

"Will you take me to the admiral's cabin? Can we get there without meeting a dozen pirates on the way?"

Hesitantly, Clayton nodded. "Yes, they'll all be on the main decks now. But . . . They'll kill me, Yankee. There's no escape from this ship for the likes of me."

"In truth," Jason said frankly, "I do not know how we will escape either. But if there is a way, then I will find it."

"Then will you take me with you?"

"It is not a prospect I relish, but yes, I will do that."

"Then we go by the number three hold. Down into the bilge and up again by ladders. They come out on the second deck where the cabin is. It's a long way round, but we won't be seen. And if we are . . ." His eyes gleamed in the semidarkness. "Better you give me back the knife. I know how to use it."

"And so do I. Come, we must hurry."

Clayton led him round a corner of the passage and through a tiny door that was little more than a hatch set in the wall. They climbed down ladder after ladder, and splashed their way forward in the bilge water and the darkness.

There was a fierce, controlled elation in Jason's heart now. Once more he was on his way to rescue the woman he loved so dearly.

CHAPTER THIRTEEN

Even in the strong wind, Admiral Sinan's victorious flagship was rolling but making no other movement. The burning hulk of the *Astride* was drifting away from her, but the *Habou* stood idle, as though she were becalmed.

The admiral was annoyed. He stood at the porthole of his cabin and stared across the water at the wreck as the waves washed over her, bringing up bodies that were tossed on the crests like playthings. Finally the *Astride* keeled over and lay for a moment on her side, and then slid majestically under the water, the flames turning to steam, the black smoke billowing up and being carried away by the wind.

And still they were not under way. Was it because Captain Mustafa Ajou was dead? His spirits rose as he thought about the demise of that despicable man. The first mate was taking over now—hesitantly, no doubt—and he was a man Sinan distrusted too, and not very competent either. Sinan knew that he himself should be on the bridge, but he could not tear himself away from what he thought of as a highly emotional and therefore alarming love affair. For the first time in his life, he wanted more than the physical satisfaction he was accustomed to taking whenever he wanted gratification. It intrigued him, amused him—and also worried him, though he would not admit it.

He turned away from the porthole and looked down on Opal.

She lay curled up on the bunk on her side. One hand

was clutching at her shoulder as she sought to cover her breasts with her arm, and the other was between her thighs as though she could shield herself from his lustful gaze.

He sat beside her on the bed, and began stroking the soft contours of her hip. He was surprisingly gentle with her. It was an unexpected side of the nature of this powerful, rough, and completely uninhibited man, a condition brought on by close contact with a young woman whose physical perfection moved him deeply, and whom he knew to be his superior in every conceivable way. This was not a thought that pleased him, but he knew that there was no escaping it.

Opal was watching him through half-closed eyes. She was in the grip of an intolerable distress. And yet . . . It came as a dreadful shock to her when she realized that she was looking at Sinan not only as her captor and tormentor, but also as a man.

Seated beside her, relaxed and at his ease, his body was very straight and controlled, his half-naked chest under the open scarlet waistcoat corded with rippling muscles, his upper arms enormous. His beard and moustache were thick but neatly trimmed, and his dark eyes flashed with humor, a humor that belied the situation entirely. Opal trembled as she fought an almost hypnotic fascination with his physical splendor, knowing that the evil in his black heart was only temporarily hidden. The realization of his uncanny magnetism was strange, and she thrust the thought away with a deliberate effort of will.

He smiled at her and said softly, "You cannot know the number of beautiful women I have enjoyed, sometimes by force but more often with a reciprocated affection that always pleases me greatly. Indeed, I cannot count the number myself, women of every color, race and creed. And they have all had one thing in common: excellence. Excellence has always been my first criterion. That means physical beauty, a beauty that can lie in the depth of lustrous eyes or in the curve of a breast or thigh. I have searched always for the unattainable—perfection."

His hand touched her breast lightly, a finger toying with

a tiny pink nipple. "And I think that at last," he whispered, "I have found it. I have never been so smitten by loveliness, a loveliness that approaches the divine and arouses me to a passion I have seldom known. A Berber goes to Paradise by killing his enemies, the infidels. But I have found my own paradise here on the high seas." He came down to earth again. "You need proof of my ardent desire for you?"

He took her hand and pressed it against the cloth of his breeches. With a sense of terrifying shock she felt the strength of his manhood, huge and strong and throbbing powerfully; she felt an overwhelming desire to close her slender fingers around it, but she did not, and when he released her she pulled away from him and lay still, trying not to meet his eyes.

He stood up and stripped off his scarlet waistcoat, staring down at her with desire in his eyes. He kicked off his high boots and rolled down his heavy stockings, then unfastened his belt and slid his breeches down over narrow hips that looked as though they were carved from oak. He stood there for a moment. She would not look at his splendid body but turned her face away from him, trying to control her tears.

He knelt beside her on the bunk, one hand at her breasts, the other at the junction of her thighs, stroking her very tenderly. He whispered, "I will not hurt you, dear Opal. But you must give yourself to me freely. If not, then I will force you, and we will both have lost a little of the pleasure." He sat back and said, "Touch me."

Opal shook her head, refusing to meet his eyes. "No."

"Hold me."

"No."

"Stroke me."

"No. I will not. Nor will I love you freely."

"Not even if I arouse you to uncontrollable passion? As I can, and I will."

His lips were on her. She shuddered and took hold of herself, and said tightly, "Jason Farn. What have you done with him?"

He straightened up, but he did not lose his smile. But the inherent evil was evident now. "Jason Farn?" he echoed. "Imagine that I am he, dearest Opal. It is an indignity I will gladly suffer. Imagine that these hands are his, that my lips are his."

He lay down beside her, and she moaned at the touch of his burning flesh. But she said steadily, "Jason. Is he dead?"

He did not immediately answer her. He was on his side, and his knee was steadily forcing her thighs apart. He kissed her breasts, and whispered at last, "How should I answer that question? If I tell you he is dead, will it release you from your foolish inhibitions? Or will you turn instead to a grief that will be even more inhibiting? Should I tell you that he still lives, and will continue to live as long as I am pleased with you? Which should it be, dear Opal? I can lie or tell the truth with equal fluency. I am a Berber, an Arab, it is very easy for me."

"The truth."

Sinan sighed. If only he could find a way into this lovely woman's favor! He said, "I wish we were talking of other things, not of a past lover, who may or may not be dead." He was still holding himself back, savoring the warmth of her thighs, not yet beginning to penetrate her, for reasons of his own. It was by a strong effort of will that she forced all physical sensation away from her, driving away her excitation as he worked on her with practiced efficiency. He felt sure that the woman who could resist him had not yet been born.

At last he said, "He is alive, and if I am pleased with you, then perhaps I will allow him to live for a while. Perhaps I will even give him a few women to love, to compensate him for your loss."

He hesitated, and spoke at last the words he had long wanted to say. "I am in love with you, Opal. A *true* love, that will not be denied. Hold me."

"No! I will not."

"Hold me, and guide me into you."

"No!"

He took her wrist and moved her hand to his body, and whispered fiercely, "Hold me and guide me into you, or he will surely die, quite slowly. And you, my dearest Opal, will watch him die."

She moaned softly as she wrapped her fingers around him. He let go of her wrist very slowly and began to stroke her again. He whispered, "That was the beginning of acceptance, I think, is it not so?"

She held her breath as he toyed with her, and thought of Jason. Was he truly still alive? In an effort to detach herself from her own sensations, she fixed her mind on him.

Is he still alive? Is he hurt? Is he suffering now? Shall we ever escape from this purgatory, as we have escaped before? Does he wonder what is happening to me? Is he crying out for me in anguish as I cry out for him?

Sinan was kneeling now between her legs, his hands beneath her, and lifting her up, placing her slim thighs over his shoulders.

There was urgent knocking at the door. She saw Sinan lift his head, furious anger in his eyes, heard him shout savagely in Arabic. But the knocking continued more urgently. Sinan swore again, ready to explode with anger. He heard the bo'sun's muffled voice. "A matter of importance, Excellency! The bashaw of Tunis is here!"

Sinan froze, still holding her up. Not moving, he called out, "The bashaw? Here? On board my ship?"

"Aboard the *Habou*, Excellency."

Sinan swore again as he lowered Opal to the bed. Then suddenly all his anger was gone and he was laughing. He leaned down and kissed her quickly and said, "In spite of all my evident faults, dear Opal, I am not entirely devoid of a sense of humor. I must ask you to wait for me. There is a matter I must attend to. But in a little while we will be together again. Contain your anxiety in patience, I beg of you."

He was certain he was winning the game he was playing with her, and yet . . . he was not at all sure that it really was a game. The realization worried him. He dressed himself quickly and bent to kiss her breasts again, although she turned away from him. He said quietly, "Very soon, my love. And this time, I will arouse you as you have never been aroused before."

He strode to the door and opened it. He had quite recovered his calm, and the sight of the bo'sun brought him back to earth from the strange paradise in which, for a while, he had found himself. He said coldly, "What? What is it the bashaw wants with me?"

The bo'sun shrugged. "I do not know, Excellency. The *Jamara* signaled us that he was coming aboard, and they lowered a boat. The first mate—" He broke off and said piously, "Since our beloved Captain Mustafa Ajou died so nobly, the first mate is in command now. He saw the signal and chose not to ignore it, as a better man would have done. And so he came aboard. He demanded immediate access to your cabin, Excellency. But at my persuasion, he awaits you on the bridge."

"Good. Your services will not be forgotten."

Bo'sun Munir fawned. "Always at your esteemed service, Excellency."

"Wait at my door. During my absence, which I hope will be brief, no one will enter, or leave."

"It shall be as you say." The bosun's eyes gleamed. There was no one aboard the *Habou* who did not know just how their admiral was engaged. Neglecting the bridge for the love of a woman!

Admiral Sinan closed the door carefully behind him, and went to meet with the ruler of Tunis. He was a man Sinan hated, yet feared too; the bashaw's influence with the bey of Algiers was very strong, and powerful heads had fallen at his whim very often. But when he reached the bridge the bashaw was not there. The first mate said, "He has gone below, Excellency, to inspect, he said, the damage to your fine ship. Though in my opinion, there were other reasons."

There were indeed other reasons.

The bashaw was a nervous, worried little man who knew that his position was a tenuous one, and whereas the other rulers maintained their power largely by their fighting abilities, he himself survived only through the efforts of his widespread intelligence service. Three times in the past year attempts had been made to overthrow him, each of them frustrated through information sent by his spies.

The spies were everywhere, in Tripoli, Morocco, in Algiers itself—even on board the *Habou.* And waiting for the admiral, wondering what it might be that was keeping him off his bridge at a time like this, he had gone off to make a few inquiries of his own. He had searched out a sailor named Serouf, a wily young man from the Tunisian oasis of Gafsa, whom he had placed aboard the flagship more than two years ago. They stood together at the stern railings of the lower deck. The bashaw said, "The *Astride* has been sunk, my good friend."

Serouf nodded. "Yes, Excellency, quickly fired and sunk."

"And yet she was carrying more than a hundred thousand pounds in gold. I wonder if that treasure lies on the ocean floor now?"

"It does not," Serouf said promptly. "Six men were detailed to find it and it was brought on board the *Habou.* It lies now in the admiral's cabin."

"And was it brought aboard secretly, Serouf? Or openly?"

Serouf laughed. "No secret at all, Excellency. Two or three score men saw it. And I am astonished at this."

"I am not astonished," Ismail Assada said, beaming. "It merely means that Admiral Sinan, though no doubt covetous of such a prize and wishing, no doubt, to add it to all the other gold he has stolen, places a higher price on his own life. For were he to report to the bey that the tribute had been lost, then he would have lost his head."

"Ah yes, of course. But there are other matters you should be informed of, Excellency. First, the thirty-two women the bey wanted captured are all on board, picked up, it seems, from a fishing boat in which they were trying to escape."

The bashaw's malevolent eyes were excited. "Ah . . . that explains, no doubt, why the *Astride* changed her course and headed for Gibraltar. I will confess that this was a question that puzzled me." He saw at once, from the smug look on Serouf's face, that there was something else. The spy said blandly, "Second, Captain Mustafa Ajou died in the battle, killed by a shot fired from the deck of the *Astride*."

The bashaw clicked his tongue. "Mustafa Ajou? He was a good man, Serouf. An Algerian, of course, and therefore not a thinking man, but still . . ." He broke off and waited, knowing that there was more to come. Serouf said gently, "The shot that killed him was fired by Bo'sun Munir."

"*What?* Are you sure of this, Serouf?"

"If I were not sure, I would not have reported it. Three of my own men saw it. One of them overheard Admiral Sinan himself giving the order for the killing. It is known that there has long been bad blood between them."

"So . . ." The bashaw sucked in his breath and thought about this, wondering how he could turn it to advantage; perhaps a quiet word with the bey of Algiers? But Serouf was smiling and saying quietly, "And there is one more item of information for you, Excellency, and it is my hope that this will bring you even greater satisfaction. The fishing boat in which the refugees were trying to escape was being sailed by a man who is known to all of us, the American, Jason Farn."

The bashaw stared; he felt that his eyes were goggling. "*Jason Farn?*"

"None other."

"And was he . . . alone?"

Serouf made an elaborate gesture. "But no, Excellency! The boat was filled with women, as I have said, so heavily laden that it is a wonder it could even float—"

"Don't play games with me, Serouf!" Ismail Assada said angrily. "Or I'll have your neck!"

The spy answered quickly, "The American had his own woman with him. The English lady whose name is not known to me, the one who escaped from the bey's harem."

The bashaw was trembling violently. "And at this moment, no doubt, she is . . . ?"

Serouf said triumphantly, "In the admiral's cabin, Excellency. And if I have done well in telling you all these momentous events . . ."

For a long time the bashaw did not speak. This, then, was the reason for the admiral's absence from his bridge! He found that he was shaking with rage, but he controlled it and said wearily, "Yes, you have done well, Serouf. There will be money. I am pleased with you."

He left the spy there, bowing and fawning and rubbing his hands at the thought of the gold. He went back to the bridge and found Admiral Sinan there, striding up and down impatiently and wondering what was going on. He embraced him warmly and said effusively, "My good friend Sinan! What a splendid battle you fought. Such excellent seamanship. I am proud of you, very proud! And are you well?"

Sinan said courteously, "I am well by God's grace, only if you are, Excellency."

"And by God's grace, I am well too. And your house?"

"It prospers, thank God. And yours?"

"Thanks be to God, mine prospers too."

"And I am honored by your Excellency's visit to my humble flagship. She is not worthy of your august presence, I fear."

"But no, my dearest Sinan! She is a splendid vessel, far better than the miserable *Jamara*."

"Forgive me," the admiral said smoothly, "that I dispute with my master, whose humble servant I am. But the *Jamara* is a ship almost worthy of your Excellency's command."

Well! There was a snide remark if ever he heard one! But Ismail Assada peered around the bridge and said, puzzled, "But your captain, Mustafa Ajou, he is not here?"

"Unhappily, Excellency," Sinan said, frowning, "the good Mustafa Ajou died bravely in the battle with the *Astride*. It grieves me deeply to tell you this. I always counted him as one of my closest personal friends."

"Then allow me to offer you my condolences, Sinan. He was indeed a good man." He brightened perceptibly and continued, "But I came here to congratulate you on the efficiency with which you despatched our enemy, Sinan! I saw you take her wind no less than three times. The *Astride* was commanded by one of England's most skilled captains, yet you outsailed him and outfought him. My felicitations, dear friend."

The admiral murmured, wishing this hated man would get back to his own damned ship, "You are most kind, Excellency."

"What a shame it is that England's tribute must have gone to the bottom! Well, in a worthy cause, I suppose."

So *this* was what he wanted to know! Sinan said, "It did not go to the bottom, Excellency. It was recovered and brought aboard the *Habou*."

"Ah, splendid! I have always known you to be a man of great merit, dear Sinan. I have told the bey so a thousand times. And now you have filled my day with the most sublime contentment." He sighed. "Well, I have been away from my ship for too long. I will be in Algiers ahead of you, and I will tell the bey that you will bring his tribute on your triumphant return. I am sure that he will arrange a hero's welcome for you." He beamed. "A thousand men on the docks, firing their rifles into the air to welcome the great Admiral Sinan! I am honored to count you as my dear, dear friend. And perhaps we should arrange a state burial for our friend Mustafa Ajou. Yes, a cortege through the streets. Is that a good idea?"

"An excellent idea."

"Led, perhaps, by your bo'sun, Munir. Well, I must be on my way."

There was no emotion on Sinan's handsome face, but his heart was beating wildly. Did this smooth spoken old fool know more than he gave him credit for? He said nothing, and kept the frozen smile in place.

"I bid you farewell," the bashaw said. "Your prestige this day has been greatly augmented." His foot on the top rung of the ladder, he turned back and said, frowning thoughtfully, "But perhaps, if I am to tell the bey that you have his tribute, I should see it?" He laughed shortly. "You know Karim Abdullah as well as I do, and the first thing he will say is, 'Have you actually seen it, Ismail?' So perhaps you would be good enough to show it to me."

The admiral said smoothly, "Of course, Excellency, and how right you are, as always." He raised his voice and called, "Runner! The bo'sun is at my cabin door. Tell him to find six men at once, and bring the tribute chest to the bridge."

But the bashaw protested, "But no, my good friend, that will not be necessary at all. It will be far simpler if we go to your cabin and . . . take a peek at it."

Sinan said, masking his anger, "I will not put you to such trouble, Excellency. I will have it brought here." He glared at the waiting runner and said angrily, "What? You did not hear my order?"

As the man turned away, the bashaw said gently, "No, wait! It is no trouble, dear Sinan, for me to go to your cabin, and that is what we will do."

The runner was shaking. His master was the admiral himself, but here was one of the rulers countermanding the orders, an eminence whose very whim was law, admiral or no admiral. The bashaw said quietly, "Take me to your cabin, dear Sinan."

Sinan knew when he was defeated. Tight with repressed rage, he escorted the bashaw to his quarters. The bo'sun threw open the door and closed it behind them.

Opal had wrapped herself in a sheet and was standing at the porthole, staring out across a wide sea that offered her no escape from her terrible predicament. She turned and saw the bashaw staring at her in feigned surprise. He said, "*W'Allahi!* By God! Do my old eyes deceive me? But no! The English lady, Opal Grant!"

Sinan said nothing, knowing there was nothing he could say. It was all he could do to control his anger.

But Ismail Assada was smiling. He turned to Sinan and said easily, "She was promised to me by my good friend the bey of Algiers, who is your master, as I am too. Allah is wise and he moves in mysterious ways to perform his wonders. You see that he has brought us together again, and his wish for our mutual enjoyment is apparent." He looked up into Sinan's lowering eyes and saw the anger there, and it pleased him. He said gently, "And so, I will enjoy her now. You may leave us, Admiral Sinan."

Sinan trembled, and bit his tongue to hold back the mounting violence in him. For a long moment he toyed with the idea of striking the bashaw down, storming up on deck and turning his guns on the *Jamara*, to be sunk without trace. . . . But no, there were spies on board his own ship, not only the bey's but the bashaw's as well, he was sure of it.

So he bowed instead and muttered, "Your servant, Excellency," and stalked out.

Ismail Assada bolted the door carefully and leaned against it, peering at her excitedly. But he could not fathom her expression as she stared back at him with a kind of shock on her face that he misread completely. It was not fear, nor even anger; rather, it was overwhelming surprise that her own emotions of a few moments ago, try as she might to control them, had almost betrayed her. The surprise quickly went, replaced by an ice-cold fury at this loathsome creature who stood there smirking at her, full of self-confidence.

Ismail Assada said amiably, "Divest yourself of that foolish sheet, dear child, and lie down on the bed for me."

He was already dropping his belt with the ornate dagger in it to the ground and pulling his long gown up over his head. And at the sight of that unappetizing body all her long-restrained temper rose up inside her and exploded.

She screamed, "Monster! Savage!" and threw herself at him, reaching out with her fingernails, going straight for his face in an eruption of passion that was beyond reason. Her anger was directed not only against him; it was also against herself for not attempting to fight Sinan as she was now prepared to fight the bashaw.

She hurled herself at him, and he fell to the ground under the violence of her assault. But now the fury was on him too. He shrieked and rolled over to reach for his dagger. She heard the dreadful sibilance as it was drawn from its sheath. She sprang to her feet with feline speed and picked up the admiral's chair, made of oak and so heavy that normally she could scarcely have lifted it. She swung it at her adversary as he stumbled to his knees with the knife in his hand. He threw up an arm to deflect it, but he could not. There was a ferocious strength in her that she did not know she possessed. She fell with the chair as it smashed into his head. He lay still.

Quite overcome with the violence of her efforts, she crouched on her hands and knees for a moment, gasping as she tried to recover her breath and her calm, trying to control her shaking.

She forced herself to her feet, swaying slightly. What now? Somewhere to hide? She went uncertainly to the door and opened it.

She stared into the startled eyes of her beloved Jason.

He too stared, and then his arms were about her and he was whispering in astonishment, "Opal, my love . . ." Over her shoulder he saw the still body of the bashaw with blood on his head, a heavy chair upended beside him. But Opal's eyes were on the pasty-faced young man who was with Jason, and she breathed, *"Clayton?"*

Jason nodded. "Yes, he is with us now."

"Oh, my love . . ."

"Come quickly. We are still fugitives aboard a pirate ship, surrounded by our enemies, who will be searching for us soon. We must hide."

He turned to Clayton, aware that Opal was looking in shock at the stump of his wrist. He was not sure how far he could trust him, but he said quietly, "We are in your hands, Clayton. Find us a place to hide till we can devise a way to escape from this hell-ship."

Far above them, a bell began to clang. Jason said quickly, "The alarm? Have they so soon discovered our escape?"

But Clayton was staring up at the companionway. He listened, and then said, his voice hushed, "Three, and three, and three. It is the order: all hands to battle stations!" His face was whiter than ever with fear. "We are under attack!"

Four men were racing down the corridor past the cabin, their naked scimitars in the hands, and Jason tensed. But with hardly a glance the men raced on, heading for the companionway and up to the deck. Jason pulled Opal quickly back into the cabin, and Clayton came in with them and shut the door. Jason said quietly, "Perhaps this is the circumstance we have been praying for. How we can turn it to account, I do not yet know. But I will find out!"

CHAPTER FOURTEEN

The *Habou* and the *Jamara* were both under attack. And the enemy was a very formidable one.

She was the *Virginia*, an American warship commanded by a captain as tough and indomitable as his ship. Captain Aloysius Breck was a sour and angry man who was only happy when he was fighting, preferably sinking the frigates of what he liked to call "those hell-blasted picaroons, the Berbers."

He had been sent here on a punitive mission by Vice President Jefferson, with explicit instructions. They were strolling together in the fine gardens of Monticello as Mr. Jefferson noted the progress of his vegetables, his consuming passion. Crouching over his Brussels sprouts and studying them intently, he said, "Take your ship, Captain Breck, close into the Algerian strands. Find one of their damned pirate villages and shell the daylights out of it. The bey has insulted us again, and this time I don't want him to get away with it. Have you heard about Bainbridge?"

Breck nodded, wondering what it could possibly be about Brussels sprouts that so interested the vice president of the United States. "Of course I've heard, Mr. Jefferson," he said sourly. "Bainbridge is a friend of mine. The bey made him a messenger-boy, called him a slave."

"A friend of yours? I didn't know. Good. The Arabs think of us as a giant, Breck, but a very flabby giant, and it's time we showed them that we still have teeth. Get out there and avenge Bainbridge, teach those savages a lesson they won't easily forget. Many of their towns are perched high on sandstone bluffs at the water's edge. Find a sizeable one, put broadside after broadside into the cliff a hundred feet or so below it, and topple it down into the sea. We can't have men of Bainbridge's stature treated with such contempt. I won't have it."

Breck said, relishing his assignment, "And any pirate ships I might find en route? I'd like carte blanche to sink them if I find them."

"You have it, Breck."

Breck was a very happy man.

And now he was even happier. The lookout in the crow's nest had called out, "Two ships on the port bow! Four degrees and fifteen miles! One Algerian, one Tunisian, both becalmed!"

Becalmed?" Captain Breck was startled. "How can they be becalmed in a wind like this? Bear down on them, helmsman."

"Aye, aye, sir. Fourteen points to starboard."

Breck said sourly, "I didn't say fourteen points. I said bear down on them."

"Aye, aye, sir, bearing down on them now, we are going to run with the wind."

"Make that fifteen points, helmsman."

"Aye, aye, sir. Fifteen points and still running."

Breck looked up at his sails and nodded his satisfaction. He heard the bo'sun's angry bellow below him. "Watch your topgallants, you misbegotten bastards! You think this is a pleasure cruise? Give me more sail up there! We are running now!"

The American was bearing down fast on the Berber ships, and aboard both of them there was panic. The *Virginia* had been identified, and it could only mean the direst calamity. They had been caught stationary in the water, the worst fate that could befall any vessel. They were both turned into the wind, their sails empty, and once she was stationary a sailing ship could not be started on her way again without a great deal of time-consuming labor.

On board the lighter *Jamara*, the men were working the

shrouds furiously. The first mate shouted, "The bashaw is still aboard the *Habou*, Captain!"

The captain was a volatile, angry man, fiercely bearded, with a black patch over one eye. He screamed, "To the devil with the bashaw! He is the son of a whore and a camel! I will not bring my ship under attack by a thirty-gun cruiser! Get those sails filled!"

On board the *Virginia*, the first mate said, "The Tunisian, sir. She's breaking away. Her sails are beginning to fill."

"Then we hit her first. And when I say hit her, I mean *sink* her, Mr. Mate."

"Aye, aye, sir."

Captain Breck strode to the rail and shouted down, "Mr. Fennell!"

The master-gunner came running. "We are ready, Captain!"

"I'm bringing us down on the port side of the Tunisian. I'll give you fifty feet, all starboard guns below her waterline. I want her sunk in the first salvo, Mr. Fennell! If I have to make a second pass, I'll have your guts for garters!

"Aye, aye, sir!"

For a mere five minutes, the two Berber ships watched the fast, relentless approach of the *Virginia*. The *Jamara*, drawing away now, was the closest, and her captain, a very frightened man, screamed, "A broadside as she passes us! Hot shot!"

A voice came back to him from below. "What hot shot? The coals are not lit!"

"Cold shot, then! A broadside!"

But it was too late. The *Virginia* swept past at no more than fifty paces, and at a very great speed. At the precisely correct moment, Mr. Fennell called out casually, "All port guns ready . . . Flares ready . . . Wait for the roll!" A half-moment of waiting, and then: "All guns, *fire*!" The flares were dropped to the powder, and fifteen of the dreaded royal cannon fired in almost perfect synchronization. The *Jamara* took all of the shot at her waterline, where they would do the most damage. Her own guns answered ineffectually as she heeled over, and Captain Breck shouted, "Is she killed, Mr. Fennell? Or do I have to court-martial you for incompetence?"

Master-Gunner Fennell was very pleased with his gunners' work. He thought of himself, not entirely without cause, as the best gunner in the entire American navy. He shouted back, "She is sinking, sir! I give her fifteen minutes, no more!"

"Your last round missed her altogether!"

"No, sir. My last round hit her rudder, where it was aimed!"

"Very well. The *Habou*, now!"

But the *Habou* was not idle. Sinan had taken over command from a first mate in whom he had no confidence at all, and he was a sailor of great skill. Waiting for more of his sails to fill and get him under way, he ordered a port salvo from all guns as the *Virginia* swept past him less than a hundred feet away. Seven of them struck home, three of them smashing into the base of the *Virginia*'s bridge, and Captain Breck swore. He did not mind too much if men were killed, but he hated damage to his beautiful ship. She ploughed on, and Breck turned to the helmsman and said, "Bring us round again at a thousand yards, head-on for the *Habou*'s prow. There's nothing there she can hit us with." He shouted down to the bo'sun, "At the end of the turn, shorten sail! Prepare the irons and nets. We will board her at the next pass."

"Aye, aye, sir!"

He called down to Fennell: "Port to port now. I want your royals to hole her, your whole cannon and demis to sweep her decks. I want a shambles aboard her. Bo'sun! The nets ready, and shorten sail at the turn. We board her now."

"Aye, aye, sir, we're ready!

The riflemen in the rigging of both ships were firing and reloading furiously. At better than twelve knots, the two ships collided. Within moments, the grappling irons were in place and the nets thrown across. Two hundred well-drilled marines were swarming aboard the pirate.

There was chaos aboard the *Habou.* More than seventy men had been killed by the initial cannonade that swept across her decks. The screams of the dying almost drowned out the sounds of the rifle fire and the clash of cutlass against scimitar.

The American warship was immensely stronger, her men far more numerous and better armed, better trained, and filled with a hatred of the Berbers that was learned from the captain. The battle was quickly brought to its end. The *Habou* had inflicted great damage on the *Virginia*; but she had also taken more than thirty heavy shot below her waterline, and was in very sore straits indeed.

Jason and Opal had taken refuge among the water barrels that had once before saved their lives. He crouched over her protectively as the gunfire thundered sporadically. Clayton was with them, and a small group of the refugee women, cowering together, seeking the security that Jason's presence seemed to offer. The Berber girl Andara came running to them. She whispered, "An American ship, no?"

Jason was surprised to see her. "Yes," he answered, "an American warship, much more powerful than the *Habou.* Where are the rest of you?"

Andara shook her head. "I do not know. We were in one of the holds, and it was burst open by cannon fire. They are looking for safety, I think."

Jason stared up at the great hull of the *Virginia* looming above them, firmly lashed to the *Habou.* His arms were around Opal as they listened to the sounds of the fighting. He said quietly, "It will soon be over. She is the *Virginia,* the best fighting ship we have, four hundred marines aboard her."

"Marines?"

He smiled and said, "It won't take long. We're listing badly. It means that we're sorely wounded. As soon as the fighting is over, we will cross over to the American. It won't be difficult; there will be nets."

He turned to Andara and said, in Arabic, "Very soon now it will be finished. We will leave this shelter. I will help Opal cross over the nets, and then I will return with you. We must search the *Habou* from stem to stern for the rest of the refugees. Some of them may have been wounded. The *Habou* does not have much time left."

"Yes, yes, I know where most of them will be. And will the American ship take us to Gibraltar?"

"I'm sure of it."

"Good."

In less than ten minutes the last of the firing ceased, and there was a welcome silence. Clayton said nervously, "I think it's time for the likes of us to be moving out, Mr. Farn. This ship will be in Davy Jones's locker very soon."

Jason nodded. The water barrels were a potent shield against danger, but it was time to leave.

Clayton held back. He said hesitantly, "And will you put in a good word for me, sir? I'm a pirate, and they won't like that."

"Under the circumstances," Jason said affably, "circumstances I will not bore you with, it might not be easy. But I will do what I can."

They crept from their hiding place and went up on deck. Opal gasped at the sight of the slaughter there. Jason's strong arm was around her as he led her over the dead and dying bodies to the first of the nets. Four armed Marines were there, shepherding the pirate prisoners across. One of them, tall and straight and proud even in defeat, was Admiral Sinan. He glared at them but said nothing, stalking aboard the *Virginia* in great dignity. A marine pushed him to hurry him along. Sinan shrugged off the hand and said coldly, "Your hands off me, scum! I am an admiral!"

But one of the marines was staring at Jason open-mouthed, and he shouted, "Jason! Jason Farn, by all that's holy!"

Jason turned as the marine broke ranks and ran to him, embracing him warmly, slapping him on the back, shouting, "Jason Farn! We all thought you must be long dead!"

Jason was smiling broadly. He returned the embrace and said happily, "Pratt! Pratt Wilson! It's been a long time, friend!"

"Three years and more! And we all heard you were dead, long since!"

"No, I do not die so easily. I'm still alive and kicking. How are you, Pratt?"

"Well, well indeed, and it's good to see you!"

Jason introduced Opal. "My wife," he said quietly. "And this is Pratt Wilson, an old and good friend from—from days I have almost forgotten."

She was wrapped in a sheet and nothing more, but he took her hand and murmured, "A great honor, ma'am."

Jason said urgently, "Have you seen the extent of the *Habou*'s damage, Pratt?"

"Aye, she's little time left. Another pirate ship to the bottom."

"How long?"

"An hour, no more. At point-blank range, our royals have made a right mess of her bottom. George Fennell is still our master-gunner, and as you no doubt remember, he's a master of his trade."

"The *Habou* is carrying thirty-two Berber women, refugees who were bound for the bey's prisons. A few of them are with us, but I must find the rest. Help Opal aboard for me, take care of her, there's a good fellow. It will take a little time to round them up, and if we only have an hour, then I must hurry. I don't want the *Habou* to sink under me before they are all safely aboard the *Virginia*."

"Good, I'll do that," Pratt said eagerly. "There are already some of our fellows below her decks. They'll help you out. And don't worry about your lady, she's among friends and in good hands."

"Thank you, friend." Jason indicated Clayton, standing nervously behind them, and said, "And this fellow is English, impressed into service by the pirates and not one of them at all. He's been a great help to us. Take care of him for me too, Pratt, will you do that?"

"Of course." Pratt looked curiously at the stump of Clayton's wrist, but he said nothing more.

"Pass the word around," Jason said. "I don't want anyone putting a musket to his head because of the clothes he wears." He embraced Opal and whispered, "Go with Pratt, my love. I will rejoin you as soon as I can."

Andara was waiting. "Show me first," he said, "where the women were being held. And then from there, we will search."

They moved off together among the bodies that littered the *Habou*'s shattered decks.

Captain Breck was in the best of moods. The wrecked remains of the *Jamara* were no more than a few floating spars, and the great *Habou*, the most notorious of all the Barbary pirates, was lashed to his hull in ruins. His own casualties had been high but not insupportable, and though the damage to his ship had been heavy, it was already under expert repair. He would not admit the extent to which pure chance had played a part in this battle; had he not found the Berbers becalmed, it might well have gone against him.

But it had been a good day, and a good fight. The prisoners were still crossing over as he stood at the railing and looked down. The line of his mouth tightened when he saw a dozen painted women, dressed in the flimsiest and oddest of ragged clothes, being shepherded across between two rows of grinning marines.

He said to the mate, his voice very cold, "Ladies of the night, Mr. Mate. The pirate ships always carry these fallen women, more shame to them."

The mate was casually good-humored, dedicated to his work, and stood in awe of no man, not even the formidable skipper. He said, his tongue firmly in his cheek, "Yes, sir. And if you ask me, Captain, we could take a leaf out of their book and ship a few whores aboard too. There's nothing like a good whore to lift a sailor's morale."

Breck scowled at him. "I did *not* ask you, Mr. Darwin. See that they're kept apart from the men. I'll have no licentiousness aboard the *Virginia*."

Darwin sighed. "Aye, aye, sir."

"Later on, I will have a word with them. It may not be

too late to turn some of them away from the shameful lust they are tainted with."

"If you wish it, Captain," Darwin said blandly, "I could do that for you. Save you the indignity, so to speak."

"There's no indignity, Mr. Mate, in turning a fallen woman from her evil ways."

"Yes, sir. No, sir."

Darwin heard a curious voice and said, puzzled, "An Englishwoman there, Captain."

Breck frowned. "Where?"

"The woman dressed in the sheet, talking to Wilson and Price."

The captain stared at her and listened. He too was puzzled. "Yes," he said, "English indeed by her speech. I find that very strange. And why should she be so curiously dressed, I wonder?" He raised his voice and shouted, "Wilson!"

Pratt Wilson snapped to attention. "Sir!"

"The woman with you. I will see her on the bridge."

"Aye, aye, sir." The captain waited, and when Wilson brought her to the gate of the bridge he scowled at her and said, "I thought I heard an English voice, girl, and it intrigued me. Are you indeed English? And if so, perhaps you would care to enlighten me concerning your presence on board a pirate ship?"

Opal was very conscious of his hostility. She said calmly, "I am English, sir, from London. My name is Opal Grant, and I am the daughter of—of the late Sir Neville Grant of the British Foreign Office. You may have heard of him."

Breck was startled. He said quickly, "Sir Neville Grant? Yes, ma'am, I have heard Mr. Jefferson speak of him most highly." His attitude changed at once, and he said gruffly, "I must ask you, ma'am, to accept my apologies for what must have seemed a brusque tone of voice. It is just that, er, well, your attire, ma'am, and your presence aboard the *Habou* . . ."

"As a prisoner, sir."

"A *prisoner*? Good God!"

"I was captured, sir, in Algiers, where I was visiting.

More correctly, I was abducted from my hotel and carried off to the bey's harem."

His voice was hoarse with shock. "The scoundrel!"

"Though fortunately I was rescued in time by a very gallant gentleman, one of your own countrymen, sir. A journalist, Mr. Farn, whose paper is the *Gazette of the United States.*"

"Ah yes, an excellent paper. But—the bey's *harem*, you say?"

"Yes indeed, sir."

"Shocking! And quite monstrous! These damned picaroons! But forgive me. If I may present myself, ma'am? I am Captain Aloysius Breck, and your servant. Please accept the trifling hospitality of my ship."

"I thank you, sir. It is a great relief, I assure you, to know that these dreadful events have come to an end."

"Then if you would accompany me to my cabin? I am sure that you are not comfortable here under so many eyes, ah, dressed as you are."

"The sheet I wear, Captain, is not of my own choosing."

"Of course not. But I will have the ship's tailors stitch up something more acceptable for you. Take over, Mr. Mate."

"Aye, aye, sir."

"Send me the casualty and damage reports when they are ready, and the list of prisoners."

He took Opal down to his cabin, offered her a seat, and said, "I do not know, ma'am, if it would come amiss were I to offer you a small glass of medicinal whiskey. It is a great cure for malaise, ma'am, and after such dreadful experiences, it might perhaps be acceptable?"

Opal replied gravely, "It would be most acceptable, Captain. Thank you."

"Good. I am not a drinking man myself, but under the circumstances, I will join you." He produced a decanter and glasses with commendable speed and poured a very small whiskey for her, a somewhat larger one for himself. "And are you hungry, ma'am? I cannot imagine that the food on board a Berber ship is either liberal or insufficient to keep body and soul together."

Opal smiled and sipped her drink. "I scarcely remember when I last ate. But it is not important at all."

"We shall shortly be serving supper in the officers' mess. Perhaps you will honor us with your presence?"

She inclined her head. "I would be delighted."

"And tell me, please, if you can. I saw a number of, ah, fallen women boarding us from the *Habou*, an abominable pirate habit and I will not speak of them. But there were a number of other women, some of them quite elderly. I find their presence very strange. Can you enlighten me?"

"Oh yes. When we escaped from the bey's palace, Mr. Farn and I, we brought with us thirty-two refugees, the relatives of certain rebels. The bey was in the process of rounding them up so that he could submit them to—to torture, in order to bring about the surrender of their men."

"The more I learn of the bey," the captain murmured, "the less I like him."

"Though there were far too many for our small fishing boat, Mr. Farn insisted on bringing them along, in the hope that we could all reach the safety of Gibraltar. We were picked up by an English merchantman, the *Astride*. She was attacked and sunk by the *Habou*, and we were all taken aboard."

"Then Mr. Farn is with you now?"

"He is aboard the *Habou*, sir, searching for the rest of the women, some of whom may be lying below decks, wounded."

The captain smiled. "He seems to be a very enterprising man, your Mr. Farn. I trust I will have the pleasure of meeting him?"

"If I may present him to you when he comes aboard? He is such a good man! His courage is quite remarkable."

The captain said lightly, "The name Farn is somehow familiar to me, though I cannot recall in what context. It's just a thought at the back of my mind. From the *Gazette*, you say?"

"Yes."

"It is published in Philadelphia, which is my home town, so perhaps I met him there once." He said, frowning, "Farn, Farn, not a common name at all . . ."

Opal said, prompting him, "Jason Farn, thirty years old or a little less, very tall and strong, and really quite—" She broke off, surprised at the captain's reaction. He was staring at her with an expression on his face that she could not understand. Was it anger? Why should he be angry?

He rose to his feet and said coldly, "When first you mentioned the name, ma'am, it seemed to remind me of some past event that would not fall into place. Now, it has done so." His voice was tight and unforgiving. "Three years ago, your Jason Farn deserted my ship off the coast of Nicaragua, and was reported to me as sailing for Algiers. And I am obliged to inform you, Miss Grant, that desertion from the Marine Corps in time of war is an offense that is punishable by hanging."

Her hand went to her throat. She stared at him, speechless. The captain put down his glass and said coldly, "I thank you, ma'am, for the information with which you have provided me. I will set aside a cabin for you. The tailor will visit you there to dress you decently. And perhaps under the changed circumstances you will not wish to join us at supper. I will have food sent to your cabin. And I must ask you not to attempt any communication with Marine Farn. He will not be allowed visitors."

She could not hold back her rising emotion. Breck strode to the door, opened it, and bellowed, "Orderly!" A seaman came running. The captain said harshly, "Take this lady to Cabin C. Tell the master-tailor to find some bunting and stitch up some more decorous clothing for her. Tell the steward she will be eating in her cabin, tell the officer of the watch that she is not to leave it. That is all."

"Aye, aye, sir." The captain said pointedly, "Good day, Miss Grant," and turned his back on her.

In shock, she followed the seaman. As she sat on her bunk in the tiny cabin, she knew that she had brought the shadow of the gallows to hang over the man she so dearly loved. She dissolved into tears. But in a few moments, she dried her eyes, lay down on the cot and began to think.

The master-tailor came in a little while. He was a quiet, friendly old man with steel-rimmed spectacles on the end of his nose. As he ran his tape carefully over her, he said softly, "It is common knowledge aboard, ma'am, that there are certain problems distressing you. Perhaps this will take your mind off them."

It was a kindly comment, but Opal shook her head. "No, I do not wish to take my mind from them. Will you tell me your name?"

"It's Barney, ma'am."

"And mine is Opal Grant."

"Yes, ma'am, we know that."

"Do you know a marine named Pratt Wilson, Mr. Barney?"

"Not *Mister* Barney, ma'am. Just Barney. *Old* Barney, they call me. Bend your arm at the elbow, please." He sniffed. "And yes, I know Pratt Wilson, a good boy."

"Will you ask him if he can visit me here?"

"If I were to do that, if he were to do it, it would mean the brig for both of us." He said softly as he took the measurement, "I could, perhaps, drop a chance remark in Wilson's hearing." With no change in the tone of his voice he went on, "I thought of running up a skirt, ma'am, in bunting. Ours is of excellent quality, a light buff in color. And perhaps a blouse of white sheeting. Now, if you will kindly hold your arms out from your sides?" She was not sure whether or not he was truly prepared to help her, and she waited while he ran the tape around her. When he was through, he said, "In an hour, ma'am, I will have something for you to wear." He turned away and mumbled, "The other matter . . . it might take a little longer. Pratt Wilson will not be able to come here, even if he will take the risk, until he is off duty, at four bells of the dog watch. That is to say, at six in the evening."

Opal said breathlessly, "But you will speak to him?"

He raised a trembling hand, as though not wanting to pursue the matter any further. "A chance remark only. And please do *not* tell me why it is you wish to see him."

"I thank you, then, Barney, with all my heart."

He beamed at her suddenly. "*Au revoir*, then," he said, his weary face lighting up. "*Au revoir*, that's French, and it means 'till the next time,' which will be within the hour."

He slipped out, looking almost guilty. She sat down again to compose her mind, and to decide what she could say to Pratt Wilson when—if—he came. "An old and good friend," Jason had said, and she had seen the pleasure sweeping over Pratt's boyish face. Surely he would help! But how? If she could only contrive a way, with his help, to see Jason, wherever he might be, and talk to him! The more she thought about it, the more her spirits rose. She would not admit the possibility that nothing could be done.

Old Barney returned sooner than he expected. He held up the long, beige wool skirt for her inspection, and said proudly, "Our best bunting, ma'am, and I hope you will like it." He showed her an unfinished white blouse. "The cotton is a little coarse, I am afraid."

Opal said urgently, "And Pratt Wilson, Barney?"

"Ah yes." He pulled at an earlobe and said thoughtfully, "I seem to remember I did chance to meet with him. And if my memory serves me, he may have mentioned something about coming here at four bells. Though of course it is quite unforgivable for a marine to enter one of the cabins, and I can't think what he would want here. But the blouse, ma'am. Will you try it on before I finish the stitching? I will step into the corridor while you do so."

So Pratt was coming after all. She could not control the beating of her heart, and as she took the blouse she said: "No, that won't be necessary. If you would just kindly turn your back?"

"Of course." He turned away discreetly to stare through the porthole. Opal unwrapped the sheet from her slender body and let it fall to the ground. She stepped quickly into the skirt. It was well cut and draped softly over her hips. She said, "And Jason, do you know where Jason is?"

"He is still aboard the *Habou*, or what is left of it, ma'am. He does not know what is in store for him, and even if he did, there is nowhere he can go now. And you will be pleased to know, Pratt says, that only a few of the refugee women are left unaccounted for."

She slipped the blouse over her head and found that it was modestly cut, high at the neck, but only pinned at the sides. She said, "All right now."

The old tailor turned and looked her over, nodding his satisfaction. "The skirt is perfect, really quite perfect. Is it comfortable?"

"Yes, very comfortable. And a great relief after what I have recently been wearing."

"The blouse, then."

He took a handful of pins from the little leather pouch at his side, tossed them into his mouth, and mumbled through them, his fingers flying swiftly as he pinned her up, "We must not have it too tight, nor too loose either."

But Opal was suddenly deeply troubled. She whispered, "The man I love is in the most frightening trouble, and here I am fussing over a new dress! It makes no sense, does it? I did not think that I was so foolish and . . . flibbertigibbety."

The old man smiled. "Not flibbertigibbety, ma'am, and it makes all the sense in the world. If a lady is improperly dressed, she is not at her best. And if there are problems to be solved, of which—I repeat—I choose to know nothing, then you must be at your best. A mere bedsheet wrapped around you is not conducive to careful thinking."

"Yes, you are right, of course." She brushed a tear away. "And thank you, sir, for the benefit of your wisdom, which I find comforting indeed."

He handed her the sheet and said, "Slip this over your shoulders and give me the blouse. It will be finished in a few minutes." He turned his back discreetly again while she changed, and murmured: "I do not believe that you know Pratt Wilson well, ma'am?"

"Yes, that is true."

"Then it may be more comfort to you to know that he is

a very determined young man, and absolutely trustworthy. You may trust him with your life. Or, in this case, the life of Jason Farn."

Opal was trembling with emotion as he left.

Between them, Jason and Andara had found all of the refugee women. Three of them had been badly hurt. They were carried aboard for attention by the *Virginia*'s medics, and the rest of them were herded below to a vacant mess hall where they were given hammocks.

But for Jason, there was a different kind of reception.

He was stopped at the gangplank by three marines under the orders of a sergeant, and marched below to the brig. There were seven small cages there, two of them crammed tightly with the prisoners from the *Habou*. Jason paused as he stared into the malevolent eyes of Admiral Sinan.

He was put into a cell by himself. He sat down on the wooden plank bed and wondered about Opal. There was great comfort for him in the knowledge that she, at least, was safe.

He lay down to stretch his long legs and closed his eyes. He heard Admiral Sinan's mocking voice from the cell next door. "You too, American? Are we all to hang together, then?"

He did not deign to answer.

CHAPTER FIFTEEN

Only a few minutes after four bells sounded, Pratt Wilson was tapping at Opal's cabin door. She opened it quickly, and he slipped inside and whispered, "If I'm found here, ma'am, I'm in trouble. These cabins are off limits. Are we likely to be disturbed?"

Her heart was pounding. "I think not, Mr. Wilson. I cannot be sure."

"A steward, perhaps, to bring you food?"

"Yes . . ."

"It will be Silo, or maybe Jenkins. Jenkins is short and very fat, Silo is tall and thin as a rake, with a nose that sticks out a yard in front of his face. If it's Silo, let him in, he's a friend. If it's Jenkins, take the tray from him at the door. Make sure he doesn't come in."

"Very well."

He said diffidently, "I don't mean to give you orders, ma'am, but this is no time to stand on ceremony."

"Of course not."

"Then first things first. We both know the trouble Jason is in, and the first order of the day is to find a way to help him."

"Yes, yes!" Opal said eagerly. "But sit down, Mr. Wilson. We must talk."

"Yes, there's a great deal we must discuss."

He sat with her on the bunk. He was a tall, good-looking youth in his twenties, slender and blond, with an unsuccessful beard and moustache and bright blue, intelligent eyes. He took her hand in his in friendship and said earnestly, "One point, ma'am, before we decide what has to be done. And that is that Jason is a good, good friend of mine. We've fought shoulder to shoulder in a score of battles, and he has saved my life a few times too. You know that he is a deserter?"

"Yes, he told me."

"And do you know why?"

"No. He had only hinted at it. I gathered he was very angry with what the marines were doing in the Bahamas."

"Not the marines," Pratt said swiftly. "This is an honorable corps and I'm proud to be part of it. But there's a bad apple in every barrel, and we had a third mate named Colby, a cruel and violent man. He was a maniac too in other ways, specially, if you'll pardon my frankness, ma'am, with women."

"Go on, Mr. Wilson."

"There was a hamlet on the outskirts of the town, and a dozen of us went there, with Colby in command, looking for one of their leaders who'd been giving us a lot of trouble. His name was Manuel Negrito. We found his hut, but he'd flown the coop, seeking safety in the jungle. His wife and daughter were still there, and his wife was armed. She opened fire on us, and Colby shot her dead."

"And Jason was there?"

"No. Jason and two other marines were under fire from the bush, and they were cutting their way into it to find their assailants. But four of us, Colby was one of them, took over the little mud shack. The girl was there, weeping over her dead mother. She couldn't have been more than fourteen years old. Colby questioned her, asking her where her father was. Fourteen years old and scared out of her wits, but she told us nothing. Colby threw his rifle to me to hold, and knocked her down with a fist to her stomach. He ripped the clothes off her, just a shift she was wearing . . ." He hesitated. "I must use harsh words, ma'am, if you are to know why Jason deserted, as you must."

Her face was white, but she said steadily, "I am not a child, Mr. Wilson."

He went on, "Colby picked her up like a sack of coals and threw her naked on the bed. He ripped off his belt and whipped her with it till the blood came, and he was shouting all the time, 'Tell me where your father is!' I wanted to stop him, but in the marines you can't stop an officer from what he's a mind to do. And Colby was striking out at her with a kind of savagery I'd never seen. And then—I'm sorry, ma'am, but I have to tell you. He took her. That is to say . . . he dropped his breeches, and he raped her. And we stood there like frightened idiots watching him. Then the door opened and Jason came in, limping. He'd been shot in the leg. He saw what was happening, and when he heard this poor child's screams, he roared like a lion and he threw himself at the third mate and dragged him off her, and he drove his fists into him like a maniac. And when Colby lay unconscious on the ground, with blood at his mouth because a few broken ribs had punctured his lungs, Jason said to me, as calm as any man you ever saw, 'Well, Pratt Wilson, it seems I've assaulted an officer, and that's a hanging offence in the marines. I've no wish to be hanged for doing what is just and right, so I'll leave you now. But do me one last favor, friend. Put this poor child's dress back on her, take her out into the jungle, and hide her. For if not, when Colby recovers his damned consciousness, he will surely kill her. So goodbye, dear friend. Forget me.' Those were the last words I ever heard him say. I heard that he found a ship and sailed to Algiers. It was the last time I ever saw him . . . until today."

"Then surely they can't punish him for *that*? The mitigating circumstances . . ."

"Oh, but they can," Pratt said. "And they will."

"But Colby?"

"Colby said he'd been hurt in hand-to-hand fighting with Manuel Negrito, that Farn came to Negrito's rescue and assaulted him. He was decorated for it."

"And none of you—?"

Pratt said steadily, "No, ma'am. To our shame, not one of us said a word, though in the corps they won't take the word of even a hundred marines against that of an officer.

We kept quiet and said nothing. And two weeks later Colby was shot dead by Manuel Negrito."

"And now, Mr. Wilson, after all this time, will they still try to punish him for what he did?"

"Yes, ma'am. They will hang him, without a doubt."

"Oh, God."

"Unless we can somehow get him out of the brig."

"And how can we do that?"

Pratt shook his head in despair. "I don't know," he said simply. "It is possible that no one, in the whole history of the marine corps has ever escaped from a warship's brig. And even if he could, we are a long way from land, much too far for him to swim. It wouldn't be easy to lower a boat for him, unseen."

He fell silent for a moment, the germ of an idea in his mind. He said, frowning darkly, "And yet . . . by tomorrow night we will be very close inshore, only a few hundred yards off the beach."

Opal was excited. "Why, that's already half the battle! But are you sure?"

Pratt nodded. "Oh yes, quite sure. Our mission is to shell one of the coastal villages, and Captain Breck has chosen to sail in very close, pound the cliffs with his cannon, and drop it into the sea. A punitive expedition. This means that we must go in perhaps as close as three or four hundred feet. It is very little for a man like Jason to swim. He is very good in the water."

"Yes, I know it."

"But the essential question remains, how to free him from the brig."

There was a knock on the door. Pratt was instantly on his feet, his body pressed into the wall. Opal said carefully, "Who is it?" The muffled voice came back to her from the corridor: "The steward, ma'am. Your supper."

Pratt knew the voice. He grinned and whispered to her, "Silo!" He threw open the door, yanked the startled steward bodily into the cabin, and the tray went flying across the floor as the door was shut and locked again behind him.

Silo whispered, "Pratt! In God's name, what are *you* doing here? It means the brig if you're discovered!"

"Ssshhh. Keep your voice down, Silo!"

Silo was already on his hands and knees picking up the scattered pieces of meat and blowing on them delicately to remove most of the floor's dust. He looked up and said, "You know what will happen to you if they find you here? Mother of God, I see you hanging from the yardarm already, side by side with poor Jason."

"Jason will not hang," Pratt said vehemently, "if we can get him out of the brig by tomorrow night."

Silo looked up at him in shock. "Out of the brig?" he echoed. "Are you mad?"

"Out of the brig."

Silo looked at Opal as though seeing her for the first time. He struggled to his feet and touched his forelock, and said lamely, holding the plate out to her, "Your supper, ma'am."

She took it from him. "Did you hear what Mr. Wilson said, Mr. Silo? We have to get Jason out of the brig by tomorrow night. Preferably when we are already close inshore. The less time he has to spend in hiding aboard, the better it will be for all of us."

"By sundown," Pratt said. "If we don't, he will be hanged, of a certainty. And there's not a man aboard who wants that, save the captain and perhaps a few of the officers."

"And will you tell me," Silo asked sardonically, "just how you propose to accomplish this impossible feat?"

"No," Pratt said. "*You* are going to tell *us*."

Silo goggled. "I am?" And Pratt answered, "Yes. We need ideas now. So talk to our closest friends, the ones we can trust."

"That means Hoskins, Brent, and Fairweather. No others."

"Good. Hoskins particularly. He's a very devious man. I'm on duty again at six bells, so let us all meet at midnight. Talk to them, Silo. Sound them out, tell them we're looking for ideas, a way to open the brig at sundown, or before. Most important, find out which guards will be there, and at what watches."

"All right, I'll do that." Silo grinned, his broad smile lighting up his unappetizing face. "And while I'm here," he said, "you want some good officers' meat, Pratt? It's smoked beef tonight."

"No. But get some to Jason if you can."

"He's feasting like a king, I did just that. And the damned Berbers in the other cells, I gave them gruel. Till midnight. We'll meet in the galley, it'll be empty then." He ambled awkwardly out.

Opal took Pratt's hand and whispered, "You have brought me hope where I thought there was none."

He nodded gravely. "There are still almost insuperable difficulties, but we have progressed. I too must leave you, ma'am. At two bells I'm up in the crow's nest for four hours."

"And will you let me know what happens at your meeting?"

He smiled. "If you'll not take exception to a visit at an unseemly hour of the morning."

"Of course not! I *must* know!"

"Then I wish you good evening. Take courage, ma'am."

When he had gone, she sat on the bed and munched mechanically on the food. She thought of Jason, and wondered how he was bearing up under this new torment.

A sudden rocking of the ship took her out of her reflections. Then there was an alarming sound, a sound of water violently bubbling. For a moment it startled her, and then she realized that the *Habou*, cut free from the *Virginia* at last, was sinking to the bottom close by. In a little while she heard the succession of heavy thudding sounds that were the ship's filling sails catching the wind as she got under way again.

She took off her fine new clothes, wrapped herself in the sheet that had been her only covering for so long, and lay down on the bunk to wait for midnight and another visit from Pratt Wilson, Jason's old comrade and her newfound friend.

* * *

Breck had spent long hours pouring over his charts, and had found the ideal target. It was a coastal village named Farsi, and there was an annotation on the map: *a factory here for the manufacture of cannon.* There was a small cove, barely a mile across, just enough room to manoeuver in, with a sharply rising headland two miles to the west of it on which a shore battery was marked: *eight twelve-pounder guns, coverage 320 to 68 degrees.* The elevation of the village was given as four hundred feet, it was on the edge of the cliff, and there were eighteen fathoms of water to within fifty feet of the shoreline.

At an officers' meeting in Breck's cabin, he stood over his chart table puffing on his favorite meerschaum pipe as he stabbed at the map with a blunt-fingered hand.

"Here is where we turn. We approach to within two miles of the coast under darkness, we turn south and enter the cove. We cruise past the village two hundred feet off shore, and we'll give them our broadside on the first pass. You'll be at near maximum elevation, Mr. Fennell, and I want that cliff pounded to pieces forty or fifty feet from the top. We'll make a total of five passes, all to port, though in my opinion three ought to be enough. There'll be almost no opposition at all."

He puffed a cloud of blue smoke up into the swinging lantern and said with satisfaction, "It'll be like shooting fish in a barrel. And then, gentlemen, we just might proceed to the island of Djidji, where that damned bey has a palace, and teach him a somewhat more personal lesson. I learned that he's abducting white women into his harem now, and I've a mind to blow it to pieces for him."

One of the junior officers said, startled, "But if it's full of white women, sir . . . ?"

Breck grunted. "Well, we'll think about it. The first order of the day is to drop that damned cannon factory into the sea. Move all your royals over to the port side, Mr. Fennell, we'll need the heaviest shot we have. And take your time. Their defenses will be two miles behind us, and all they'll have on shore will be a few muskets to fight us off with." He made a little joke for their amusement. "And their scimitars, of course."

He could not have been more wrong.

Only two weeks before, the bey had written a petulant letter to Admiral Sinan. It said, in part:

> . . . and I learn to my astonishment that our prime cannon factory at Farsi appears to be quite undefended. A battery of only eight guns to protect it? And two miles away? There might be room in the cove for a frigate or two, and Allah in his wisdom has given us room enough on the cliffs for a thousand guns. See to it, my friend and my son, in the knowledge that the love between us is better than the love of women. . . ."

Sinan sent out orders to his subordinates. And now there were fourteen twelve-pounder guns on the edge of the cliff at Farsi, and seven small frigates, very heavily armed, riding at anchor in the cove.

Six bells sounded aboard the *Virginia*, eleven o'clock at night, and Captain Breck was restless. He had slept for an hour to refresh himself for the coming mission, but there were still more hours to pass before they would reach Farsi. But the movement of the ship was steady and controlled, and he knew that the second mate was in competent command on the bridge. He went to the door and sent his orderly for the bo'sun.

He sat down at his desk, wrapped in thought and staring into space. When the bo'sun came he said, "There are some ladies of the night aboard my ship, I believe, from the *Habou*?"

"Yes, sir. Fourteen of them. Pirate whores, sir."

"They are being cared for, I presume? And treated correctly?"

"Oh yes, sir. I arranged hammocks for them in the number four hold."

"And they are being fed properly?"

"Yes, sir, they had a good meal at four bells." He added apologetically, "I told Silo to feed them officers' food, sir, I hope that's all right. Some of them looked half-starved, like they hadn't seen decent food in months."

"Yes. That was correct."

"Thank you, sir."

"And they have not been—molested in any way?"

"Oh no, sir. I've got a guard on the hold."

"I won't have any Gallic frivolity aboard the *Virginia*, bo'sun."

"No, sir, of course not."

"Shameless women."

"Yes, sir."

"Using their bodies in Satan's work. That is all, bo'sun."

"Aye, aye, sir."

When the bo'sun had gone, wondering what was on his skipper's mind, Captain Breck sat for a long while thinking of those fourteen sad creatures whose only purpose in life was the use of their wicked bodies to satisfy all that was degrading in man. There had been one young girl, he remembered, who could not have been more than fifteen years old, a doe-eyed waif of a child with skin the color of burnt amber, and dark unkempt hair that hung untidily over her bare shoulders. She had been dressed in a kind of shift of coarse white cotton tied over her shoulders with string, and so loosely fitting that from the bridge above her he had clearly seen the nipples of her smooth and gently budding breasts, only a trifle paler than her lovely face.

The captain went to his bookshelf and took down his Bible. He opened it at the first page and read the inscription:

To my son Aloysius, in the hope that the Good Lord will guide him in all things.

Amos Richard Breck, Captain of the Good Ship *Fortune* and now at the point of Death. October the Third, in this Year of Our Lord, 1772.

He thought of his dead father for a moment, the man who had kept him in the path of righteousness. Then he tucked the heavy Bible under his arm and left his cabin. He went down the inummerable steps and ladders to the number four hold. The guard there saluted, opened the hatch for him and closed it behind him. He was a young, cheerful boy of some nineteen years, with a shock of unruly hair and bright, humorous eyes.

The captain climbed down the ladder and saw that there were six or seven tallows burning—a fine waste of government property!—and that all the startled, expectant faces were staring up at him. To his horror, two of the women were lying together in a hammock, naked and clutched in each other's arms. He roared at them, scarcely understanding what they were doing, "Shame on you! Hussies! Clothe yourselves at once!"

There was not one among them who understood a word of English, but his tone was imperative and they wrapped their rags around their bodies and hurried to him, wide-eyed and frightened. He shuddered when he thought of the sin that was on them all.

He opened the Bible and set it down on a tea chest that was just the right height, the height of a pulpit. He cleared his throat and said sternly, "I will now read to you from the Bible. Come, gather round me."

Nobody moved, and he gestured with his arms and said again, "Come! Gather round."

They all moved in on him, serious and solemn-eyed, squatting in complete subservience at his feet. He looked them over. He found the lustrous doe eyes of the young girl he had noticed before right in front of him. That loose-fitting shift was wide open, and he could clearly see her breasts. He said harshly, "Cover yourself, child! In the name of the good Lord, cover yourself!"

She stared at him, not understanding, and threw a frightened look to the woman beside her. "*Aish bu'ul,* what does he say?"

The woman gestured hopelessly. "How should I know

what he says? But there is a light in his eyes. He wants you."

The captain placed both his hands on his own chest and said loudly, "Cover yourself! Cover, *cover*!"

"Ah . . ."

Light dawned on the young girl. She quickly slipped the strings down over her childlike shoulders, pushed the shift down to her waist, and sat there with her young breasts pointing up at him. Her hands were in her lap, her eyes demurely cast down.

"No!" the captain wailed. "No, no!" But she did not know what *no* meant, so she did not move, wondering what he wanted. She looked up at him with wide, uncomprehending, innocent eyes.

He wanted to tear his look away from her, but he could not. He took a firm hold on himself and said, as calmly as he could, "Then instead . . . tell me your name, child. Your name, your *name*!" He thought that if he spoke loudly enough, they could understand him. He pointed to himself and said clearly: "I am Captain. Me, Captain." He pointed at her. "You?"

"Ah! *Na'am*, yes! My name is Zowra."

He tore his eyes away from those pointed breasts. He could not bring himself to touch her. He placed his hands on either side of his Bible for moral support, cleared his throat and said, "I will now read to you words of great wisdom."

He took his gold-rimmed spectacles from his pocket and adjusted them carefully on his nose. Then he began to read. But soon he broke off and stared down at the child Zowra in horror. She had risen to her feet and was slipping the cotton shift down over her bare hips, a little hesitantly because she was not sure what was required of her.

He said hoarsely, stammering, not taking his eyes from her slender naked body, "These . . . these are the words . . . the words of the Prophet Hosea, who was . . . was married to Gomer, a harlot. He lived . . . lived in a time of great turbulence. . . ."

Zowra dropped to her knees in front of him and reached out to touch him. She found him hard with the strength of a man who had lived too long in celibacy. He felt her slender child's fingers closing about him, and began moaning uncontrollably. Her hand was at the leather straps of his breeches, unfastening them, reaching down to grasp his nakedness. He screamed, "No! Away from me, woman!"

He gathered himself together furiously, grabbed his Bible and ran, clambering up the ladder and hammering on the hatch till it was opened. The guard was there at once, staring at him and wondering what had happened to put his captain in such a frenzy. With his breeches unfastened, too. But the righteous Captain Breck paid him no attention at all as he ran in overwhelming frustration to his cabin, there to throw himself on his stomach on the bunk and grind himself into the mattress in the search for shameful release.

The young guard said aloud, "Well! And I wonder what all that was about?" He tucked his musket into its accustomed hiding-place, raised the hatch again, and climbed down the ladder. He looked around at the women and said cheerfully, "Hullo, girls, everything all right? It's me again."

Smiling broadly, he looked them all over. He saw Zowra, still on her knees, slim and amber-colored and very lovely, her black eyes wide with an emotion he did not understand. He reached down and touched her straggly hair.

"You're a real pretty one," he said. "How is it I missed you the last time around? All right, girl on your back."

Understanding nothing but the intent, Zowra lay down on the wooden floor and spread her slim thighs to receive him as he lowered his breeches, lay on top of her, plunged inexpertly into her.

In the throes of his passion, quite unable to control himself, he whispered hoarsely into her ear, "Marvelous, bloody marvelous. You're all right, whatever your name is."

He tried desperately to hold back the moment of fulfillment as she thrust up her loins to meet him. Two of the other women, starved for a kind of love that was at least affectionate, had stripped off their rags and were crouched beside him, hoping for their turn, fondling him as he loved her. The men they had always known had been brutal and quick, but here was a man who was gentle and kind and appreciative, carefully holding back his own explosion until it met their own, and he did not even beat them.

The young guard looked at the two other girls and caressed them, savoring the soft touch of their flesh. He said, a little sadly, "My name's Henry. There's not one among you who understands a word I say, is there? Well, never mind. I love all of you." He gasped as Zowra brought him to his satisfaction, and said, trying hard to recover his sanity, "Not the kind of love a man has for his mother or his sister, is it? But it's still love." He laughed at his own little joke, and they all laughed with him, because something good had been said, though they did not know what it was.

And the *Virginia*'s number four hold was suddenly a place of great happiness, where the wretched and oppressed and lost had found a fleeting moment of contentment.

CHAPTER SIXTEEN

The *Virginia* ploughed on in the darkness, forcing her great prow into the seas with an ominous rushing sound. Shortly after one o'clock in the morning, Opal was prowling in her tiny cabin like a caged panther, wide awake and impatient, when Pratt came to her again, slipping furtively through the door and closing it quickly behind him. In the pale light of the tallow that swung from side to side with the rolling of the ship, his good-natured face was pale and drawn, and there was little sign of hope on it.

He whispered, "No satisfying news yet, ma'am, I'm afraid. Except that I sneaked down to the brig and spoke with Jason."

Her heart leaped. "You spoke with him? And how is he, Mr. Wilson?"

"He's in fairly good spirits, and worrying only about you."

"Oh God! I can't bear to think of him alone down there! And has he been hurt?"

"No, ma'am. There's no one aboard this ship who'll lay an unlawful hand on him. It's only the course of the law that we have to worry about, and that's a big enough vexation, I'll confess. But I told him there were comrades on the outside who are trying to help him—no, *determined* to help him! And it cheered him up considerably."

She was bursting to hear the news. "And the meeting with your friends?"

He sighed. "There are six of us in on the secret now—

Hoskins, Brent, Fairweather, Silo, a Frenchie named Marsac, and myself, and though we found no good answer yet, I left them still debating. That Marsac has a good head on his shoulders, and he came up with the idea of overpowering the two guards down there and just hoping they wouldn't see who it was knocked them out cold, and then getting the keys. Hoskins thought we could make up masks to cover our faces. We're all dressed alike, so they'd never be sure who it was. But Jason says no, the guards are both armed, of course, and someone might get hurt or even killed, and he won't allow that. But whether Jason likes it or not, we're holding on to that as a sort of emergency plan in the hope that something better will come out of all the talk. And it will, ma'am, I promise you. One or two of us like to think we're very smart when the need arises, and we'll find a way to break him loose."

She felt he was talking just to comfort her, and she said slowly, "And then, Mr. Wilson? Assuming that we can find a way to get him out of the brig, what then? If he jumps overboard and swims to the shore . . . You spoke of an attack on a Berber village. Does that not mean there will be Berbers on the beach, perhaps in great number? He would find himself in grave danger of being captured again, and by a still more dangerous enemy."

Pratt nodded grimly. "That may be so indeed, ma'am," he said. "But we'll cross that bridge when we come to it."

It was small comfort, but a little was better than none at all. She said, knowing this man was a good friend, "I love him so dearly, Pratt. There's a tight, cruel clutching at my stomach when I think of the danger he's in."

He told her about the imminent shelling of Farsi. "Any moment now, you'll hear our guns right above your head. They make a terrifying din, ma'am, that echoes clear through the ship, but pay no heed to it at all. It's not us that's getting hurt. Those savage Berbers have nothing at all there to hit us with."

But he was quite wrong.

There was the sound of creaking timber, and a heavy roll as the *Virginia* changed her course. He said, "We're turning into the bay, ma'am, an opening in the reef less than a hundred feet across. It means mighty skilful sailing. And they'll be sounding battle stations soon, so I'd best be on my way. Just remember, there's nothing to be frightened of at all."

"I'm frightened only for Jason, Pratt."

Then there was a distant clanging sound of a bell not aboard their own ship. It was quickly taken up by others, some of them closer, some far more distant. Frowning, Pratt leaped to his feet and strode to the porthole to stare out into the darkness. He whispered hoarsely, "Jesus! Three frigates there, no, four of them! And they said the bay was empty!"

The alarm bell on board the *Virginia* was already calling all hands. Pratt ran to the door and looked back. To her surprise, he was grinning broadly, and he said, "But don't worry, ma'am, it takes more than frigates to harm a great ship like ours!"

He slipped out. Opal stood at the porthole, straining her eyes against the night. She could see the silhouette of the rocky shoreline very close, and there was a red glow high up on the cliff where a score of giant charcoal burners were flaring, their ragged flames leaping up and lighting up the sky.

On the bridge, Captain Breck swore softly. There was little need for his glass at such close quarters. He glared around the inlet and said, "I make it six frigates in all, Mr. Mate, and every one of them at anchor, so we'll just try not to pass along their beams."

"Seven, Captain," the mate said. "One more under the lee there."

"I see it. We proceed with our objective as planned."

"Aye, aye, sir." They were both gloating. It was axiomatic in seafaring circles that a vessel caught at anchor, requiring a very long time to fill her sails and get under way, was a sitting duck.

Breck leaned over the railing and bellowed: "Mister Fennell!" The master-gunner was already there below him, knowing what the orders would be now. The captain called out, "Your royal cannon are still for the top of the cliff, Mr. Fennell! You'll order fire at will with the whole cannon and the demis as targets of opportunity present themselves. I want at least half of those frigates sunk before we leave the bay."

"Aye, aye, sir."

They were sailing close inshore now, and there was the sporadic rattle of musket-fire from the Barbary pirates' decks. Some of the heavy guns sounded, and half a dozen cannonballs came at them, one or two of them thudding into the *Virginia*'s massive hull. And then, as though from the heavens above them, the skies erupted.

The Algerian commander of the new shore battery was quick to heed the warning of the frigates' bells, and all fourteen of the twelve-pounder cannon at the top of the cliff were blazing away with a particular ferocity that could only be described as Berber. The commander galloped his iron-grey stallion along the rows of cannon, screaming, "All guns fire at will! I want that ship blown out of the water!"

Firing a heavy cannon was a slow and laborious business. First, the gunny sack of black powder had to be dropped down the muzzle and rammed home tight with the rod. Next, the thick wadding was firmed down. Then, the cannonball itself, and finally the touch-powder was placed in the pan and fired with the flare. Five, six, sometimes even seven times out of ten, the touch-powder would ignite the main charge and send the iron ball whistling on its way. And there was great danger to the gunners themselves. If the touch-powder did not function properly the first time around, then the red-hot ball could burn through the cloth wadding and simply blow the gun up. But these men were experts. Only one of the fourteen guns disintegrated by premature explosion, killing the four men who tended it.

The target was a relatively easy one, moving very fast but two hundred feet below them. Much of the shot was overshooting the *Virginia* to land harmlessly in the water beyond her, but a great deal was crashing down onto her decks. And Captain Breck's great ship began to suffer very severe damage.

Her crew was highly trained and diligent. Breck stood in silence on the bridge, knowing that there was no need for orders. He was very calm. He watched two of the red-hot balls burning into his deck as the pumps went to work on them, saw the stretcher bearers running to pick up the wounded. The gunners were at their cannon in the embrasures, holding their flares ready for the roll of the ship, not waiting for orders from Fennell or anyone else. He felt a great sense of pride; he knew that he had trained his men well.

They were coming up to one of the enemy frigates. The pirates were high in the rigging, their loaded muskets ready. As the two ships drew close the half-inch lead pellets began crashing into the bridge around him. He did not move, but waited patiently, and as the distance shortened speedily and they passed her only yards away and full on the beam, eight of Fennell's demis blasted at point-blank range into her hull, a foot below the waterline. The frigate heeled over so quickly that her topmost sails and lines swept along the *Virginia*'s deck. Shouting men were there at once with their knives, hacking at the ropes. In moments, the Berber heeled over and sank behind them.

Breck said amiably, "Very nice work, Mr. Fennell. Do that again for me a few more times, if you've the mind for it."

Pratt Wilson, chewing on a musket ball to form it as he ran, raced down the companionway, hoping the bo'sun would not see him. He scuttled down the corridor and tapped at Opal's door, throwing it open. She stared at him as he shouted, "Are you all right, ma'am? Yes, I see that you are. I'll be back!"

She had no time to say a word, and could only gasp. He ran on, dropping swiftly down the ladders to the number one hold, splashing through ankle-deep water to the brig. A corporal of the guard had joined the two sentries there. Pratt pulled up short. The corporal, a man he did not much like, said angrily, "What the devil are you doing down here, Wilson? Get back on deck where you belong!"

Lying brazenly, Pratt said, "They want to know if we've been holed down here."

The corporal scowled. "*Who* wants to know?"

Pratt answered blandly, "Well now, Corporal, I think it was the second mate, but it could have been the third. Someone just shouted at me, 'Get below, Wilson, for a damage check,' and the truth is, Corporal, I don't know who it was. Someone yells at me loud enough, I do as I'm told. I'm a marine."

"Oh." The corporal sniffed. "Well, you can see for yourself, there's water coming up from below us. We're holed in the bilge by the looks of it. But the pumps are keeping up with it, so it's nothing to worry about, not yet."

Pratt moved to Jason's cell, studiously ignoring his good friend, and gripped the iron bars as he stared at the water on the floor, deep to the span of a man's hand. He said cheerfully, "Looks like all the prisoners are going to drown, doesn't it, Corporal? Of course, that's probably no worse than being hanged, though I can't be sure about that."

"We don't allow things like that to happen in this man's Corps," the corporal said coldly. "So get back on deck and tell them that if I have to move the prisoners, I'll send for an escort."

"I hope you get it. There's a lot of trouble up there. The bay's full of pirate frigates, which we're sinking one after the other. But they've got a thousand cannon up there on the cliff. And come to that, Corporal, they sounded all hands on deck a long time ago, so what are *you* doing down here?"

It was the guard's first duty, on that signal, to assure the security of the prisoners, but the corporal did not feel he owed any explanations to a mere marine, and he ordered angrily, "On your way, Wilson."

Pratt hurried off, knowing that the problem had almost been solved for him if he could only work out the mechanics of it. He stopped at Opal's door and knocked again. He said quietly, "There's no time for long explanations, ma'am, but I wanted you to know at once. The good Lord came to our rescue, and the first part of our endeavor seems to be at hand. We'll have Jason out of the brig in a very short time now."

Opal could not contain her excitement. She herself was doing nothing! "Oh, Pratt, will you tell me how?" She was close to tears. "And most of all, will you tell me what I can do?"

He laughed suddenly. "What you can do, ma'am," he said, "is stay in your cabin. You're very safe on this deck. And be assured that your friends have the problem well in hand."

She replied almost angrily, "But I do not want to be safe while he is in danger! I am not just—just a weak woman, Pratt, I am a woman in love! And I want to help!"

Pratt said firmly, "No, ma'am. Jason would have my neck if I allowed you to run the slightest risk. And if you were to appear on deck now in the middle of a battle, you think the captain would not see? He would send you below again, and put a guard on your cabin, and no good would be done at all! No, ma'am. You must stay here." His eyes softened. "Yes, I know that it's hard to stand by and wait. But this is a time for patience and restraint. But I will keep you informed. And don't worry about the good *Virginia*. We've taken some damage, and we'll take a great deal more before the night is out. But we're a man-o'-war. We'll not be hurt beyond our capacity."

He closed the door and ran up to the deck to find the bo'sun. He fired a shot from his rifle at a frigate as it swept past, just to show that his mind was on the job, and as he reloaded, ramming the wadding and the chewed bullet down the long barrel, he heard another broadside from Fennell's demis and saw the Berber ship almost disintegrate. He heard the master-gunner's fervent yell, "That's the third of them, Captain! Get me closer on their beams and I'll sink the rest of them for you!"

But the shore battery was firing furiously at a target that was circling the confined waters below, and there was chaos on the *Virginia*'s decks, with fallen spars and rigging everywhere, and nearly a dozen fires burning and hissing as water was poured on them. The bo'sun was beside him suddenly, swearing volubly and demanding, "And where the devil have you been, Wilson?"

"The corporal of the guard called me below, sir," Pratt replied promptly. "Number one hold is flooding, water coming up from the bilge, and the cells are in danger of flooding."

The bo'sun scowled. "A bunch of damned Berbers, and they're all going to hang anyway."

"And Farn, sir."

"And he'll hang too. But it's not part of marine tradition to let our prisoners drown like rats."

"No, sir."

The cannon on both sides were roaring, and the night air was filled with the acrid smell of smoke. The *Virginia* was holding her course steadily, east to west along the shoreline and then laboriously turning for another run, though two of the pirate frigates had found their wind and were buzzing around her like mosquitoes, being expertly sailed in the narrow waters of the bay. The bo'sun tightened a rag around an arm that had been shattered by a musket ball, his face white with pain.

"Take two men, Wilson," he said. "Move the prisoners to number two hold and batten the hatch on them."

"Aye, aye, sir." The wheels in Pratt's fertile mind were turning furiously. He said, feigning apprehension, "Only two men, sir? There are more than a score of those barbarians."

"You're armed," the bo'sun said, "and they're not. I can't spare any more guns. And while you're here—Is your knife sharp?"

"I can shave with it, sir."

The bo'sun turned his back and pulled down his heavy woollen shirt. "There's a bullet there," he said, "lodged just under the skin by the feel of it. Cut it out for me. I've no wish to die of lead poisoning."

"Over here, then, where there's light. Have you anything better than water in your flask?"

The bo'sun grunted as they moved to a cannon embrasure where the gunner was waiting with his flare as his powder-man rammed the sack of gunpowder down the barrel. He said, "When you've been at sea as long as I have, boy . . ."

"Yes, sir."

Pratt took the proffered flask after the bo'sun had emptied half of it down his gullet, and drank a gulp of the whiskey himself. He did not relish what he had to do now. He held the blade of his knife in the gunner's flare for a moment or two, turning it carefully to cleanse it, and began digging with its razor-point into the bo'sun's shoulder. He said as he worked, "If I've got only two men to move the prisoners, sir, can I take men I can trust?"

The bo'sun was biting his tongue till the blood came, but he said suspiciously, gasping, "Tell me . . . tell me who you can . . . can *not* trust aboard this fine ship, Wilson."

"Yes, sir. What I mean is, we don't want any of them to escape, do we? Can I take Hoskins and Fairweather with me?"

The bo'sun stifled a moan and took another long swig from his flask. He said impatiently, "Hurry it up! I don't want to be here all night over a damned bullet in the back. I've work to do."

"Yes, sir."

He prised, and the lump of lead plopped out and fell to the deck. Pratt took the flask and poured whiskey over the wound. Taking a deep breath, the bo'sun said, "Find it for me, Wilson. Give it to me."

Pratt picked it up, an ill-shaped lead ball more than half an inch across. Had it been better chewed and therefore more efficient, it would have killed him. The bo'sun took it from him and said, a little shamefacedly, "I always save them for my missus. She likes to collect mementoes like this."

"Yes, sir."

"All right. Take Hoskins and Fairweather. Move the prisoners to number two, batten them down in there. And I want you all back on deck as quick as maybe."

"Aye, aye, sir." Pratt hurried off, wiping the blood from his knife and sheathing it again at his belt.

The *Virginia* was making her third pass, and cannonballs were still pounding into her. On the bridge, Captain Breck stared up at the cliff, wondering about the obstinacy of hard sandstone that should have shattered long ago but would not, it seemed. For the third time in less than two hours, Fennell's royals spoke their dreadful thunder and eight more heavy iron balls crashed into the cliff, fifty feet below its summit. And then the captain watched open-mouthed as a flaming mass of charcoal, one of the furnaces of the factory, came tumbling down the cliffside into the sea. It was followed by another cascade and yet another as the whole of the crumbled plateau and its factories rolled down into the boiling sea like lava from a volcano.

He could not contain his emotion as he heard the excited cheering from the decks. Not trying to hide the triumph in his voice, he shouted, "Well done, Mr. Fennell, very well done indeed! By God, sir, I salute you!"

The helmsman was already spinning the wheel for his turn, and the captain, watching the fiery deluge still tumbling down, shouted, "For my satisfaction, Mr. Fennell, how many rounds?"

"Forty-seven, sir!"

"Then another sixteen on a single pass at the battery up there! We've destroyed their damned factory, let us destroy a few of its products too! Have you the elevation?"

"Yes, sir!"

"Then go to it."

The shore battery, most of it further along the cliff edge in three separate segments, was still in furious action, though four of its guns had been lost with the furnaces. The helmsman said stolidly, "Permission to take us one hundred and fifty feet further offshore, Captain, to help Mr. Fennell with his elevation."

"Permission granted. Do that, Helmsman."

Pratt Wilson found Hoskins and Fairweather kneeling in the scuppers watching the approach of a Berber frigate, waiting for her to come within range. Hoskins turned to him and said, "We can turn this battle to advantage, Pratt, though I don't quite know how."

Pratt grinned in the darkness. "But I do," he said happily. "You and I, my friends, are going to move the prisoners out of the brig because the cells are flooding, on the express orders of the bo'sun himself, and what better authority can we have?"

Fairweather's eyes gleamed. He said, laughing softly, "We'll open only Jason's cell. Let the damned Berbers drown. We hit the guards over the head—"

Pratt interrupted him. "No, we don't," he said emphatically. "Once the door to Jason's cell is unlocked, a word to him is all that is needed. We're taking him with all the other prisoners to number two, and if we can't contrive an escape along the way—then we all deserve to hang too. And when the time comes, as it will, we can tell them that there were only three of us and we had our hands full with the savages and Jason somehow slipped away in the darkness. Take my word for it, it won't even go too hard with us. A week or so on bread and water, no more than that. The bo'sun said, and I give you his own words: 'I can't spare any more guns.' Doesn't that mean he knows we'll have a difficult time holding them all in check?"

It made good sense to both of them. Hoskins nodded. "A boat," he said instantly, and Fairweather answered him, "What boat? We're less than three hundred fathoms offshore. He can swim to the beach and make his way from there wherever he wants to go."

Pratt remembered Opal's admonition: "There will be Berbers on the shore in great number." He shook his head. "No. Jason cannot land on Algerian soil now, there'll be a Berber behind every rock. We have to give him the stern dinghy."

Fairweather aimed his musket as the frigate ploughed past them. He fired at a pirate in the rigging and shouted, "I hit him, I know I hit him!" He began ramming wadding and powder into his musket again, turned to Pratt and said sarcastically, "You think we can steal a dinghy in the middle of a battle and not be seen? Pratt Wilson, you're a madman, I always knew it."

But Hoskins said eagerly, "There's chaos aboard now, everyone looking out for himself and rightly so, too. No one will see us."

"Not *us*," Pratt said. "*You*. Can you do it alone?"

"I can launch a man-o'-war alone if I have to."

"We're making better than twelve knots, remember. It won't be easy."

"I can do it!"

"Good." Pratt shouldered his gun. "Then give us half an hour. I want it trailing behind us half an hour from now."

"It will be there. You can count on it."

Pratt looked at his other partner in this conspiracy and said cheerfully, "Then come with me, Charlie. We have the bo'sun's orders to carry out. We're supposed to move the prisoners."

They hurried off together.

A duel was going on now between the *Virginia* and the strong battery atop the cliff, and there was dreadful mayhem on both sides. The opposing teams of gunners had both found their range and were attempting to obliterate each other. In a battle of this kind, a shore battery, without the movement of the waves to contend with, was at an immeasurable advantage. But Captain Breck was a very stubborn man. He shouted down: "Mr. Fennell! How many sixty-three-pound shot do you have left?"

The voice came up to him from the confusion on the deck: "Ninety-two, sir!"

"And for the whole cannon?"

"Eighty-seven! And two hundred and thirty for the demis!"

"The riflemen?"

"Powder and shot in plenty!"

"Then we will have another pass, Mr. Fennell."

The mate said mildly, "We are listing badly, Captain." Breck answered him testily. "I am not blind. Have the bo-'sun trim his sails accordingly."

"He has so been ordered, sir."

"And make this a tight turn. A strong list to port will help you considerably. Just try not to capsize us in the endeavor."

The second mate was hurrying up from below. He reported breathlessly, "We're holed in four places, Captain, the timbers cracked in three others. We're shipping a lot of water."

"Repair crews?"

"At work, sir."

"Good. Then this will be our last pass."

"Aye, aye, sir." He was a Catholic, and he crossed himself unobtrusively before slipping down the ladder to give his orders. He was thinking: "Mother of Christ, we'll never last out the night, not with that madman in command."

Pratt Wilson and Charlie Fairweather had reached the brig. The corporal of the guard had gone, called to other urgent duties, and there was only a single sentry there now, standing up to his knees in water and sure that his last hour had come. His name was Porter. He was fingering his musket, worrying about the score of Berbers packed into the flooded cells and screaming imprecations at him; he was quite sure they were all going to die.

Pratt took charge immediately with the superiority of a strong man over a weak, and said, mocking, "What's the matter, Porter? Did you think we'd leave you here to drown? We're moving the prisoners to number two."

Alarmed, Porter looked at Fairweather and back to Pratt. He said, stammering, "What, just—just the three of us?"

"Just the three of us. Give me the keys."

"Three of us against twenty or thirty savage Berbers?"

"We're armed," Pratt said, echoing the bo'sun's comment, "and they're not."

"I don't like it."

"Then I'll tell you how we do it. Go to the top of the ladder, Porter, and watch the prisoners as they climb up to the next level. Charlie and I will let them out, and we'll shepherd them up to you, up the ladder one by one. Have your musket ready at all times, and watch them like a hawk. When we all get to the top, we'll take them along to number two and batten the hatches on them."

"I still don't like it."

"There's nothing you can do about it, Porter, unless you want us all to drown."

"Very well. But if you get too close to them they'll overpower you for sure. So why don't you let Farn out first, have him unlock their cells, while you two stand well back, away from them and out of their reach, or your guns will be useless. It's the only way, Wilson."

Pratt said gravely, "That's an excellent idea, Porter."

The guard handed over the keys and moved off to climb the ladder and take up his position in the passageway above it. He was frightened, but he was glad to get off that menacing third level, where the water was rising, almost halfway up their thighs now.

Jingling the keys to show the Berbers that they were being let out, Pratt stood by the two cells and shouted, "Quiet, you savages! We are leaving this place now, and any one of you who tries to escape will be shot. There are three good riflemen waiting to shoot you down and throw you to the crabs! Is there anyone among you who's civilized enough to understand English?"

Close to the bars, Admiral Sinan said quietly, "I understand you perfectly, sailor."

"Then tell your fellow savages what I just said. If anyone tries to escape, he will be killed instantly."

"Rather than wait for the gallows?" Sinan asked scornfully. He turned away and spoke in a low voice to some of his followers, explaining to them exactly what they should do.

Pratt went to Jason's cell and whispered to him, "Listen carefully, dear friend. When you reach the top of the ladder, Porter, who is not one of us, will be watching the Berbers very closely, he is terrified of them. Slip away quickly, run to the stern. The stern dinghy will be in the water.

Climb down the painter and cut yourself adrift. And then wait till the *Virginia* has outrun you, find the compass in the locker, and set a course of two hundred and seventy-one. It will take you straight to Gibraltar, where you will be safe."

Jason clutched his hand through the bars and said, "And Opal, Pratt? I must know where Opal is."

"Your lady," Pratt said impatiently, "is in her cabin. She is safe, no harm can come to her now."

"Which cabin, Pratt?"

"In God's name, does it matter? Cabin C, on C Deck!" He unlocked the barred door, gave Jason the keys, and said, "There are only three of us to handle these savages, so wait till I tell you, then let them out." He gestured to Fairweather and they stood well away with their rifles ready.

As Jason fitted the heavy key into its lock an awful thudding sound immediately beside them told of a heavy ball that had crashed into the hull below the waterline. It had found a weak spot where the planking had been damaged earlier. They stared as the timbers began to split and a trickle of water became first a strong spout and then a rushing torrent. It was rising fast. The Berbers were screaming out their panic. Jason shouted in Arabic, "Sinan! Calm them down, for God's sake, or none of us will get out of here alive!"

Sinan answered him furiously, "What, am I your ally now?"

Jason had no recourse but to throw open the doors, and they poured out frantically. Pratt Wilson called out calmly, "Porter! They're coming, watch for them now!"

The three marines waited till the last of the Berbers, fighting his fellows for a place on the ladder, was almost to the top. As Jason climbed quickly up after them he saw that the Algerians had seized on the opportunity Allah had sent them. There were only three guns, which took more than half a minute to reload, even in the hands of an expert; three shots, no more, and three of them would surely die in their fight against the infidel, and thus be assured of a place in Paradise. They were rough, cruel men, and barbarians, but they were not without courage and the odds were greatly in their favor. Moreover, their admiral had told them, "At the top of the ladder, that is where we make our move."

Three of the Berbers wrestled Porter to the ground and were struggling to get his gun. Jason hurled himself at them and saw Pratt and Fairweather coming up, heard the two shots they fired, saw them swinging their muskets like clubs as they piled into the fight.

Many of the Algerians were racing for the decks, there to dive overboard into a sea that was their own, but not all of them. Jason found himself on the ground with a pair of arms wrapped around his knees and strong hands at his throat, trying to throttle the life out of him. He looked up into the fiercely triumphant eyes of Admiral Sinan, and as he broke the hold a booted foot crashed into the side of his head. As he fought to retain consciousness he felt himself being tipped through the opening again, back into the flooding hold he had just left. He clutched at the lip of the hatch for support, but there were heavy boots stomping on his hands, and he fell. As he splashed into deep water and tried to focus his eyes he saw the hatch slam down above him and knew that he was trapped in a hold that was rapidly filling with water.

Was the *Virginia* sinking? And was the woman he loved so fervently about to join him in a watery grave?

The cold water revived him. He searched his mind desperately for the location of the second and third hatches, knowing that by now his fellow marines, well trained, would be battening them down too, to control the flooding. The hatches were watertight for just this purpose.

He swam fast and found both of them, only a foot or so above his head, but they were fastened securely. He held onto a ladder and hammered on the underside of one of them, raising his voice and yelling for someone, anyone, to come and let him out.

But he knew that over the continuing sounds of the battle, the thunder of the cannon and the rattle of musket fire, he could not be heard.

He knew, too, that he had little time left. The water was rising fast.

CHAPTER SEVENTEEN

The *Virginia* was now faced with a terrifying calamity. One of the Algerian vessels, the *Bahri*, had been set on fire by the Berbers' own cannonade from the cliffs. No less than four of the glowing cannonballs had landed on her deck, one of them burning its way rapidly down to the small hold in the stern where the gunpowder was stored.

The captain had been killed and the first mate had taken over and was urgently trying to raise the wind so that he could beach his ship and save her guns. But the *Bahri* had been stationed near the narrow opening that led to the sheltered cove to the east and the wind was in the northwest. It meant a long haul to the east till the sails could fill and give her enough freeway for the use of the rudder, and she was burning furiously in three different places. But as they passed the eastern extremity of the gap, the *Bahri* blew up.

More than half the men on board were killed, either by the fearsome concussion or by the flying timbers that smashed into their bodies. The survivors, many of them wounded, leaped into the sea to swim to the safety of the shore or the reef. The frigate went down stern first into the water, the flames turning to steam and smoke as she hung there, buoyed up by the air trapped in the forward holds. Her masts and sails were on fire. She was almost dead center in the cove's entrance, on the verge of sinking there.

As the *Virginia* swept along the shore, the sound of her cannon and the fury of her rifle fire were deafening. Many of her complement had been hurt or killed, and she was listing dangerously. Captain Breck surveyed the damage unmoved as the mate said quietly, "Burning wreckage by the reef, sir. Our way out is blocked."

"I see it." Breck took his glass to examine it carefully. "She'll soon sink, Mr. Mate," he said, "and the way will be open again." He unrolled his chart to check the depth of the water at that point. "Six point four fathoms. We'll pass over her safely when she's gone down."

"With two feet to spare, perhaps," the mate said with a sigh. The Captain answered him coldly, detecting his unease, "And we'll be at full speed when the time comes. Whatever obstruction remains, we'll blast our way through it with our weight and our speed. Do we have a casualty count?"

"Eight men killed, sir, forty-three wounded so far, about half of them badly."

"Then we are doing well. Six barbarian frigates sunk or damaged beyond repair, to say nothing of their foundry. Yes, it is a good score, and a small price to pay, on balance." He handed the telescope to the mate. "Tell me how long that frigate will last."

The mate studied the burning *Bahri* intently. "It's not easy to make an estimate, Captain, it all depends on how securely her forward hatches are battened down, how long the air in them will last, how quickly the fire will open them. But at a guess, less than an hour."

"Then let our last hour in this cove be a profitable one. As we wait we will make one more assault on the shore battery and go after the remaining frigate."

The thunder continued.

Below decks, the Berber prisoners had long since sought safety in the water—except one. Admiral Sinan strode confidently along the dimly lit corridors, knowing with arrogant certainty that he was absolutely safe till he chose to show himself topside. All hands were on deck, and it was deserted down here. He had overheard Pratt Wilson telling Jason of the precious cargo in Cabin C, and the very thought of it drove him like a man possessed.

He found the cabin quickly, and paused for a moment efore softly trying the latch. It was fastened on the inside. . muffled voice could be heard from inside, a man's voice. Ie frowned, looked both ways down the corridor and saw iat it was still empty. He went to the tallows and pinched iem out with finger and thumb, then moved back to the oor and pressed his ear against it in the absolute darkness. Ie heard the low voice say, "And Lord alone knows where e went, ma'am."

It was Fairweather.

He had been knocked unconscious in the melee at the op of the hold's ladder, and on recovering had found himelf alone. Bleeding badly from a cut at the back of his ead he had gone looking for Jason, sure that he would nd him here in Opal's cabin. He said uncertainly, "I ieard Pratt tell him where he'd find you, ma'am. I can't hink what could have happened to him. So I'll continue ny search."

He went to the door and unlocked it. When he opened it, or a brief moment he wondered why the candles had been nuffed out. Then there was a monstrous blow to the stomich that doubled him up in pain. He felt himself being hrown bodily back into the cabin, and as he fell he drew he knife from his belt, but a powerful hand seized his wrist and swung his arm up viciously till it came out of its ocket. He heard Opal gasp, and saw in the reflected gleam of the cabin's lights that his unknown assailant had he knife. Its blade streaked up and came down to silence he shout that was forming in his throat.

Admiral Sinan picked himself up off the dead body and shut the door. He turned to Opal and smiled very gently, and said mockingly, "So, dear lady, it seems that fate has thrown us together again. And this time, permit me to assure you, she will be kinder to me than she has been in the past."

Opal stared in horror at the bloodied body on the floor. But as she opened her mouth to scream, Sinan was on her, pouncing like an animal. His heavy hand gripped her face cruelly, stifling her; his arm was around her waist, swinging her off the ground. His lips close to her ear, he said softly, as though time mattered nothing to him now, as though the furious thunder of the guns above them did not exist, "An officer's cabin is a very private place in the midst of a great battle, no? What say you?" He put her down on the bunk, holding her tightly still.

She could not speak, nor could she force his huge hand away from her mouth. She stared at Fairweather's body. He was a friend of Jason's and therefore of hers, who had tried so valiantly to help them both! He was lying in a pool of his own blood, his throat ruthlessly cut by this loathsome man.

Sinan went on, sounding amused now, "I do not know, dearest Opal, how much time we have together now. But let us make the most of it."

Fairweather's sharp knife, red-stained, was still in his hand. He laid the edge of it across her throat and whispered, "No one will hear you if you scream. But we will have silence now."

Opal trembled and held her breath. Her eyes were wide with horror. Smiling easily, Sinan put the knife away and said, "No one will disturb us here. *All* hands are on deck. Below decks, where we are now, there is no one to help you." He laughed softly. "Perhaps more importantly to you, though not for me, know also that your Jason Farn is dead."

She caught her breath and began to moan. He took his hand from her mouth and murmured, "Is it cruel of me to tell you this? I am sure that it is, but I must! For now there is no one to come between me and the woman on whom I have set my heart. Your lover is dead! He is drowned like a rat in a trap."

Opal sobbed, and could not hold back the tears. She was in shock. She cared nothing that his fingers were at the buttons of her blouse. There was an image in her mind that distracted her.

It was an image of the hotel in Algiers. She was entering her room, leaving at her door a very charming young man whom she hardly knew, who had said to her courteously,

"My name is Jason Farn, ma'am. If I may know yours?" And then his sudden bursting in at the sound of her screaming. . . . There was the image of the two of them perched on the railings of the *Habou*, when she was staring down fearfully into the churning sea she was supposed to jump into and did so only because his arm was around her, as they escaped from the hell-ship that had become her prison. . . . She was clambering down a vine with him from the Bey's harem, and he was whispering, with moisture in his eyes that he tried hard to hide from her, "Have they harmed you, my love?"

And most of all . . . that night in the great blue cavern where he had first taken her, when she had thrown her naked thighs around him to hold him deeper inside her as he whispered in her ear, "My love, my love, my true love now. . . ."

The tears coursed down her cheeks as she thought of the man she loved so dearly, and she was scarcely conscious of her bared breasts, the blouse tossed carelessly aside as he worked the skirt down over her naked hips. She felt the light touch of fingers, and then lips, and she heard a whispered voice, "Part your thighs for me, my love. I do not wish to force you." But the words were those of Sinan, not of Jason who was dead, and she moaned, "No, no! I will not!"

The voice was even softer now, the voice of an ardent lover, not a man who moments ago had sliced a knife across the throat of a good man who had come to help her. It was saying gently but impatiently, "I am in *love* with you, Opal! And these are words that I have spoken to no woman before, ever. Do you understand what I am saying? I am in love with you! I want you to live with me for ever, to be the favorite of all of my women. I have a house in the Casbah, a most beautiful house, the house of a man of quality, and you will be happy there, my love. Moreover, I promise to avail myself of your services two, three, even four times every week. You are the choicest of all my women. Open your thighs for me."

She gasped, "No! No, no, no!"

"Then I will force you!"

"I will not give myself to you!"

"Then I will take you against your will! My patience is not as strong as my desire for you, and if I am to die this minute, I must enjoy you before I go to my ancestors. I will die for the love of a beautiful woman, even though I should be swimming fast for the shores of Algeria. Your eyes are the eyes of a desert gazelle, your lips a budding rose, your breasts are soft and yet firm, the smoothest I have ever kissed, and your thighs are beyond compare. . . ."

He held her tightly and said fiercely, "And I will *make* you want me!" His lips were at her breast and his hand was at the satin of her loins, insidiously caressing her. He was a man of great power and physical beauty—and a vicious murderer.

He was naked beside her. When had he removed his clothes? When had he removed hers?

Was it while Jason was running like a hunted animal with the Libyan bandit, Osman? While he was searching out the harem in the bey's palace, or clambering up onto its balcony? While he was confined miserably in the brig, thinking only of her? The touch on her flesh was the touch of a feather; the thick hair of his beard was rough on her skin. That hard, pulsating muscle was against her side. She said aloud, her voice choked with her suffering, "Jason, my Jason, my only true love . . ."

Suddenly, all of that close and terrible contact was gone. Opal's eyes were closed, and when she opened them she saw that he had risen to his feet, a look of fury on his face. He knelt on the bunk, his powerful thighs straddling her, the muscles on them like corded ropes, and he said harshly, "Very well. If it will not be with your consent, it will be without it."

She stared up at him in horror; the reality of the moment struck her like a physical blow. He said coldly, "Your Jason is no more, a corpse. Forget him, and think only of me."

He forced himself towards her. She wept and tried to turn her face to the wall.

* * *

But Jason was not a man to accept death without a fervent struggle, and he was still alive.

It was not easy for him in the pitch darkness of the hold, but he knew what he had to do. He dove deep and swam underwater along the hull, knowing when the rush of seawater hit him that he had found what he was looking for—the jagged timbers of the hole through which the ship was taking on water. Then he surfaced quickly. There were only a few inches of air space above his head. He rested for a brief moment to get his breath back, then filled his lungs and dove deeply again, straight to his means of escape.

He forced himself through the aperture and hung on, knowing that if he let go precipitously he would lose the ship altogether, and this was not his intention. He tried to work out in his mind his exact position, and concluded that above the waterline and not too high over his head, the channels would be braced on the outside of the vessel—the board planking bolted there for spreading the lower rigging. But the ship was running fast, sweeping him along with it, and he was not sure if he could reach it. She was listing heavily. Surely the braces would be very close to the water?

But his lungs were bursting and there was no time for more thought. He let go, kicked out strongly, and *hoped.* As he shot to the surface he saw that the channel-stays were immediately above his head, moving, with the ship's great speed, very fast out of his reach. He threw up his arms and caught one of the wooden ties, letting it drag him along furiously till he could gather his strength and pull himself up onto the boards.

He did not wait. He clambered swiftly hand over hand up the lower ropes of the rigging and swung himself aboard. He was appalled at the damage there.

The once orderly deck was littered with fallen spars and shrouds, lit here and there by fires which were not being doused fast enough. The base of the bridge was a shambles, and men were lying dead or wounded everywhere. The

guns were still firing, shattering his eardrums as he ra
past them to the companionway.

The bo'sun was lying on the stairs, grotesquely spreadea
gled in death, his ruddy face ashen, his eyes wide and stai
ing, his mouth twisted in a kind of waxen grin. There wer
others he remembered from the old days, Henshaw, Smith
Marsac. And at the bottom of the steps he found the one
handed Clayton, dead too.

He pulled up short to see Pratt Wilson hurrying up t
greet him, limping from a bullet wound in the thigh. Prat
cried hoarsely, "In God's name, Jason, where have yo
been? We've been searching the ship for you from stem t
stern."

Jason demanded, "Opal?"

Pratt's face was tight and drawn, but he grinned an
said happily, "Opal's in her cabin, right as rain. Fair
weather is with her. He went to see if you'd found her."

Jason hurried off like a man possessed, but Prat
stopped him. "Wait! Calm down, man, and listen to me!"

Jason turned, and Pratt went on, "The stern dinghy's ir
the water, trailing behind us."

"Ah, you're a good friend, Pratt." He took a long deep
breath, shook the confusion from his head, and said, "And
you're hurt."

Pratt shrugged. "Nothing. I took the bullet out long
ago." He hesitated, and studied his friend's face shrewdly.
He knew, with absolute conviction, that Jason would never
leave the ship without Opal.

He said softly, smiling, "You're determined to take her
with you, aren't you?"

Jason nodded. "Yes, Pratt, I am. If ever you feel the
pangs of love as I feel them . . . Yes, I will take her with
me. She would not wish it otherwise. It is because the love
between us is not mine alone, but *ours*." He looked around
him in the darkness and said, "For God's sake, Pratt, is
this ship ever going to survive?"

Pratt nodded confidently. "She's taken damage as bad as
this before. Yes, she'll survive." He pointed. "You see that
flaming wreck out there?"

The *Bahri* was lower in the water now, still burning. Pratt said, grining broadly, "That's one of the Algerians, hit by the Berbers' own red-hot cannonballs. She's right in the middle of the gap in the reef, which is our only way out. Until she sinks we're blocked in here, Jason. So the skipper is just cruising up and down and blasting the coastal batteries until that damned frigate sinks and we can pass over her—hopefully I tell you, it's not a nice prospect."

"I'll need a good knife," Jason said, "to cut us adrift when we board the dinghy."

Pratt's clasp-knife was in his hand immediately. "Take mine. Carry it with you always, Jason, as a memento."

"I will, and I thank you, Pratt, for all you've done for us. We'll meet again, in Gibraltar."

"You'll be there ahead of us. In the state we're in we'll not make more than three or four knots."

"Then look for us at a tavern called the Swan and Sugar-Loaf. That's where we'll be waiting for you."

"Be on your way now to your lady."

The two men embraced and Jason went below, his heart pounding and his step light, to Cabin C. He tried the latch and found it fastened. He knocked on the door and called out, "Opal! It's me, Jason! Open up quickly!"

He heard her piercing scream, threw his weight into the door, and burst it off its hinges.

It was almost a reprise of his assault on the door of Opal's room back in Algiers, so long ago. But now, his mortal enemy Sinan was alone, and it was man to man.

Naked as the day he was born, Sinan still had the knife. He balanced athletically on the balls of his feet, his muscles rippling in the candlelight as he waited for Jason's charge. The knife was weaving in front of him in a circular motion that seemed to be an invitation.

Opal sat up on the bunk, her lovely eyes on fire. Jason was conscious of Charlie Fairweather's dead body lying between them, but he would not take his eyes from Sinan's, knowing that every iota of his attention was required against this formidable enemy. He could not even reach into his pocket for Pratt's knife for if he did so he would be dead, and there would be no hope for Opal at all.

Out of the corner of his eye he saw her gather herself on the bunk and leap suddenly onto Sinan's broad back, her arm around his throat and her long legs scissoring his waist. She was screaming in a paroxysm of rage that awed him momentarily. He shouted, "No! Leave him to me!"

Sinan's blade swung up high for an expert thrust behind him that would surely have killed her instantly. But the momentary deadlock had been broken, his attention distracted by a threat he had not expected, and Jason reached for Sinan's wrist with both his hands and swung him around. Opal leaped clear as they both fell to the floor, and Jason took the weapon arm across his knee, bore down on it with all his strength, and snapped the arm in two. He dragged his opponent to his feet and slammed his fists repeatedly into that muscular chest, hearing the ribs crack with the force of his blows. As Sinan stumbled, Jason threw all of his weight into a final punch at the side of his neck, just below the ear. It was a blow to shatter granite. The Berber admiral crashed into the cabin wall and slid down it to the floor.

Jason was white with fury, unable to contain himself. He picked up the fallen knife and raised it high, but he heard Opal shriek, "No, Jason, no!"

She grabbed at his arm with surprising strength, trembling. She whispered, "No, there has been enough killing."

He stood motionless as a statue and tried to force the all-consuming rage away from him. At last he lowered his arm and dropped the knife to the floor. He looked down at Sinan's motionless body and said quietly, "He may indeed be dead. I neither know nor care."

Opal's arms were around him, the tears streaming down her cheeks as she shuddered uncontrollably. Her heart was bursting with mixed emotions: shock and anguish, relief and great love, emotions that tore at her savagely as she tried to take hold of herself. She sobbed, "Oh Jason, Jason, Jason . . ." seeking to reassure herself that he was really there.

He held her for a moment, and said softly, "Come. Put on your dress and we will leave now. There is a boat."

She nodded. He helped her into the blouse and skirt. He looked down at the dead body of his old friend Fairweather and asked quietly, "Was it Sinan? I must know."

"Yes. It was Sinan, I saw it." She could not drive the horror of it from her mind, nor would the shaking leave her. She said again, hoarsely, "I saw it."

"Then come." His arm was around her as they went out into the darkened corridor and up the stairs of the companionway. The ship was still fighting, still taking damage from the battery. No one paid them any attention as they ran in the clouded moonlight to the stern.

Pratt Wilson was there, waiting for them. He took Opal's hand in his and said, "You see, ma'am? Even a battle like this has its bright side, bloody though it may be! Jason, over the stern with you quickly. Grab the painter and haul the dinghy in close. I'll help her down to you."

Jason embraced him again. "Charlie Fairweather, Pratt. He's dead. Killed by the Berber admiral, Sinan."

Pratt's face went white. He said harshly, "And where is Sinan now?"

"In Cabin C. If he's alive, he'll be unconscious for a long time, I think. But don't let him get away, Pratt. A brace of ropes around his arms and legs till the battle's over. And then tell the third mate. Whatever his other crimes may be, he murdered a marine."

"I'll do that. But go now."

"Till we meet again, then."

Jason clambered swiftly down over the stern to where the trailing dinghy was bobbing furiously in a rushing sea, hauled hard on the painter till it was in close, and leaped aboard. He stared up in the darkness to the stern rail looming high above him, and saw Pratt helping Opal down. She jumped and fell to the bottom of the boat, and he slashed quickly at the rope before they could overturn with the violence of the motion, picked her up and held her tightly.

The *Virginia* was speeding on her way, leaving them alone on a dark sea. He set her down gently on the stern bench, raised the sail swiftly and fastened the sheet. He took the tiller and forced it over, and swung round to gather the wind and steer the dinghy to the remnants of the flaming wreck that marked their way out of the bay. His arm was around her as he steered past the dead *Bahri*, its fires almost out now.

"We have a stout boat under us now, and there is a good wind that will serve us well. Soon, my dearest, all this will be a memory."

"A memory never to be forgotten."

"It is true. But Gibraltar lies ahead of us . . . safety at last."

Opal raised her head and brushed the tears from her eyes. "And most of all," she whispered, "we are together again."

"Again, and for ever."

They passed close to the charred hull of the *Bahri*. The high waves rose up to meet them. They were in open water now. The sound of gunfire diminished as the great shadow of the reef receded from their sight. Opal asked quietly, "And the *Virginia*, Jason? Will she not sink?"

Jason shook his head. "No. That Captain Breck is a hard, bigoted man, but he's also the best sailor we have. No, she won't sink, he won't allow it! I promise you, very soon now you and I will sit together high up on the Rock of Gibraltar and watch her limping into the shipyards for repair."

He held her tightly and caressed her. Behind them, the *Bahri*'s last flames were being extinguished as she slid slowly to the bottom.

And further still to the east, the red-gold streaks on a gray horizon heralded the dawn.

CHAPTER EIGHTEEN

The first mate, the glass to his eye, sighed with relief.

"Captain! The Berber frigate on the reef has gone down. The way out is open to us now."

"Ah . . ." Breck said contentedly. "Then we will presently break off this engagement, Mr. Mate. I feel we have acquitted ourselves well and taught the enemy a lesson he will long remember. What is our casualty count?"

"Twelve men dead, sir, seventy-one wounded. Damage to the ship is considerable, but we're holding our own. Two of the holds are flooded, but they're battened down and the pumps are keeping the sea at bay."

Breck was a very fair man, and he said, not hiding his pleasure, "I congratulate you, Mr. Mate, on finding men to work the pump at such a difficult time. I will admit, it *has* been difficult for us."

"Not men, Captain," the mate said easily. "Women."

Breck stared. *"What?"*

"Women, sir. The whores and the refugees alike. All the Berber women have been taking their turn at the pumps these last three hours, freeing the men for more pressing duties. And, I will say, doing it willingly, and with great energy."

"Well!" The captain was flabbergasted. He said wryly, "It is not often, I feel, that women come to the help of the United States Navy in time of battle. I commend you for it."

"Thank you, sir."

The captain moved to the wheel and looked at the compass. They were in the middle of their turn. "Helmsman, you will now take us out to sea, on the course that will give us the greatest speed through the reef. We have a wreck to smash through that may, or may not, easily break up on the impact."

"Aye, aye, sir."

Behind them, as they completed the turn and maneuvered into position for a fast run on a tight starboard tack, the few guns left of the shore battery were still firing, but all of the shot was dropping into the sea far short of the target. The mate was waiting for an order, and when it did not come, he said diffidently, "We are well out of their range, Captain. May I sound the stand-down?"

"You may not. All hands are on deck, I assume?"

"Yes, sir."

"Then there remains one final duty." Breck strode to the rail, gripped it firmly, and looked down on the deck. Not one of the many fires that had started was still burning. In the clouded moonlight and the faint rays of grey light from the east he could see a multitude of white faces staring up at him. The men were waiting, exhausted, for the stand-down.

He called out clearly, "This is your captain. Hear me!" The silence was acute, broken only by the distant cannonade.

"Hear what your good efforts have accomplished this night! I bleed for the dead and the wounded, but death and injury are part of a good fighting man's heritage and must be accepted. We have destroyed an entire Berber cannon factory, dropping it down into the sea, and we have destroyed at least half of a major shore battery!" A cheer went up, and over it he shouted, "Moreover, we have sunk seven barbarian frigates! It has cost us dearly, but the great *Virginia* has won yet another battle, which will long be remembered in the annals of American naval history!"

The cheering was deafening. A solitary voice yelled,

"God bless you, Captain Breck!" His heart was swelling with pride. He shouted, "It is through *your* efforts! And because of those efforts the name of our ship will never be forgotten as long as men can read of the exploits of our great naval heroes! I salute you one and all!"

The cheering went on and on. He turned away and said calmly, "You may now sound the stand-down, Mr. Mate."

"Aye, aye, sir."

The mate rang the bell, and they both watched the dark waters ahead of them. They were moving on a course for the reef at a very commendable speed. The helmsman said stolidly, "Passing over the wreck in one minute, sir."

They waited.

When the crunch came, it was violent and shuddering. It threw them off their feet. For a brief moment it seemed as though the great *Virginia* might yet be stopped by a ship long dead. But her dreadful list had lifted her keel a full two feet higher than it would normally have been, and both her speed and her weight were great. The filled sails strained and the masts creaked, and then she lurched forward suddenly as, below her, the charred remnants of the *Bahri* toppled over and gave way.

The cheering on the decks was renewed as she entered the high seas. Breck said smugly, "I believe the course is two hundred and seventy-one, helmsman."

"Aye, aye, sir, two hundred and seventy-one."

The Berber battery, hopelessly out of range now, was still keeping up a desultory fire; like a ship under full sail, a Barbary gunner could not easily be stopped when he was well under way, even though the iron balls were being wasted. On board the ship they could even hear the faint, distant shouting as the survivors yelled at each other in triumph, each convinced that it was his particular cannon that had finally driven the intruder off.

The third mate had come to the bridge and was whispering with the first, and Captain Breck scowled. He did not like secrets aboard his vessel. He said testily, "What is it?"

"The casualty count, sir," the third mate replied. "Not twelve men dead, as we supposed, but thirteen. One more body has been discovered."

Breck nodded. "Thank you. That is all."

"No, sir. I mean, with due respect, sir. The thirteenth man was not killed by cannon or musket fire. His throat was cut."

"What?"

"Yes, sir. Marine Fairweather, sir, his throat cut from ear to ear."

The captain roared, "*By whom*?"

"By the Berber admiral, Sinan, sir, who was a prisoner, and escaped with all the other pirates when the brig flooded."

Breck's face was convulsed with his anger. "They *escaped*?"

"Yes, sir. They jumped overboard and swam to the shore."

His voice was like a sharp blade. "Admiral Sinan too?"

"No, sir. The admiral is our prisoner, bound hand and foot. He was found in the cabin of the English lady, who has disappeared."

"A lady can hardly *disappear* from a ship at sea. Search for her, find her, bring her to me. I wish to be assured of her safety."

"Yes, sir. And the Berber admiral, sir?"

Captain Breck said coldly and deliberately, "He murdered an American marine. Hang him. *Now*."

"Aye, aye, sir." He scuttled down the steps to carry out his orders.

The first mate was using the glass again. He said quietly, "A dinghy ahead of us, Captain. Four points on the starboard beam and one mile distant."

Breck was deeply concerned about Opal. If the wretched Berber had been found in her cabin . . . What could he have been doing there? She had been a prisoner on board Sinan's ship. Was she also dead then, her body perhaps tossed overboard or down into one of the holds? And in

God's name, he was responsible for her! The blood drained from his face as he pondered what might have happened to her. He glowered at the mate and said harshly, "I am not overly concerned at the moment with a damned fishing boat. I have other vexations."

"Not a fishing boat, Captain, but a dinghy, very much like one of ours. Moving faster than we are, on much the same course. There are two people aboard, though I can't see who they might be. I don't think they're Berbers, sir. One is a woman."

Breck snatched the glass from him and focused it. Against the overcast western sky he could see very little. Then the dinghy came into his vision, carried up on the crest of a great wave, to hang there for a moment before disappearing again into the trough. He held the glass steady and strained his eyes. There it was again. And one of the figures was indeed a woman. As the boat held on the wave for an instant, he saw her look back, her white face so distant that he could not really be sure at all. As the waves swallowed them up again, he knew, and a great sense of relief swept over him. The other figure, then, could be no other than ex-marine Farn.

Captain Breck grunted loudly. He snapped the telescope shut and handed it back, and said stolidly, "All of our efforts now, Mr. Mate, to bringing this sorely wounded ship to the yards in Gibraltar."

"Aye, aye, sir."

The *Virginia*, more dead than alive, ploughed on.

On board the dinghy, Jason had opened up the well-stocked locker.

He found a seven-gallon oak cask of water, four three-pound sacks of dried salt cod, two smaller sacks of smoked dried pork, a box of hard biscuits, and a basket containing a dozen ripe limes. It provided a veritable feast for them, and they found that they were ravenously hungry. They relished every tough morsel.

The sun was well up over the horizon now, casting its

golden sheen on the sail. Jason had lashed the tiller to hold their steady course. The sky was a brilliant blue, and all the dark clouds had been replaced with scudding drifts of white cotton. The coastline was far, far distant, a smudge of purple mountains to the south of them, and soon they lost even this reminder of Algiers.

Their arms were around each other as they sat together in the dinghy's stern. Jason asked quietly, "Are you happy, my love?" He placed a gentle finger under her chin and tilted up her face to kiss her. "Soon," he said, "we will be in Gibraltar among your people. We are making good speed, and in less than a day and a half we will see that great fortress looming up ahead of us."

"And the *Virginia*? Are you sure that she will go there too, Jason?"

"Yes. Those are the only shipyards in the whole of the Mediterranean that can repair the damage she suffered." He smiled. "Why do you ask? Are you so anxious to see the *Virginia* again?"

"Yes. To assure myself that all those good men are safe."

"They will be."

She said, worrying about it, "In the excitement of the moment, I did not even thank Pratt Wilson for all that he did for us."

Jason laughed. "He knows that we will meet again. There is a tavern where you and I will be waiting for our good friends Pratt and the others. . . . And I will ask your forgiveness, my darling, if we celebrate our freedom a little injudiciously. But there is a matter of pressing importance we must attend to first, within moments of our arrival."

"And that is what, dear Jason?"

The stern of a wildly tossing dinghy among the waves was not the easiest place to do it, but Jason dropped to one knee, took Opal's hand in his and kissed it.

"Will you honor me, my darling Opal, with your hand in marriage? My love for you is boundless, and I feel that it is shared. If you accept, as I devoutly pray you will, I will be the happiest man in all of Christendom."

She felt she was melting. She slipped off the seat and knelt beside him, her arms enfolding him passionately; she could not find the words to answer him. At last she whispered, "Yes, oh yes! I love you so much, dear Jason."

"For ever and ever, in love and in marriage . . ."

"Till death us do part."

Their arms were tight around each other, and they sat down together on the polished mahogany seat by the tiller as Jason kept an ever wary eye on the sail that was their lifeline. He said, smiling, "And will you come and live with me in my home in Virginia?"

"Anywhere with you, dearest."

"They are fine people there. You will quickly find good friends in a new country that may, at first, be strange to you."

"If it is your home, I know that I will love it there."

"You will not miss your own home?"

Opal fell silent for a while. She said at last, sighing, "London . . . it is the greatest city in the world. But our house there holds sad memories for me, conflicting memories that disturb me deeply. I think I will never set foot in it again."

There was a longer silence now. Then Jason said softly, "Yes, your father. It is a very heavy cross to bear."

"And yet, once he was such a good man!"

"We have left behind us the memories of Algiers. We must leave the memories of London behind us too. There is a whole new world to encompass us, Opal. Together."

"Oh, Jason . . ." Emotion rose within her. His hand slipped under her blouse, touching her soft breast. He pulled her gently down to the hard bottom of the boat and lay beside her. For a long time he quietly caressed her and relished their closeness, knowing that all he desired in the whole world was here with him now.

Opal's slender fingers traced the muscles of his powerful chest, and soon slipped down under his belt to fondle him.

He freed himself from the confines of his clothing, and slowly eased her skirt up over her hips. He played with her for a while, and then rolled over on top of her and entered her smoothly as she gasped out her desire for him. He paused, contained within her, as his eager lips found her breasts, before he began that fervent thrusting that drove her to the borders of frenzy.

Ecstasy overtook them both at almost the same moment. They lay breathlessly still in each other's arms until it had passed.

They slept in the heat of the day. When he awoke Jason was conscious of a slackening in the sail as the wind changed slightly. He withdrew from her and heard her murmur, only half awake, "No, do not leave me, Jason . . ."

He kissed her and whispered, "I must, for a very brief moment."

He adjusted the sail and the tiller's lashings, and lay down beside her again, his hands moving delicately over her. The hours passed in their mutual passion. As the night began to fall he gave her his shirt to keep her warm. She crouched at his knee as he manned the tiller against the vagaries of the night winds.

The moon came out and crossed the heavens. Jason saw that she was asleep, a smile of pure contentment on her lovely face. The wind changed again, as he had expected, and he trimmed his sail accordingly, trying not to disturb her as he moved.

When the sun came up she awoke with a start and reached up to throw her arms around his waist, clutching at him desperately as she whispered, "Oh, my love . . . I dreamed that you had left me!"

He leaned down and kissed her lips, and said gently: "Never, my darling!"

She was still in the limbo between sleep and full wakefulness. She murmured, "I dreamed that you had left me for a Berber girl named Andara."

"Andara?" He had almost forgotten her.

"There was a look in her eyes when she spoke with you.

You talked only Arabic, and I did not understand. But I was sure that she craved your love, as I crave it too."

He embraced her warmly. "Andara too is a memory," he said. "There is no woman on the face of the earth who will ever come between us." He laughed suddenly, remembering. "Yes," he said, "Andara wanted to join what she thought was my harem, and she was greatly disappointed when I told her that not only did I not have one, but also that I had no urgent plans for one. I told her that there was only one woman in my life, which she found very hard to understand. I told her that I loved only you, and to the point of desperation." He touched her cheek and said gravely, "And what I told her was the truth. No other woman, Opal. Ever."

Opal smiled and laid a hand on his cheek. She whispered, "If your love is as great as mine, dear Jason, there will be room for no one else in your thoughts, as there will be no room in mine either!"

She brushed the sleep from her eyes, and ran her fingers through her hair. A new and more serene day had dawned for them, far from the trials and dangers that were behind them now. The blue water was all their own. There was no other vessel in sight on the limitless sea.

The morning passed, and the afternoon. They loved each other again and again and again. There was nothing to disturb their serenity. The peace of the wide sea was absolute. And when the sun was halfway down, a gull flew over them, screeching wildly.

Jason excitedly stared out to the western horizon. And there, only twenty miles or so away, a great gray rock was rising out of the sea to welcome them, seeming to beckon them, to call them to its strength and its safety. It was tall and imposing in the light of the late afternoon, with the sun standing over its high twin peaks.

Opal climbed to her feet and stood beside her lover. The wind wafted her long hair about her lovely features, driving her blouse and her skirt against her slender body. Her arm was around him as they stood together, balanced and swaying with the motion of the dinghy.

Jason said triumphantly, "It is Gibraltar! And for us, the beginnings of a new life together."

The little dinghy, the property of the United States government, sailed on steadily to the British rock that was to be their deliverance, and the means to their eternal happiness.